MW00461603

Space Thing and other stories

An Accumulation of Dooms to Distract the Masses

Ran M. Baffle

Beg to Differ Press

First edition.

Published by Beg to Differ Press.

https://begtodifferpress.ca

Cover art by Valentina Testa

Print edition ISBN: 978-1-7388864-0-1

eBook edition ISBN: 978-1-7388864-1-8

For Frances and Marion

Dooms

Sudden Life

T he first time I died was when I took my Ducati Superleggera motorcycle for a short flight off the edge of a highway on the Pacific coast. Unfortunately I have no first-hand reports of the nature of the afterlife to offer, no revelations from the Great Beyond. My last memory prior to the facility is, in fact, of seeing a huge boulder rushing toward me and wondering what kind of rock it was. Then it struck me, quite literally: it was a granite glacial erratic.

The next thing I knew, I was lying in a bed in a white room. Waiting at my bedside was a young man with a long, coiffed beard and a tight mohawk. He wore a plastic tag on his white coat, bearing a phoenix logo and the name Magnus. I took this as proof that he was not an angel. He glanced up from the tablet in his lap and realized that I had regained consciousness.

"Hey there. Welcome back," Magnus said.

"Where am I?" I asked, originality not being my top priority at the time.

"You are at the Phoenix Cryonics facility. Specifically, you're in the Reintegration Room of the facility which, trust me, is a far better place to find yourself than the Disintegration Room."

I stared at him in bewilderment.

"That's my little joke," he explained, deadpan. "So anyway, you died." He did air quotes around this last word. "Fortunately, we were able to get you into cryopreservation within a viable time frame. That's the good news. The bad news is that although you did sign up for Full Body Preservation Plan, your actual body at the time of transition wasn't really in a preservable state, per se, so to cut a long story short, and a long person short, we only froze your head. At this point I'll just remind you that, according to your contract, Phoenix Cryonics is not obligated to offer any refund or discounts if such circumstances should arise beyond our control."

My bewilderment only increased. "Cryonics worked?" I asked, making no effort to conceal my incredulity.

"I know, right?" He guffawed and shook his head. "Believe me, no one was more surprised than us. Very few freezies—sorry, very few clients—ever make it back." He waved his tablet at me. "But, the old nanobots have done their stuff in your brain and I have green lights across the board here. Well, more or less. You may experience some memory loss, some visual and auditory hallucinations, and some nausea, but there is a silver lining there in that you no longer have a stomach with which," he consulted his tablet before finishing his sentence absentmindedly, "to vomit."

I couldn't help but notice that Magnus' beard and mohawk were various shades of blue that seemed to move in slow swirls, reminiscent of the brushstrokes of a Van Gogh painting. Fascinatingly, the effect remained fixed in position when the man's head moved behind it, as it were, like the design was projected on. I stared at it for a moment, wondering if it was a hallucination or not, then snapped myself out of it.

"How long?" I enquired, warily.

"All of these side effects tend to gradually fade away over a few weeks to a few months. Usually."

"No. How long have I been dead? Preserved? A freezie?"

"Ah," he said and consulted his tablet. "That would be one hundred and eleven years, by my calculation. And it says here you declined to shell out for the family plan, so everyone you once loved is now dead. My condolences."

As you might imagine, this was a lot to take in, and I was struggling to keep up. "You said something about my body?" I remembered.

"That is correct. Your original body was not fit for preservation after your accident, so we moved you onto the Neuro Plan. However, there is good news! Thanks to our Gold Partners at Kindred Cybernetics, we have been able to fully equip you with a new ex-demo torso and basic limb system from the KC Adequate series. On a temporary basis, of course. Kindred Cybernetics: Together, we can build the best you."

And with that slogan, he threw back the white sheet covering my body to reveal my new anatomy, all white and blue carbon fibre.

"Oh," I said, and passed out.

***

For the next three days I recuperated. Magnus and his colleagues gave me counselling and physical therapy, if you can still call it physical therapy when you're just a head. Tiny airborne medical robots buzzed around me constantly, monitoring my progress. Lawyers had me sign papers that I barely read and helped me activate the revival trust that I had set up during the same optimistic period that I'd signed the Phoenix contract, over a century ago.

They fine-tuned my new body, configuring and calibrating it endlessly. They taught me how to use it, how to charge it and how to maintain it. The body was a loaner, a basic model that I could test drive until I picked out one of the more expensive customized systems. Or at least that's what Kindred Cybernetics was betting on. It seemed a pretty safe bet, as they appeared to be the only game in town and I didn't fancy spending the remainder of my second life as a severed head in a jar.

Then, without further ado, they ejected me into the world of the future. It was underwhelming, to say the least. It turned out that the facility was in an industrial park on the edge of the city, surrounded by other equally anonymous and utilitarian-looking buildings, all white and grey boxes squatting warily behind high fences and bristling with threatening signs and conspicuous video cameras. As I briefly scanned the sky for flying cars, I noticed that the clouds seem to have a subtle but eerie green glow. No hover taxis, though. So much for sci-fi, I thought.

A distinctly earthbound blue and white van bearing the Kindred Cybernetics logo pulled up beside me. The driver was a young lady in her early twenties, dressed in corporate pale blue coveralls and with cropped blonde hair and round, green-tinted glasses. She introduced herself as VV.

"You're here to look after me, I understand," I said.

"I'm here to look after that," she said, indicating my body. "The hardware. You're just along for the ride. Which reminds me."

She produced a small remote control from her pocket and pressed something, and I was suddenly illuminated from within. An animated Kindred Cybernetics logo scrolled into view on my chest panel, followed by half a dozen little animated characters sporting various artificial body parts who proceeded to dance energetically around my abdomen to some unheard music. This brief performance culminated in the dancers freezing mid-leap, and the slogan *Together, we can build the best you* appeared. Then the cycle started over again.

"Wow," I said. "Classy."

"Don't worry, you can't turn it off but it's smart enough to deactivate itself when appropriate."

"That's a relief. I thought I might look foolish for a second."

"Hotel?" she asked.

"Hotel," I confirmed.

"No self-driving car?" I asked, tentatively maneuvering my unfamiliar new body into the passenger seat of VV's vehicle.

She snorted. "Self-drivers are for old folk. No offence."

"None taken."

I fumbled around for my seatbelt for several seconds before I realized it didn't exist, and we zoomed off abruptly, rapidly achieving a speed that once upon a time would have sent my stomach into my throat, back when I had those organs. Within a minute we were recklessly merging onto a vast highway, each of the countless lanes packed with traffic hurtling onward at death-defying velocities. I decided to attempt conversation to distract myself from the high probability of imminent death.

"So, does VV stand for something? Or is that your whole name?"

VV smirked. "My name is Violet, but everyone calls me VV."

"Why?"

"It's a nickname. Violet Violence."

"Ah," I responded, nodding. "Cool." So much for distractions.

Suddenly VV pulled left, changing lanes and cutting off a black six-wheeled truck that was the approximate size of a tank. I heard a horn blaring furiously and a moment later the aerodynamic panzer was roaring up beside us on my side. Large, blood-red digital letters appeared across the side of the vehicle in some death metal font.

WAKE UP ASSHOLE, it read, followed by TIME TO DIE.

The driver lowered his tinted window to glare at us. He was bald and his scalp was covered in tattoos, but I was too far away to distinguish them clearly. The weapon he was waving at us was too large to miss, however.

"Is that guy threatening us?" I asked. The answer seemed obvious but I held out some hope that I was still hallucinating.

VV looked over casually. "The guy in the taunter truck? Nothing to worry about. I've seen bigger guns."

"I was hoping I'd avoided the whole Mad Max dystopian future."

She looked at me, puzzled. "I don't know what that means," she said. And with that, she put her foot down and we thrust forward, steering abruptly right to cut off Panzer Man a second time.

"What are you doing? Can I at least get my money's worth out of this life before you kill me again?"

VV laughed. "Relax. Didn't people drive this way back in your time?"

"Not if you wanted to keep your license, no."

She looked puzzled. "How do you mean, license?"

"You're not licensed to drive?"

VV looked at me like *I* was the crazy one. "No one licenses people to drive. This is a free country. We self-regulate."

At that moment I was startled by a loud crack. Looking to our rear I watched with horror as Panzer Man fired his gun into the air above us. "He's shooting at us! Shouldn't we call the police?"

She guffawed. "Why? Will you relax? They're just warning shots. Anyway, this is us." She pulled right across several lanes of traffic and took us down the exit ramp. Panzer Man made a sudden course change in pursuit and within seconds he was tailgating us despite our alarming speed.

"He's right behind us," I informed my escort.

"I hope so," VV said smugly. She jerked the wheel hard to the left, abruptly changing lanes again. I looked back just in time to see Panzer Man get swallowed by the road in the lane we had just left.

"What the hell just happened?" I blurted. "Where did he go?"

"Looks like he found a hole in the road," explained VV, non-chalantly. "A pretty big one. It's been there for a couple of weeks now, I think. The state really should get that fixed, but you know how it is."

She did a double-take in my direction and raised her eyebrows. It was only then that I realized I had gripped the car's grab handle so hard with my artificial hand that I had ripped it from the ceiling.

***

Somehow VV got me to the Reznor Hotel in one piece; or technically in two pieces, I suppose. Despite feeling self-conscious, I strode through the lobby with my head held high as if it was perfectly natural for it to be perched atop a walking advertising billboard. Glancing around, that seemed to be true: no one paid me any attention. The woman at the reception desk seemed equally indifferent to my appearance. I checked in for a week to start, and she gave me a price in dollars. When I expressed surprise that they were using old-fashioned dollars as currency rather than some newfangled cryptocurrency, she looked fleetingly offended.

"We're not criminals." she objected, before gesturing to the elevators with her own artificial hand and sending me on my way to my room on the 237th floor.

When I reached the room I couldn't find the slot for the keycard anywhere. On closer examination I realized that it wasn't a keycard at all, just a card indicating my room number with a little icon suggesting I place my eye to the door sensor. What I had assumed was just a peephole in the door turned out to also be a retinal scanning device (though how the hotel knew what my retina was supposed to look like was a mystery). After trying both eyes against it, widening my eyes with my fingers and making multiple undignified facial expressions, the thing still refused to open. Fortunately, a passing housekeeper had mercy on me and opened the door, swiping her master keycard against the room number.

"Happens all the time," she assured me.

It was somehow comforting to find that mid-range hotel rooms had barely changed in the last century. I dropped the bag that the facility had equipped me with and flopped—or rather, crashed—onto the bed. The Kindred logo went dark on my chest and I sighed with relief. The large screen in the room was expecting me, greeting me by name and advertising all the hotel had to offer. It also detected my Kindred hardware and informed me that I could, if I so wished, control all the devices in the room just by thinking about it. The Kindred techs at the facility had enthused about the raft of third-party integration features, but honestly, I had enough new things to adapt to without giving myself a headache trying to get my robot body to communicate with the toaster. I picked up the remote control and went old school, drifting arbitrarily through the video streams.

A fat man brandishing a bible threatened me with the fires of Hell unless I send him money. Too late, buddy.

A news report about orphans that I soon realized was a commercial selling orphans. Nope.

Pornography. Hardcore. Not interested, for depressingly obvious reasons.

A game show where the contestants participated in increasingly life-threatening stunts in the hope of winning life-saving medical procedures for themselves or their loved ones. A real tearjerker.

An alleged documentary about a billionaire's sexual exploits in space, produced by an exploitative billionaire. Classy.

A commercial for a chain store called Jesus Saves. Free crucifix with every automatic weapon for a limited time only!

An infomercial solicited investments in mineral exploration on asteroids. You too can be rich enough to have sex in space.

A writhing mass of bodies, squirming and pulsating. For a moment I thought it was more pornography, then I realized that these naked men were smashing each other's heads in. Hard pass.

Another commercial, this one for Morgan's, a restaurant specializing in a niche market cuisine. The camera lingered sensually over the various naked body parts of a group of beautiful, happy young people as the jaunty jingle reached its climax: *Mmm–organs! We are what you eat!* sang the smiling livestock. I fumbled the remote in my haste to change channels.

A news report. A real one, this time: Anarcho-capitalist terrorists destroy a police cruiser with an IED. Two officers down. The police chief implored viewers to donate funds. A new report finds that the majority of teenagers cannot identify continents on a globe, with a significant percentage protesting that the exercise is unfair because the Earth is not spherical. Air quality is forecast to reach critical levels again downtown, so don't forget those respirators, folks!

The next item involved one Aurelia Fropp. Ms. Fropp had only recently purchased her new legs from Kindred Cybernetics when they spontaneously combusted due to overheating whilst she was out running, and she was forced to wade into a nearby pool to extinguish the fire. Although she had avoided any burns from the flames, she consequently had to be hospitalized due to chemical burns from the polluted water. The reporter said Kindred had failed to respond to their questions about the safety standards of their products.

I turned off the TV with a deep sigh. I pressed the panel on my chest and the power drawer slid out softly, revealing the two batteries, one of which was redundant. I switched the active battery to the full one and glanced at the little status panel below. Back to full power, all green lights, including the perfusion device that kept my actual head alive. I removed the depleted battery, closed the panel and grabbed the Phoenix bag. No recharging cable. I knew exactly where it was: it was plugged into an outlet in my room at the facility. Fortunately the battery life was a couple of days. I would have to get a spare from VV in the morning.

I showered my head and slept, dreaming of fleshly bodies on fire.

***

The next morning I was awoken by the skeuomorphic ringing of an old rotary telephone. I forced my eyes open and tapped the small phone screen that was built into my forearm. It was Magnus from Phoenix.

"When possible we like to match up our newly revived clients with some old hands," he announced, excitedly. "Someone who transitioned around the same time as you. We find it helps with acclimatization. VV will take you out to meet your revival buddy."

Twenty minutes later I met VV in the lobby.

"Is that the hotel's robe?" she asked.

The illuminated logo shone through the fabric but it was better than wandering around naked, so to speak. I had VV take me to a clothing store and grabbed some of the long tunics and loose pants that seemed to be all the rage before we headed off to our meeting. It was a long drive. The city seemed to go on forever, and I started to wonder if there was even any space between cities anymore. Eventually the skyscrapers and the sprawling malls fell away, followed by the suburbs as we advanced into an increasingly desolate landscape. The buildings became increasingly deserted, derelict, and devastated, in that order, as if we were being drawn toward the scarred epicentre of some dreadful holocaust.

"This Hannah friend of yours likes to keep her distance from other people, eh?" VV observed.

"What makes you think she's my friend?" I asked.

"Well, she called Phoenix and enquired about you by name. Offered her services. Magnus didn't mention that?"

"He did not."

"Well, I guess I just ruined the surprise." She smirked. "Apparently she saw you on a Kindred commercial and recognized your face."

"I'm on a Kindred commercial?"

"Of course. Remember all those little bug bots buzzing around you at the facility? They were Kindred's cameras. That fancy system you're riding around doesn't come for free. You signed the waivers."

I sighed and stared out the window as I tried to remember any Hannahs from my former life. I came up blank, so the joke was on VV as far as I was concerned. I decided to change the subject. "So what happened out here? Was there a war I missed?"

VV snorted. "Man, there hasn't been a war for ..." she shook her head slightly as if the rest of her sentence was unknowable. "Centuries," she decided.

I considered correcting her for a moment but didn't want her to digress.

"This is industrial stuff, mostly. Industrial accidents. There were a few nasty ones out here a few years ago. You know," she said with a shrug, "explosions and stuff."

We were driving through a veritable wasteland now, the few structures that were still standing nothing but ruins. Up ahead I could see a void among the remains, possibly a massive crater in the earth—you know, industrial stuff—but then the road we travelled curved away and the void passed from view.

It was just then that I caught a movement in my peripheral vision. Small figures were dashing in and out of the ruins. There was a loud thump as something hit the roof of the vehicle. "Shit!" I exclaimed, and checked the wing mirror. Children were chasing us and throwing debris. VV remained unruffled. "What's the story with the kids?" I asked her. I was full of questions today.

"Oh, gangs of them like to roam around these derelict areas. They're kind of feral."

"Where are their parents? Don't they have school?"

She shrugged. "Parenting is self-regulated. Education is their call. But take my advice." She turned to show me her serious expression. "Don't let the little fuckers near you."

***

"You don't remember me at all, do you?" Hannah Carfax asked me, as she handed me a coffee with a curious wink. I placed it on the small table between us. It smelled fantastic and I yearned for a digestive system.

VV had been right: the lady did like to keep her distance. It had taken us quite some time to track her down, finally finding her sitting outside of her large RV, parked on the grounds of an old theme park, beneath a huge, rusting rollercoaster. VV told me that this place had been abandoned before she was born, due to contaminated water or some such "industrial stuff". The rotting sign over the seized-up, open front gate read GRAND RANDLAND.

Hannah was middle-aged, give or take a century, and unlike myself appeared to be in excellent physical shape. Her shoulder-length black hair carried a streak of grey, and her intelligent green eyes seemed to be disassembling me in order to see what made me tick. I could have saved her some time: it was a lithium-ion battery.

She had invited me inside, and VV had moved to follow us. "Not you," Hannah had said, without so much as a glance or a break in her stride.

VV had complied with just a roll of her eyes. I observed, however, that she had chosen to await my return beside one of the trailer's open windows.

"I'm sorry," I replied. "You're not ringing any bells."

I looked around the room for a clue as to who this woman was, or who she had once been. There was a pile of what appeared to be film scripts on the desk. "You're a writer?"

"I'm a rewriter," she replied. "I rewrite old movie scripts, to make them more authentic to human nature."

"How so?" I asked, intrigued.

"Well, for example, I rewrote *Terminator 2*. In my version, Arnold Schwarzenegger's android gives up protecting John Connor and spends his time on social media instead, because Judgement Day is years away so really, who cares?"

"I see," I lied, nodding knowingly.

"I also rewrote *Armageddon*. That movie where misfit blue-collar oil drillers are sent into space to destroy a huge asteroid that's on a course to hit the Earth? In my version, Bruce Willis is assassinated on the launch pad by a conspiracy theorist who believes the asteroid is a false flag operation engineered to allow the government to take our guns away."

"Wow," I said. "So, people pay you for this?"

"No," she said, matter-of-factly, and pressed right on. "Right now I'm working on *The Postman*. Did you ever see that? With

Kevin Costner? Probably not, few people did. My version has Costner's post-apocalyptic postman realizing that his mailbag is full of scams, pornography, and penis enlargement ads so he shoots himself in the face."

I nodded, not quite sure how else to respond. "And were you a writer before? Is that how I'd know you?"

"No," she said with a slightly sad smile. "I was a scientist. You and I never actually met in person. But once upon a time I was an avid user of the social media platform you founded. As a consequence of which you may have seen me on the news." With that, she removed her hair, revealing the familiar blue and white carbon fibre of a Kindred Cybernetics neural prosthesis beneath. The unit had replaced most of one parietal bone but was completely undetectable once she replaced the exceptionally realistic wig.

"Ah. I see. That Hannah Carfax," I said grimly.

"None other."

"Right. I remember now. The anti-science conspiracy theories. The scientist witch hunts. The doxxings. The violence. I thought you were dead," I added, idiotically.

She raised her eyebrows.

"I'm so sorry about what happened to you, Hannah. Back then, I—well, I was misguided. I thought free speech was all. Whatever the cost."

Hannah shrugged. "Turned out that the cost was higher for some than it was for others."

I nodded, unsure of what else to say.

"I read that afterwards, you had everything on your platform deleted," she said.

"Much to the chagrin of the shareholders, yes."

"And then you deleted yourself."

"Which caused less chagrin, yes."

"And yet here we are," she said, gesturing in the vague direction of the city. "You often came over as inhuman, back then. And now look at you. You barely are human. Welcome to the future."

I stared out the window, chewing my lip. "You think I'm somehow responsible for this?"

"I think you were one of many unwitting architects of it."

"Is that why you wanted to meet me? To tell me that?"

She shrugged. "I just wanted you to be aware," she said slowly, "that someone remembers."

I nodded. "So you live in a derelict fairground?" I said, breaking another silence with what now felt like pathetic small talk.

"No. I roam. I don't like to stay in one place for too long. It's not safe. But meeting you at a derelict fairground seemed appropriate, somehow. How's the coffee?"

"It smells fantastic, but I can't drink, sadly."

"Oh, I know," she said, and took a sip from her mug. "I just wanted to remind you of what you're missing."

Even though I knew it was impossible, my artificial body suddenly felt very tired.

***

After my unexpected stroll down memory lane with Hannah, I felt like laying low for a while. Maybe I would spend some me time in the fetal position under the bed. I had VV drop me back at the hotel and I settled into my room for a long sulk. I turned on the news; always a day-brightener.

"Kindred Cybernetics held a press conference today to deny that the recent spate of failures in their Adequate line of body upgrades and augmentations was any cause for alarm," the reporter was saying, with a distinct note of cynicism in her tone. "There have now been more than a dozen reports of Kindred systems overheating and even bursting into flame. The spokesperson for Kindred, Arya S. Wolfskillet, stated that there was no need for any refunds or recalls, and any bugs would be rectified with the new firmware update. All users of Adequate systems are advised to install the update as soon as possible, and anyone still experiencing issues after updating should simply turn their legs off and on again."

Right on cue, my forearm communicator beeped with a message informing me that a new update was downloading. A digital progress bar started slowly crawling across the little screen. That reminded me: I had procured a universal recharging cable from VV. I plugged one end into the outlet and attempted to connect the other to my spare battery. It didn't fit. I turned it upside down. It still didn't fit. The universal recharger required a compatible adaptor.

I checked my current battery level. It was at half. I wondered for a moment what would happen if I ran out of juice entirely. Well, I'd be immobilized, obviously. And I wouldn't be able to communicate. And the perfusion device that fed my head would stop working. That would be bad, I'd imagine. It looked like I'd have to leave the comforting isolation of my room after all, and take a walk to a store to find myself an adaptor. I glanced to see how the Kindred update was doing. The little blue bar's progress was barely discernible on the screen. This would have to be an unhurried walk.

***

Down on the street outside the hotel, I headed toward the Kindred Cybernetics retail outlet that we had driven past earlier in the day, and took the opportunity to absorb my surroundings a bit. I watched through the window of a bustling Curmudgeon Coffee store as the uniformed and strapped baristas went about their business, each casually carrying a conspicuous sidearm in a colour-coordinated holster. I strolled past a fast food joint called Cronenburger that was selling some kind of weird, genetically engineered meat products, signs proudly declaring that their freaky fare was now almost entirely sawdust free. Politicians competed for my attention and my vote from animated billboards, grimacing and gesticulating in endless loops as they promoted their chosen conspiracy theories, raged against elites, slandered their rivals or made it rain digital banknotes. I gave a wide berth to the pungent garbage that had accumulated in drifts at frequent intervals along the curb, some of which were being rifled through by homeless families. A dead mime artist lay in the gutter. At least I assumed he was really dead.

I wondered if I would ever get over this feeling of culture shock. I wondered if I was absorbing this world, or if it was absorbing me.

"Plastic freak," someone close by shouted.

It took me a few seconds to realize that this unprovoked pejorative might be directed at me. Plastic freak: that was my identity now. Not millionaire tech entrepreneur. Not philanthropist. Not even amusingly anachronistic but dashing Buck Rogers–type character. Plastic freak.

"Are you addressing me?" responded the woman a few paces ahead of me. She turned her electronic eye on a stocky fellow with extravagant red mutton chops who was drinking with his buddies at the foot of a statue of Adolf Hitler, and I realized with some guilty relief that I wasn't part of this confrontation after all.

"You're the only plastic freak in the vicinity," he shot back, and I shoved my cybernetic hands into my pockets self-consciously. Mutton Chops had stepped out to block the woman's path now, his friends flanking him, beer bottles in hands.

"You're very rude," the woman said, showing no fear on the half of her face that wasn't plastic.

"I'm just telling it like it is. It's called free speech."

"Well, you've exercised your rights. Good for you. Now get out of my way."

"How about *you* get out of *my* way? Humans don't make way for machines. We were here first, and we don't appreciate being spied on by robots." The man unzipped his hoodie to reveal a T-shirt emblazoned with the slogan FUCK KIN-DREAD PSYCHO-ENGINEERING.

"Listen," the woman said with exasperation. "This is a prosthesis. I lost half of my head fighting anarcho-capitalist terrorists. You're welcome. Believe me, I have better things to do than spy on the likes of you."

"Oh, cry me a river," piped up the second man, a tall skinny fellow in a punch-me hat. "Oh wait, you can't, can you."

All three of the crew forced exaggerated laughter.

"You can't stop me going about my business. You're infringing upon my personal freedom," the woman said.

"I can't? Who's going to stop me? Kindred robots have no authority over me."

"Not yet at least. We're still free and self-regulated pure humans," added the skinny one.

"In fact," continued the third man, who was bald and somehow familiar, "you are infringing upon our personal freedom to stand here without being spied on."

The woman seemed to notice something about this man and reached a decision. "Okay. Have it your way," she said, spinning around and walking back the way she had come, which turned out to be from a vehicle parked just metres away. She opened the trunk and delved inside, as her gang of tormentors looked on with amusement.

"That's right, go back to the lab, Frankenstein!"

"Fuck Kindred!"

"Plastic freak!"

After a moment the woman closed the trunk and proceeded to walk calmly back in their direction, with what looked like a small rocket launcher in her hands.

"What the hell?" Mutton Chops exclaimed as the woman pointed the weapon at the group.

Deciding that discretion was the better part of valour, the third man spun around to make his exit and ran right into me. Our eyes met and we recognized each other at the same instance: it was Panzer Man, the road rager I'd last seen plummeting into an abyss on the highway. At this distance I could finally make out his head tattoo: a clenched fist with an anarchy symbol on it.

"I know you!" he snarled accusingly, but I was already moving in the opposite direction. I heard a boom behind me and felt a pressure wave pushing me forwards, almost throwing me off my feet. Someone started screaming, and I felt a strong urge to get the hell out of there. Right on cue a cab pulled up directly in front of me. An elderly couple clambered out and looked around at all hell breaking loose, their expressions indicating that they were already regretting exiting the vehicle. I slipped into the car behind them before they changed their minds. It was a self-driving taxi.

"Hi there! And where are we going today?" it asked chirpily, unconcerned about the chaos that was erupting around it.

I thought for a second, then told it where I wanted to go.

Then I told it twice more, enunciating precisely before it understood my accent and registered my destination.

***

En route, I got a call. It was Magnus.

"There have been some developments regarding your contract with Kindred," he said.

"Oh?"

"VV reported back to them about your meeting with Hannah Carfax. Your conversation with her raised some red flags for them, so they did some research into your background. They are concerned that your problematic history of suppressing free speech will reflect poorly on them."

I couldn't help but laugh out loud at this. Oh, sweet irony. "So what does that mean? They want their body back?" I quipped.

"Yes. They'll be reclaiming the system immediately, I'm afraid. Strictly speaking, I'm not supposed to be divulging this, but, well, I feel responsible, to some degree."

I took a deep breath. "Okay. I appreciate that, Magnus. So, what happens now?"

"VV is on her way to repossess Kindred's property as we speak."

"But she doesn't know my location," I said, then doubt struck. "Does she?"

"She can track your Kindred system."

"Of course she can," I said, and my heart sank. "So what happens to me? What happens to my head? I'm not going back to the facility, Magnus."

"Going back to the facility is not an option," Magnus agreed. "We only cryopreserve dead people. You are clearly alive. Freezing you would be tantamount to murder."

"So what then?"

"Kindred are not monsters. They will probably just remove your cranium and place it in a jar somewhere," he informed me nonchalantly.

"A jar?"

"Yes. A life support jar, obviously."

"Where? For how long?"

Magnus hesitated. "Probably in a warehouse. For an indefinite period."

"Magnus," I said, "I'd rather die. Again."

I ended the call.

***

I had the taxi stop and wait in a parking lot next to an ocean lookout. There was no one else there. I checked my Kindred system; my battery power was down to five percent and my anti-spontaneous-combustion update was at ninety-nine percent. It had been at ninety-nine for some time now. Was it done, and the progress bar hadn't caught up? Was it stalled? Or was it still waiting on that crucial final unit of code?

I got out of the car and walked cautiously over to a bench. I tried to breathe deeply of the fresh coastal air, then remembered I had no lungs to fill. I took a seat and admired the view. The sun was starting to set, and the sky was turning a blood red; the beautiful but unnatural red of aerosol pollution.

The cliff edge was only about twenty metres away, behind a low guard rail. Beyond that, the jagged rocks at the edge of the Pacific, perhaps even that same glacial erratic I had once become so intimately acquainted with. There was movement in my peripheral vision, and turning back to the parking lot I saw a blue and white Kindred Cybernetics vehicle cruise quietly in.

I ducked behind a rocky outcrop and watched. I couldn't see who was at the wheel behind the tinted windshield, but I knew. It was VV. Violet Violence. And she was here for me.

I weighed my options. If I stayed put, my battery would run out of juice, and I'd be brain dead in minutes. Alternatively, VV and Kindred would find me first, and it would be next stop: jar city. If I attempted to traverse the hundred metres or so back to the car, the unpatched Kindred system might turn me into a fireball, and even if VV extinguished the flames in an attempt to save the valuable hardware, I dreaded to think what would be left of the old noggin. Hell, even if I made it, where would I go?

But in the end, I knew I was just procrastinating. I had come to this specific place for a reason. I had tried suicide around here once before, in another lifetime, when I hadn't really even believed in Phoenix, and they had dragged me back and thawed me out into this world that I didn't fit into. I was an anachronism; a human glacial erratic. I wouldn't make that mistake again. This time there would be no contract, and nothing left to freeze. Just a return to oblivion. This time I would be self-fucking-regulated, and I'd be going head first.

I looked from the van to the guard rail, and from the guard rail to the progress bar. Almost there.

Ninety-nine percent.

Zombie Logic

"Zombies," Roland protested, "do not fucking stage dive."

He slouched on the duct-taped sofa in the small apartment's living room, his laptop computer on the adjacent coffee table. The armchair opposite him was occupied by Brandon, Roland's friend and housemate, who had his own computer resting on his crossed legs. Neither young man had seen a shower for at least a couple of days now, personal hygiene having been an early casualty of the lockdown.

Brandon's response amounted to a disinterested grunt.

"Seriously, man. Check this one out," Roland persisted.

Brandon's instant messenger app pinged. He sighed and took a break from browsing his social media to click on the link he had received.

The link led to YouTube, and a cell phone video, apparently taken by an audience member at a rock show, shaky and intermittently obstructed by raised fists and devil horn signs. Some obscure death metal band that Brandon didn't recognize was on stage, an illegible jagged band logo adorning their backdrop, the vocalist prowling back and forth, growling gutturally and unintelligibly into the microphone that he appeared to be devouring.

A few seconds in, a heavily tattooed fan could be seen climbing onto the stage and wandering around dazedly for a moment, completely ignored by the band, before he abruptly decided to bodily throw himself back into the audience with no regard for his well-being or that of the people he landed on. He was promptly swallowed up by the heaving mass of metalheads and disappeared from view. A moment later another two individuals appeared from stage left. This pair of interlopers appeared to have clearer motivation and the first of them fell upon the lead singer, whose grunts turned to panicked cries as the attacker's jaws snapped at his face. Meanwhile, the other uninvited guest suddenly became aware of the existence of the audience and, following in the footsteps of his tattooed predecessor, dived into the sea of undulating bodies, saliva streaming from his jaws. There was a fleeting glimpse of a Gibson Flying V hurtling over the crowd toward the camera before the video cut out.

"I don't know, man," Brandon finally offered, stroking his goatee. "Maybe the undead dig death metal. Who knows?"

"It's just a fact," Roland said, and pushed his glasses up the bridge of his nose as if to emphasize his expertise in undead affairs.

The alleged zombie videos had been accumulating since before the pandemic was officially declared, peaking immediately before the lockdown had been instituted three days ago, and the two housemates had watched most of them, there being little else to do. Almost as soon as any new amateur or professional coverage of the alleged plague was uploaded, the comments below it would flood in as a host of self-appointed debunkers set to work to expose yet another component of the insidious and sprawling zombie hoax conspiracy. The attacks were staged, they said; the witnesses were fools or shills; the scientists and experts were puppets, under the control of masters whose identities varied but whose nefarious motivations always boiled down to the vindictive suppression of freedom.

Brandon fleetingly pondered getting up and doing something else, maybe reading a book or brushing his teeth, before surrendering to the gravitational pull of the website's algorithmic black hole and clicking on the thumbnail of the next recommended video.

This one was dashcam footage from a car cruising slowly down a country lane after dark. An ambulance entered the frame, parked askew at the edge of the road, engine running, headlights on. Moving shadows disrupted the light that shone through the rear windows. The vehicle was rocking. The video had been wittily entitled "If the meat wagon's wobblin', paramedics be gobblin'".

Brandon shook his head and sighed. Just one more, then he was done.

The next video appeared to have been captured by a video doorbell, the convex image showing part of the porch and driveway of a house. A white truck slowed to a halt on the street and sat there idling for a moment before a young woman got out of the passenger side, leaving the car door open as she walked hurriedly toward the camera, all the time looking around her warily. She homed straight into something off-screen, and as she headed back toward the car she could be seen holding a package.

Suddenly the front door of the house across the street was flung open and a middle-aged woman wearing nothing but a large Ultimate Fighting Championship T-shirt barrelled through it and into the street at full tilt. Brandon could almost hear her screams despite the absence of audio. Hot on her bare heels was a wild-eyed, feral-looking gentleman, completely naked save for the fresh blood he was wearing on his chest and chin.

The porch pirate stopped in her tracks and watched with her back to the camera as the UFC enthusiast succeeded in making her escape, her pursuer having been distracted by the substantially easier prey that was stationary and holding a large box. Meanwhile, the getaway driver in the white truck decided that all of this was more than he had signed up for and took off in a hurry, passenger door swinging.

As realization slowly dawned on the porch pirate that she might have a problem, she dropped her prize and ran back toward the house, frantically banging on the door and yelling for help. No one was home, and no help was forthcoming. In a heartbeat the naked man was upon her and her face, wide-eyed with terror, was rammed into the camera, bringing the clip to an abrupt end.

"Fuck that!" Roland declared, and Brandon started, having been unaware that his housemate was lurking over his shoulder. "Did you see that bastard sprint? Real zombies don't run!" Roland continued, clearly personally affronted.

Brandon raised his eyebrows. "Real zombies?"

"You know what I mean," Roland said, defensive. "Authentic zombies."

"Didn't they run in *Dawn of the Dead*?" Brandon said with a disingenuous smirk.

"They ran in the inferior *remake* of *Dawn of the Dead*," Roland shot back, taking the bait. "They definitely did not run in Romero's original *Dawn of the Dead*. As Romero said, zombies do not run. They'd fall apart if they ran. That's just logic."

"And Romero is the authority on zombies? Didn't Professor Romero have his zombies break down doors and literally tear people limb from limb? I'm not sure I follow the zombie logic there."

Roland sighed. "Whatever, dude. The point here is that there's no consistency with these assholes," he said, pointing at the screen. "Some run, some walk, and apparently some stage dive. Not only is it a hoax, it's a sloppy, half-assed hoax. It's an insult to our intelligence. Only an idiot would believe this is a real zombie plague."

Whump!

Something slammed against the door to the apartment, hard enough to make it rattle on its hinges. Roland and his roommate both stared at it, train of thought immediately derailed.

"What the fuck was—"

Whump!

This time the impact was followed by a groan; a deep, animalistic groan that set the hairs on Roland's neck erect.

"Pretend to be out," Roland suggested.

"Shit, the door's not even locked," Brandon blurted at the same time.

Whump!

And then another groan, followed by a single, drawn-out word, ending with a hiss.

"Braiiinssss!"

Roland and Brandon exchanged looks of realization as the door swung open violently and a large, long-haired fellow in a faded Manowar T-shirt staggered over the threshold. He stopped and slowly turned toward the two residents, then sighed with exaggerated disappointment.

"No brains here," said the intruder.

"Lars, you fucker," responded Brandon.

Lars, their upstairs neighbour, laughed loudly. "Wait, did you piss yourselves? Don't tell me you guys believe this corny zombie horseshit."

"Of course we don't," Roland replied. "They move all wrong."

"Yes. We know. It's a hoax." added Brandon.

"It's a fucking disgrace, is what it is. It's an absolute outrage. So, are you guys ready to go?"

"Go where?"

"To the protest! They're cropping up all over the place. There's one downtown at noon. The people are taking the streets back. Fuck the lockdown! It's time to fight back!"

Brandon and Roland shrugged in unison.

"Sure. Why not?"

"Alright! Fight the power! Let's go kick some fake zombie ass!" Lars declared with bravado, and like characters in a Stephen King novel, they would all be dead by midnight.

***

"Well, I don't see any zombies," Roland said. "Do you?"

It was not long before noon on a Saturday, but the streets were deserted as the three men cruised into town in Lar's battered old van.

"I don't see anyone" Lars answered. "It's post-apocalyptic out there. It's like *Twenty-Eight Days Later*."

Roland rolled his eyes. "There were no zombies in *Twenty-Eight Days Later*," he said slowly as if explaining to a child.

Lars threw him a knowing look. "Exactly," he said.

The only other vehicles they encountered were headed to the same destination they were, and they found themselves following a battered truck sporting an array of inspiring bumper stickers: THE SHEEPLE SHALL BE SHORN, THE PARANOID SHALL INHERIT THE EARTH and CATS: TOOLS OF THE DEEP STATE.

"Hardcore," whispered Roland, impressed.

"Here we go," Lars said, pulling up across the street from the park where a couple of hundred or so people had converged. The three men left the vehicle and wandered closer to the milling throng. Several protestors were brandishing placards, and Brandon read a few of the slogans: ZOMBIES ARE A HOAX, SAY NO TO THE UNDEAD AGENDA, THE ONLY REAL ZOMBIES ARE THE MEDIA, and THERE'S ONLY ONE RESURRECTION (JESUS).

"These people are serious," Brandon said quietly to Roland as they stepped around two large fellows wearing tactical vests over their plaid shirts, assault weapons slung across their chests.

"You think the zombies are real?" asked Tactical Vest One, adjusting his tactical helmet.

"Don't care," grunted Tactical Vest Two as he patted his weapon lovingly. "Zombies, liberals, all the same to me."

From atop a car a bald, bearded man with an angry face addressed the crowd through a megaphone. "Welcome, my friends. I'm happy to see that there are still citizens brave enough to defy the tyrants in government and come together to stand up for our rights!"

The crowd applauded in self-congratulation.

"What I don't see," he continued, "is any zombies!"

The crowd booed on cue.

"Nor do I see any werewolves or vampires!"

Roland considered pointing out that the speaker was hardly likely to see any vampires in broad daylight but decided that this wasn't the right audience.

"Why do you think that is?" the speaker asked the crowd.

"Because they don't exist!" the crowd answered obediently.

"Because they don't exist," agreed the speaker. "Zombies only exist in movies. What we do have, is liars. Liars in power who take us for fools. They want us locked down. They want us cowering under our beds like children, afraid of the nasty monsters. Why? So they can have free rein to impose whatever laws they like. So they can take away our freedoms with impunity. First, they take away our right to assemble. Then they'll take away our right to bear arms. Next, who knows? Maybe they'll introduce the metric system!"

The crowd booed and bellowed in outrage at this, though an increasing number were becoming distracted by the roar of a vehicle approaching the scene at some speed. The vehicle skidded around the corner into view, revealing itself to be a police van.

"Oh, here they come now," announced the speaker, "to protect us from the zombies." He spat the last word with heavy sarcasm, and a few members of his audience laughed.

Someone started to chant the word *freedom*, and within a few repetitions the rest of the crowd had picked it up, all eyes on the approaching police vehicle. The van braked abruptly in the middle of the road, jerked forward a few metres, and then barged into the same opinionated truck Lars had followed earlier, prompting a loud expletive from a gentleman somewhere in the thick of the gawking crowd. After a short breather, the van then reversed and bumped onto the curb before finally coming to rest, the engine still running, the hazard lights blinking. The defiant freedom chant quickly petered out, replaced by a bewildered silence as the protestors watched in anticipation.

Something thumped loudly against the back of the van from the inside, and a moment later the rear doors burst open and a blood-drenched cop flew out and onto the pavement as if the van had given birth. The officer staggered to his feet and looked around as if in a daze, squinting to focus through hemorrhaged eyes.

"How can we help you, officer?" the speaker enquired through his megaphone.

The dazed cop turned quickly, looking for the source of the voice. He found the crowd and started limping toward it, as another three police officers appeared from the back of the van, equally bloody and dishevelled.

"What fake fuckery is this?" said the speaker as the ragged cops approached the crowd of protestors, some at a decrepit shuffle but others moving more energetically.

One protestor broke ranks and strode determinedly to meet the oncoming officers. He was wielding a placard that bore the words NO SURRENDER TO LOCKDOWN TYRANNY. "Zombies are a hoax!" he yelled at them. "We will not be oppressed! Freedom! Free—urgh!" He was cut off as the leading cop pounced on him, thrashing and gnashing frenziedly. The placard fell to the ground and the protestors nearby began trying to push their way through the crowd to escape. The other cops had reached the crowd now and started attacking anyone within grabbing range. The protestors scattered, some fell and were trampled, and panic set in.

"Maybe we should head back to the van," Brandon suggested.

"Where the fuck is Lars?" Roland said in response, looking around desperately for Lars, keeper of the van keys.

"Shit," Brandon said, as a cyclone of violence seemed to be moving toward them through the crowd. As the people dispersed he could see figures writhing just metres away. A female officer had attached herself to a disarmed Tactical Vest One, who was staggering around trying to shake her off as if she were a rabid dog, even as she gouged and champed at his flesh.

"Is this real?" Roland asked no one in particular before being shoved aside as Tactical Vest Two strode purposefully toward the skirmish. He aimed his rifle at the couple engaged in their bloody dance and started shooting, the loud reports reverberating around the park and exacerbating the panic. The lady officer and her victim both hit the ground as one, but not for long. Tactical Vest One, now drenched in blood both from the cop's attack and from the bullets, staggered to his feet and looked around with bloodshot eyes through broken wrap-around sunglasses. Tactical Vest Two paused, taken aback at this turn of events, before regaining his composure and raising his weapon again. Too late. His former friend hurtled toward him and sent him flying, his finger still on the trigger, bullets ripping randomly through the crowd.

In Roland's peripheral vision he saw someone fall and turned to see Brandon flailing around on the ground, blood spurting from his thigh.

"Fuck!" Brandon cried as he tried to staunch the flow of blood. "I've been shot. I've been fucking shot, Roland!"

"Oh shit. Brand, we need to get out of here, like now!" Roland said, dragging his friend to his feet and ignoring his pained protestations.

Somewhere in the chaos someone was screaming unintelligible words through a megaphone as the two men careened down an alley. Brandon's arm was around Roland's shoulder as Roland struggled to support his severely limping friend, and they barely made it around the corner and out of view of the street before they crashed to the ground at the rear of a Curmudgeon Coffee store, Brandon crying out in pain as he grabbed his knee and rocked back and forth on his backside, tears rolling down his cheeks.

Panting heavily, Roland started to shush his friend frantically. "Keep it down, man, they'll hear us," he pleaded, then he paused as he noticed movement further along the alleyway. Some thirty metres away, two people were kneeling over a third person, sprawled and lifeless. The pair, a man and a woman, appeared to be enthusiastically devouring their colleague.

"Seriously, shut the fuck up!" Roland urged in a quiet but insistent voice.

"Fuck you man, I'm losing a lot of blood here," Brandon replied at an uncooperatively high volume, before seeing the expression of horror on Roland's face and following his gaze. The feasting female was already looking their way, her lower face smeared with blood but her eyes still ravenous. Roland leapt back to his feet and put his hands under Brandon's armpits, immediately starting to drag him in the opposite direction.

Brandon grunted in pain. "Jesus Roland, wait a second, let me get up will you?"

"Sorry, man, but we've got to move right now. They saw us and I don't know what kind they are."

"What do you mean, what kind they are?" Brandon asked.

"You know, Romero zombies or remake zombies."

As the two men watched, the gore-encrusted woman stood up slowly, followed by her equally blood-drenched friend, and both suddenly broke into a run, sprinting toward the fresh meat.

"Shit! Remake, man. Remake!" screamed Roland, dropping Brandon back to the ground. Brandon screamed in terror, flailing around behind him to grab back onto his roommate, but Roland was already out of reach and running as fast as his unscathed legs would carry him.

"Roland, help me! Help me, you bastard!" Brandon raged as he crawled away from the oncoming living dead, leaving a thick trail of blood from his gaping leg wound.

Roland didn't look back. He sprinted back to the street by way of another alley, slowing at the intersection of the street and peering around the corner cautiously.

The crowd was gone, the cops were gone, but the van was also gone. He cursed Lars quietly through clenched teeth, gripping his head with both hands in frustration as he looked up and down the street, feeling panic clawing its way out of his chest. Then he spotted it. The van was still there. It had moved several metres and was now double-parked, but it was still there. From his vantage point he couldn't see if the vehicle was occupied; he was behind it and the side and rear windows were tinted. He needed to get closer. He took a deep breath and started walking, slowly and vigilantly, making his way toward the van, all the time looking around him for danger. He spotted something lying on the sidewalk ahead of him, and it took him a moment to organize the shape of it in his mind. It was a body. The body of a bald man, a megaphone still grasped in his bite-mark-covered hand. It wasn't moving, but would it? Would it sense his presence and attack? He abruptly veered to his right and onto the road, placing parked cars between himself and the dead rabble-rouser.

As the distance between Roland and the van diminished, he began to circle it cautiously. There was no sign of Lars. That was unfortunate. How likely is it that the keys are in the ignition? he wondered. Then as he came around to the passenger side, he saw the sliding door was wide open.

"Yes," he hissed to himself.

Roland moved to step inside, but Lars was there after all, suddenly blocking the doorway, looking straight at him and his blood spattered clothing.

"Oh, thank fuck, Lars. I was afraid we'd lost you. Oh, don't worry, this isn't my blood. This is Brandon's blood. I'm okay. Not bitten. I'm not bitten. But we've got to get out of here. The zombies are real, Lars. They're fucking real!"

Lars's expression changed suddenly to one of contempt. "Nice try, crisis actor," he spat and slid the door closed with a thud.

"Wait, what? What?", Roland said, confused. He tried to open the door but it wouldn't budge. He grabbed the passenger door handle but that too was locked, and he saw Lars, now in the driver's seat, starting the engine and hitting the gas hard, giving Roland the finger as the van rolled away.

He turned at a moaning sound and saw Brandon approaching. A significant portion of his friend's face was now missing, but on the bright side, his leg didn't appear to be bothering him anymore. This was evident because, as if to add insult to imminent injury, Brandon was running at full tilt toward Roland.

"Asshole," Roland whispered.

One Foot on Fraxxik

"**W**hoa, where did you get these, Sean?" asked Amber Vance, examining the featureless, matte black headphones in her hands. "They're intense. They're like a black hole in the shape of a pair of headphones."

Sean Massey snorted as he pulled on his boots. "Yeah, they look cool, but they don't work, sadly. The previous tenant left them behind. I found a box of 'em on the top shelf of the closet," he jerked his head in the direction of the plain cardboard box now in the corner of the bedroom.

Amber, sitting cross-legged on Sean's bed in just a Motörhead T-shirt, placed the hefty over-ear headphones on her head for size. "Won't the previous tenant want them back?" she asked loudly, unaware of her own volume. "They feel expensive."

Sean shrugged. "It was a guy called Stratton, and he did a runner. The landlord told me all about it when I moved in last week. I think he was sussing me out. My illustrious predecessor disappeared owing several months' rent. Landlord got rid of what little stuff the guy left behind, but I guess he missed the box of cans."

Amber raised her eyebrows. "Weird. So how many pairs do I get?"

Sean Massey looked sheepish as he donned a leather jacket. "Well, firstly, they don't work, and secondly, they're not mine to give away. Technically."

"Such honesty. It's sickening, frankly."

"I know. I should seek help," he said and kissed her. "I'm late for work. Lock up when you leave, and I'll see you Friday."

"You will?" Amber asked. "What for?"

"To give you a good seeing to, of course."

"Oh?" Amber said, "Are you going to get someone in?"

Sean guffawed as he left the apartment.

Amber sighed, flopped back and yawned loudly. Rolling off the bed and onto her feet, she stretched and proceeded to seek out and gather up her clothes. Various old LP records had found their way onto the bedroom floor, and she scanned their sleeves idly. She liked to tease Sean that working at Medical Records—*Life support for lovers of vinyl*—cost him more money than he earned there, even with his employee discount. She was at least vaguely aware of some of these artists: The Penfield Mood Organs, Aversion Therapy Overkill, Die Backpfeifengesichter, and Chekhov's Gun, but the final slab of obscure vintage vinyl was new to her: *The Entrails of the Last Priest* by Skeleton Clock. The sleeve featured the band posing around what appeared to be a huge, monstrous stone head in a jungle, whereas the back exhibited the band in all of their seventies proto-metal glory, with three-quarter-length leather jackets, long frizzy hair and droopy moustaches. She replaced the LP and distractedly inspected some of Sean's other things as she dressed; abstract black and white photos on the wall; a splayed open copy of an Iain Banks novel on the nightstand; an unusual iridescent green ball on the desk. But her token resistance was short-lived, and her eyes drifted casually over to the box in the corner, as she'd always known they would.

***

That evening, back in her modest apartment, Amber dropped the disposable chopsticks into the aluminum container and placed the lot on the coffee table. She relaxed into the couch with her Japanese beer and stared at the TV screen. The popular fantasy show called *The Heft of the Haft* was on, but she wasn't really in the mood for warriors and monsters. It was a different kind of axe she had a hankering for, she thought, and smirked. She muted the show with the remote and went on her own quest to find her cell phone. Locating it on the table by the door, she started the tricky business of choosing the right music to harmonize with her mood. She decided on some classic Dio era Sabbath and was about to send "Neon Knights" to the wifi speakers when she remembered Sean's stealth headphones. "Ooh," she cooed to herself as she rummaged through her backpack on the floor.

She dug out the borrowed headphones and sat in the comfy old armchair to puzzle out how to get the two pieces of technology to talk to each other. She found a row of invisible, low-relief buttons on the edge of one ear cup and pressed the first in line. The button adopted a slowly pulsating turquoise glow, and her phone went abruptly silent.

"Connected," she heard a reassuring female voice announce inside the headphones, and her music magically shifted to the cans.

"Whoa," she said to herself. "Nifty." Eagerly, she placed the headphones on her head.

She found a volume button and cranked up the sounds. The sound quality, in her admittedly non-audiophile reckoning, was excellent. Experimentally, her fingers found the adjacent button. "Bass effect on," the headphones lady declared, immediately followed by "Bass effect off". A press of the next button resulted in a similar declaration that she'd located the noise cancellation feature, and indeed she detected the tell-tale muffling of lower frequencies. She turned it off again and explored the next button.

"Teleportation on," said the headphones lady, and with a whooshing sound Amber found herself in an alien world. A world where shafts of light from an auroral sky infiltrated the lofty canopy to illuminate the majestic forest far below. Where swaths of blue and orange fungi colonized the rot, rocks and roots of the forest floor and clambered up the trunks of the looming white-barked trees. Where something dark and malevolent patrolled the glowing green mists that drifted ponderously between the ghostly old-growth columns.

"What the fuck!" Amber cried as she yanked the headphones off her head and threw them onto the floor; the floor of her familiar living room.

"Teleportation aborted," said the dispassionate voice.

Amber got up from the chair and walked a few steps away before turning around and staring accusingly at the headphones with her arms folded. For their part, the headphones lay on the carpet like a shadow, innocently playing music to themselves. She picked up her phone and paused the music, then suddenly she was hit by a wave of intense nausea. Dropping the phone into the pocket of her hoodie, she dashed over to the coffee table where she promptly returned the Chinese food she'd eaten minutes earlier to its aluminum container. She then took a moment to dispose of the evidence and compose herself, before resuming her accusatory glare at the headphones with even greater intensity. When she'd exhausted this she stepped boldly forward and picked them up again. She examined the buttons on the side, finding her way back to that last evil button with her fingertips. Gingerly, she held the headphones at arm's length and pressed the button. It lit up, and the music cut out, but nothing extraordinary occurred. She placed them back on her head.

"Teleportation on," the voice said, and with a whooshing sound her apartment quickly dissolved into the strange forest again, like a transition in some psychedelic movie.

"What. The. Fuck," she reaffirmed in a hushed tone. She seemed to be alone now; whatever dark presence she had sensed earlier was gone. Perhaps it had just been her imagination, she thought. Perhaps all of this was imaginary, in fact. She took a deep breath. The air was breathable. Fresh air, at that, not the sweet-and-sour-pork-infused air of her apartment. The air temperature was warm, at least in the high twenties Celsius, she estimated. She placed her palm against the ghostly white bark of one of the looming old-growth trees that surrounded her. It felt coarse, firm but with a slight yield, and warm from the sun. She took a few tentative steps forward. There was a slight spring to her step on the moss-covered surface but the ground felt solid. It felt real. She listened. She could hear the rustling of the leaves in the trees, and the faint crunch of fallen leaves beneath her feet as she walked. If this was a hallucination or some kind of virtual reality it was so vivid, so authentic-seeming as to be indistinguishable from the real thing.

She wished she had brought her phone so she could record her surroundings and then remembered that she had dropped it in her pocket. She felt its bulk and paused as she withdrew it only to find it was completely dead, though she knew the battery had been at least fifty percent charged before she had left the apartment. She returned it to her pocket with a sigh and resumed walking.

She looked upward as she walked, at the trees towering above her, all of them over eighty metres in height, she estimated, and five or six metres in trunk diameter. The densely packed, thick branches clustered together in the higher reaches like inverted root systems stretching for the clouds, giving an impression of a giant's umbrella that had been blown inside out by a hurricane fit to level mountains. For a moment she imagined what vast fruit might plummet from the darkness between those high boughs and pulverize her head, and she shuddered.

Looking around, the woods stretched as far as she could see. There was no sign of any civilization or animals, just the majestic ghost trees with their thick, searching roots partially exposed in the ground, patches of brightly coloured fungi clinging on here and there. Something else on the ground caught her eye: something nestled amongst the leaves. She crouched down and picked it up for a closer inspection. It was a spherical rock, about the size of a tennis ball, its iridescent green surface shimmering when the sun caught it. Looking around the immediate vicinity, she spotted several similar specimens strewn around randomly. The rock was familiar somehow.

There was a roaring from high above and she stared upward, trying to locate the source of the sound through the dense forest canopy. Dropping the rock, she slipped the headphones off to better locate the sound's origin, only to immediately be overwhelmed by another wave of nausea and dizziness, and she hastily reseated the headphones as they were. Removing them while they were activated—whatever activated meant—was hazardous, she started to realize, like yanking out a USB cable from her laptop without ejecting the device first. One risked corrupting the software, and in this case, she postulated, she was the software, and she was corrupt enough already, thanks.

Resuming her search for the source of the reverberating rumble, she thought she caught a fleeting glimpse of something between the silhouetted foliage; some sort of dark object moving through the shimmering sky, something mechanical, and although the view was too brief for her to work out exactly what she was looking at, she was spooked now. Someone or something else must reside in this place, and she hadn't been invited. What if the headphones stopped working? What if she were trapped in this alien world? She felt panic rising in herself, and before she knew what she was doing, her fingers found the button, and whoosh, she was home.

***

Amber's excitement was stalled by the disappointing sound of Sean's voicemail greeting. She paced as she grudgingly left her message.

"Sean. Why didn't you tell me about the headphones? I know you've been to that place. I saw the weird green rocks, like the one in your bedroom. Call me."

She hung up, then stood staring at the phone—which, oddly, had revived on her return—and immediately started second-guessing herself. That had really happened, right? She'd really, literally been teleported—yes, teleported, she committed to that word—to another place. Another planet? Another dimension? What did that even mean, though? What was "another dimension"? She saw them a lot in Star Trek and Red Dwarf but she wasn't sure those depictions were scientifically accurate.

She needed evidence.

She navigated to the camera on her phone and set it to record video, carefully propping it up against the beer bottle on the coffee table with the lens pointing toward the armchair. Then she sat back down, put the headphones back on her head, took a deep breath, and hit the magic button.

Back in the white woods again, she crouched down and collected one of the pretty round rocks from its bed of dead leaves. She looked down at the object in her palm, gripped it tightly, then with one last 360-degree look around her, she pressed the button again.

"Teleportation off."

She found herself sitting in the armchair, still gripping the rock, her knuckles white with tension. She'd brought it back. Physical proof that this wasn't some deranged hallucination. She breathed a sigh of relief. Now to check the recording. She grabbed the phone, knocking over the empty beer bottle in the process but ignoring it as it rolled onto the floor. She stopped the recording, then played it back.

The video showed Amber stepping back from the camera, sitting in the armchair and placing the headphones on her head. She watched herself take a deep breath and press the button. Blue light danced across the headband between the two sides of the headphones for a second, and then, poof, she was gone.

"'Holy shit," Amber whispered.

The camera had continued to record an empty chair for a couple of minutes and Amber watched every second of it, anticipating her own return, and rolling her new rock between her fingers. She became conscious of her anxiety and tried to shake it off. After all, it wasn't as if she didn't know how this movie ended. She saw the cushions of the chair form a slight indentation as if occupied by an invisible person and then watched her past self materialize on the screen to perfectly fill the space. The Amber in the video was clutching her shiny round rock like a prize.

The phone rang. Startled, she involuntarily let out a short scream, then immediately felt stupid for overreacting. The screen informed her that one Sean Massey was calling. She took a beat to compose herself before answering the video call.

"Hey," she said.

"You need to return the headphones, Amber," Sean said tersely, his most serious facial expression filling her screen.

"What are they, Sean?"

"They're headphones, Amber," he responded with the briefest of hesitations.

"Uh-huh. They're not just ordinary headphones, though, are they? I know you know what I'm talking about, Sean. That place?"

Several seconds passed before Sean spoke again. "You need to return them, Amber," he said again. "That place isn't safe."

"Okay, but what is it? And why didn't you tell me about it?"

"I didn't tell you because you'd have either thought I was insane, or you'd have believed me and insisted on seeing for yourself. But it's not safe."

"Is it a parallel universe or something?"

"I don't know. What does that even mean? I'm yet to encounter my evil doppelgänger with a goatee, so I'm not even sure if parallel universes are a real thing. Maybe it's another planet? I'm not sure if that's more rational or less. I really don't know."

"How many times have you been there?" she asked.

Another pause. "A few times."

"Shit, Sean. If it's so dangerous why do you keep going back?" she demanded.

"I don't know. Because it's wild. You've seen it. You know. The whole place is like the cover of some seventies prog rock album. Like Roger Dean shit. I saw a ruin there, the head of some ancient god or something, and it's exactly like the one on an old album sleeve by a band called Skeleton Clock."

"How is that possible, Sean? Were the band aliens or something? David Bowie, I could believe, but Skeleton Clock?"

"I don't know, Amber. How is any of this possible? It's all insane. Maybe we're both insane. Maybe it's mass hallucination. Anyway, I'm not going back there again. I've seen objects in the sky there. I've heard distant explosions. There's something not right there, Amber. I'll destroy the whole box of headphones, or I'll sell them to a mad scientist on eBay or something. Whatever. Bring the pair you have back, okay?"

"Okay. Okay. I'll return them tomorrow, okay? I won't use them again. Not to visit Headphones World. Not even to listen to Skeleton fuckin' Clock. Happy?"

***

The next day she returned to Headphones World. One last time, she had said to herself. She would return the headphones to Sean, for sure, but first, one last visit to the white woods. When else would she have an opportunity like this? To experience something that was quite literally, possibly, magical? Something that was certainly literally awesome. She had had awesome experiences before, of course. Sex could be awesome when done correctly. Iceland had blown her mind when she had visited it back in her student days. The hairs on the back of her neck still stood up when she listened to Iron Maiden's "Phantom of the Opera". But this was something else. This was awesome in the all-but-lost, undiluted definition of the word. And she needed to get one last hit of that unique awe whilst she could.

But this time, the awe she experienced inclined more toward the Old Testament dread variety.

When she arrived, the view before her was different. For a moment she thought she must have arrived in the night, for her view was of nothing but darkness. It made sense, she thought—as much as any of this made sense, anyway—that this place might be in a different time zone, possibly even orbiting a different star. Then, looking at the sky, she realized it was day here after all, but she was in a deep hole. A crater. Quickly, she scrambled up the black dirt of the slope before her, but even back at ground level it was clear that this world had been transformed almost beyond all recognition.

Directly in front of her one of the mighty white trees was on fire. Orange flames licked and danced their way higher up the trunk, blackening the bark and carbonizing the wood in their wake. Beyond the burning tree were dozens more that had already been devoured by combustion, now only fractured charcoal husks surrounded by dismembered and fallen limbs, charred and smoking. The ground was soot-black and sticky with tar, and the air was thick with the pungent, choking smell of smoke.

The death of the trees had birthed a new landscape and exposed a new vista, allowing Amber to see further than before, and a large boulder in the distance caught her eye. It appeared to have been carved. Intrigued, she made her way closer to the rock, and as she did so she realized that this was no boulder; this was a sculpture. A massive stone head laying on its side. But the face of this slain giant was not a human one; it was the fur-covered face of some fearsome animal, a short ridge or mohawk atop its head, furious eyes deep-set above its short but deep muzzle, its mouth open in a roar or warcry, displaying fangs the length of her forearm. She wondered if the head had once been attached to a body, in which case the original statue could have gone head-to-head with Christ the Redeemer, and she knew which of those her money would be on. Judging by the tree roots that had crept across its face, this brute had lain here for decades or longer, glaring furiously at the suffocating forest as it was reclaimed by nature.

Amber recalled the sleeve of Sean's Skeleton Clock LP.

She was about to walk around to inspect the other side of the ruin when she was distracted by a sound that she had not expected to hear in this place. A woman screamed. Amber spun in the direction of the sound and, shielding her eyes from the sun, scanned the blasted forest for its origin.

From this vantage point she could see the edge of the forest, and beyond it, a building. The building seemed to belong there, as if it had been sculpted from rock by the wind over thousands of years, all smooth surfaces and gentle organic curves. With some trepidation she approached it, her curiosity overriding her caution, and it soon became clear that this was no simple caveman's domicile. The undulating, sand-coloured walls supported multiple tall windows of some kind of high-tech glass material, opaque from the exterior but slowly shifting between pearlescent colours. In a few places the smooth walls gradually flowed into patterns of hexagonal tiles—perhaps vents or solar panels, she speculated—that could have been formed by naturally occurring fissures if not for their borders channelling streaking pulses of blue and red light.

There was a human body sprawled on the ground not far from the building's doorway. Amber stood for a moment, a few metres away, partly in shock, partly to watch for breathing or other movement, but also fascinated by the presence of another person here, albeit a dead one. He was in a prone position, with his head turned to one side so that Amber could tell that this was a young man, eyes open but unseeing, an expression of confusion frozen on his face. There was a charred circular hole between the man's shoulder blades as if he had been shot in the back as he ran for the woods. The hole was still smoking.

Amber touched her headphones, reassuring herself that she hadn't somehow lost them and that she still could, if required, hit that button and be home in the blink of an eye. Taking a thorough look around her, she ventured further toward the building. The circular doorway appeared to be missing a door, and as she leaned forward to peek inside, her head was filled with the smells of burning and copper.

There was another dead person inside the house. An older woman lay on her back in the entrance chamber, at the end of a trail of blood that marked the path she had crawled in an attempt to escape whatever horror had befallen this place. She had succumbed to the partial evisceration she had suffered just a short distance from her goal. Amber followed the trail of gore back into the adjacent room, where it ended in a slick of blood in the centre of a minimalist white space. Red footprints, both human scale and much larger, led in and out of the grisly pool. A chair against the wall was occupied by a man who had no head above his jaw, an abstract painting in blood spatter stretching up the wall behind him. A human forearm lay still twitching in the corner as if trying to attract the attention of the absentminded owner that had mislaid it. Another person was kneeling by a vast, smashed wall-mounted screen, their gender indiscernible through the blood that still flowed from three deep gouges across their face, the one unruined eye wide open and turning to look at Amber.

And amidst all this horror, this carnage, literally the last man standing, was Sean Massey.

Sean didn't look well. His hands were clamped over the cups of his headphones as if he were trying to wrench them off but they were somehow screwed to his skull. He was writhing with the effort and didn't appear to notice Amber's arrival at this macabre scene. His presence seemed unstable, somehow, his entire body fading in and out erratically as if it were shifting through a spectrum of corporeality.

"Sean?" she prompted in a faltering voice. She didn't know what one is expected to say in the middle of a surreal bloodbath so asked the most basic question on her mind. "What's happening?"

Sean's eyes met hers for one second before his gaze slid to something over her shoulder. "Amber, run," he said.

Amber once again sensed the malevolent presence from that first time in the forest, and with a dream-like compulsion, she turned to finally confront it.

The thing that loomed behind her resembled a rearing bear, but no ordinary bear. This was a mutant militia grizzly bear, towering over her, wearing something that back in the real world (which felt very far away right now) might be called a tactical vest, stuffed with unfamiliar electronic devices and various metallic toothed and curved blades. A stumpy black and red striped rifle-like weapon was strapped to its thigh. It wore a full-face reflective mask, above which Amber could see a blue mohawk protruding. The creature's arms were disproportionately long, muscular and covered with blue-grey fur, and at the end of each one were gloved hands big enough to pulverize a human head, the thick fingers tipped with large claws, glistening with fresh blood.

Amber found that the skill of moving her limbs had temporarily abandoned her and she stood paralyzed before the beast, staring at her reflection in the mirror that obscured its face, and in her peripheral vision she became aware of its long arm arcing backwards as if readying a blow that she felt sure would remove her head from her shoulders, and she wondered if she would remain seeing even as she was decapitated.

"Please recharge headphones," a familiar voice said from very far away, and everything vanished.

***

Amber smiled what she hoped was a neighbourly smile at the old gentleman exiting Sean's apartment building as she slipped past him and into the lobby before the heavy door closed on her. It had been hours now, and Sean still wasn't responding to her messages or to her persistent leaning on his buzzer, and her patience had run out; she needed to know that he had made it home in one piece. She rode the elevator and arrived at his apartment, rapping relentlessly on his door for a full half minute before she decided to try the handle. It was unlocked.

"Sean?" she yelled. When no answer came, she did a quick sweep of all of the rooms, ending with the bathroom. Sean wasn't home.

"Well, shit," she said to herself, and wandered into the bedroom. There, on Sean's nightstand, was his cell phone. It came alive when she lifted it, displaying multiple notifications of messages and missed calls, all from her.

Somewhere far away, someone said her name.

"Amber?"

The hairs on the back of Amber's neck rose, and she was suddenly more aware of her heartbeat. "Hello?" she said to the empty room. Again she ran around the apartment, checking the rooms, this time throwing open closets and looking behind open doors, but she was still alone. As she returned to the bedroom, she heard it again.

"Amber, help me."

"Sean? Where are you?" she asked desperately.

Leaning down, feeling slightly ridiculous, she looked under the bed, discovering nothing but some discarded socks, but as she straightened she saw movement on the bed; a depression was forming in the mattress, as if from an invisible weight, and then there, translucent and unstable, sat Sean. He still wore his headphones, and he still wore the look of panic that she had seen on him in the massacre house.

"Sean! What's happening? Come back!"

When Sean spoke his voice faded in and out with the solidity of his body, like a radio signal being tuned in.

"I can't. The headphones are broken. That thing in the house
..." Sean's voice faded to inaudibility.

"Sean? The thing in the house, what was that?"

"That thing in the house," he said again, fading back in. "It
whacked me pretty good. I got away, but, the headphones are
on the fritz."

"Okay. How do we get you back?" Amber asked.

Sean stared at her for a moment before shrugging slightly and
shaking his head hopelessly. "I don't know," he said, but then
looked thoughtful. "Unless ..." he started, but his voice quickly
faded away again along with the rest of him, the mattress quickly
regaining its former shape.

"Sean?" she screamed at the empty space. "Sean! Unless what?
Sean come back here!"

Amber spent the next few hours pacing and fretting in the
bedroom but Sean declined to make another appearance. She
considered sleeping there, just waiting for him to return, but
that seemed so pathetically passive, and even if he did come back,
then what? She couldn't help him, at least not from this end.
Not from this end, she realized, and suddenly she had a plan.

***

When Amber awoke in her own bed late the next morning, she
was somewhat surprised that she had managed to sleep at all.
After all, Sean was still lost somewhere on an alien world—or
at least part of him was. But at least she was doing something
constructive now. She had made another jaunt after leaving

Sean's apartment and would make more if she had to, though the memory of that heavily-armed monster still filled her with dread.

She reached for her phone and checked for messages. Nothing. She sighed and called Sean's number, pessimistically anticipating his frustrating voicemail message, though she had placed Sean's cell on charge by his bed last night, just in case.

Someone picked up after a single ring.

Her heart leapt, and she held her breath, listening intently to the silence on the other end of the line. After five seconds her patience ran out.

"Sean?" she said.

Several more seconds elapsed before she heard the voice. It did not belong to Sean.

"Sean's not able to come to the phone right now," said the deep voice, slowly. "In fact, he's not able to come to this planet."

"Who is this?" Amber demanded.

"We need to talk, Amber. Face to face."

Amber thought quickly. Whoever this stranger might be, he knew who she was and seemed to know something about Sean and the headphones. Despite her apprehension, it was almost a relief that another person might not only share this knowledge but might even know what the hell was going on.

"Okay. When?" she asked.

"Right now. I'm waiting in your living room."

***

Amber stood with her arms folded, shifting her weight from one foot to the other as she regarded the uninvited stranger in her apartment. The man was sitting on an office chair that he had pulled out from her desk. Even when seated she could tell he was a tall man. He was bald, exposing the scar that ran down the left side of his scalp to his ear, which was missing cartilage from the helix. He had dark circles beneath his bloodshot eyes, and at least a couple of days of salt-and-pepper beard growth on his face. He wore a crumpled grey suit and scuffed black boots. An incongruously bright turquoise holdall sat on the floor by his feet. Amber recognized it as belonging to Sean.

She tried to decide what to say, as a disorderly queue of questions formed in her mind: Who are you? How did you get in? Where is Sean? Though she knew that this last was just a pusillanimous way of asking if Sean was still alive.

But then the decision became moot, as the stranger spoke first.

"I believe you have something that belongs to me," he said quietly.

"I don't know what you're talking about," she responded. "Like what? Who are you, anyway?"

"Stratton," he said, and stared up and to his left as if trying to recollect. "Edward. Edward Stratton."

"The man who used to live in Sean's apartment?"

"The very same. Three months—or was it five? It's not important. Some time ago, I went away. On business. Due to unforeseen circumstances, my return was delayed. Imagine my surprise when I finally came back and found someone else living in my place. All of my stuff, gone. Almost all of my stuff, anyway.

The only thing I cared about—a box of headphones I'd hidden for safekeeping—was somehow still there. A miracle. Alas, I was soon to be disillusioned. You see, when I had left the apartment, the box had contained nine pairs of headphones. Now, there were only six units. I know your friend Sean had one pair. So, by my calculations, that leaves two pairs unaccounted for. Now, judging by your messages, you appear to have been close to Sean. So I thought you might be kind enough to help me find my property."

Amber shrugged and shook her head, the corners of her mouth turned down, but she tensed as she watched this Stratton character reach inside his jacket and withdraw a folded knife. He held Amber's eyes as he proceeded to unfold the blade from the handle, then from somewhere he produced the iridescent rock that she had delivered from Headphones World, the souvenir that had slipped her mind until now. Suddenly Stratton thrust the steel of the knife into the heart of the rock, and the rock started to bleed, a thick green liquid oozing from the incision.

Amber watched with a combination of dread and disgust as Stratton held the rock—or the nut, or the egg, or whatever it was—over his mouth and drank from it eagerly.

Amber bit her bottom lip and considered her options. She could withhold her headphones until he helped her—until he helped Sean—or at least until he had shed some light on this whole situation, but she was finding his intimidation tactics more effective than she would like to admit, and she wasn't keen on the idea of calling his bluff. Besides, she had another card to play if necessary. She retrieved her headphones from beneath the armchair and placed them on the desk next to Stratton.

"There. Your precious headphones," she said, and pointed to them. "What are they, anyway? Really?"

Stratton folded the knife and stowed it away, staring at her for several seconds, as if deciding whether she was deserving of the knowledge. Having reached a decision, he shrugged.

"They are a kind of doorway. They create a shortcut in space and project the wearer through it. As soon as they are deactivated the universe notices that you aren't where it left you and drags you right back to where you belong. They're useful for brief excursions, but the technology is not designed for prolonged use," said Stratton, idly studying Amber's headphones. He seemed to weigh his next words carefully. "The effect is like that of a drug," he continued reflectively. "Only the trip you experience is physical as well as psychological. Like any drug, when the high wears off you return to reality, and like any drug, too much of it can be detrimental to one's health."

Stratton fell silent again, staring in Amber's direction, but not at Amber. She had heard the phrase "thousand-yard stare" before but had never really understood what one was until now.

"What is that place?" she said, compelled to break the silence. "That world, on the other side of the doorway?"

"Fraxxik. That place is called Fraxxik. It's my home."

"You're not from Earth?"

"I am not, but I was stationed here. The Frax have been living amongst humans for centuries," Stratton said. "Observing. Studying. Primarily in the context of cautionary anti-patterns."

"So, did you guys build the pyramids or something?" Amber asked, unsure herself whether she was being sarcastic.

"That would have been the Egyptians," Stratton replied, not attempting to hide his condescension.

"When I went there, to Fraxxik, was there a war, or something? There was this creature—"

"Fraxxik has been invaded by a race we call the Crusaders. Long ago they enslaved the Frax. It took years to overthrow them, and now they have returned. They aim to impose their self-aggrandizing religion on all civilizations they encounter, and they do not like to be defied. That was the cause of my prolonged absence from Earth. I was helping my people fight back. But it was futile. And I had already been wearing the headphones for far too long."

Stratton paused and pressed the heel of his hand against his left temple and clenched his jaw. "But, we digress," he said through clenched teeth. "Have to stay focussed, Stratton. Stay on task."

Amber watched him with increasing apprehensiveness. He ran his hands over his face and took a deep breath.

"There is still one pair of headphones unaccounted for. So tell me, Amber Vance. Where is the skeleton clock place?"

Amber caught herself even as she drew in breath to say "Don't you know?" Perhaps these Frax people were so multitudinous as to be unaware of one another's existence, or perhaps Stratton's brain was too frazzled to make the required connections, but he was clearly unaware of the significance of Skeleton Clock. Amber knew exactly what Stratton was alluding to; it was the message she had scrawled on Sean's bedroom wall in huge letters, the message she hoped he couldn't miss if and when he next tried to corporealize there again. The message telling him where to find the headphones that would replace his defective set and bring him home.

GO TO SKELETON CLOCK PLACE FOR HEADPHONES

"I don't know what that is," she said, and tried to quickly change the subject to cover her lie. "Where is Sean now? How is he?"

"Well, how was he when you saw him last?"

"When I saw him last he seemed to be trapped in some kind of limbo. That Crusader thing had damaged his headphones. He couldn't get home. Is he still there? Can you free him?"

"Oh, I already have freed him," Stratton said, and slowly unzipped the turquoise hold-all. From within he withdrew another pair of headphones, with Sean's head still suspended between them.

Amber's hands flew to her mouth and her eyes widened. "What the fuck," Amber declared. "You murdered him. You murdered Sean."

Stratton wobbled his head slightly from side to side, considering. "Technically, perhaps you're right. But he was as good as dead already. Or worse. The fact is, there was no coming back from the state he was in. He was dead the moment the headphones were damaged. His signal was corrupted. The only way out of it was to shut him down."

"So you cut off his head?" Amber asked, incredulously.

"Well, funny thing, I couldn't get the headphones off his head." He shook the severed head around by the headphones a bit in demonstration, much to Amber's horror. "They're fused to his skull, somehow. Curious. But, regardless of their condition, I needed to retrieve them. I could not risk them falling into the hands of the Crusaders, you see. Which brings me back to my question. Where is the final pair, Amber Vance?"

Before Amber could respond—she might as well tell him the truth, what did it matter now?—she heard a deep rumble, slowly increasing in volume, like an oncoming earthquake.

Stratton heard it too and rose slowly from his seat. "Something is coming through," he said.

Amber felt that feeling of dread that had threatened to suffocate her in the massacre house rising rapidly in her chest. The armchair she had sat in when she had last jaunted groaned and creaked as if under pressure, and with a crescendo of fabric splitting and wood splintering it collapsed in a cloud of dust. The ceiling above the chair cracked and plaster dust rained down. Amber's hair blew back as air rushed away from the focus of the chaos, where something large started to fade into existence.

Something that was roaring with self-righteous fury.

"What did you do, Amber Vance?" Stratton yelled over the cacophony. "What did you *do*?"

What Fresh Hell

Hello and welcome to *What Fresh Hell*. My name, as I'm sure you are aware, is Keith Glover, and I'm thrilled to finally have the opportunity to provide commentary for what I think it is fair to say is my most famous, or perhaps I should say my most infamous, film. This has been a long time coming. *What Fresh Hell* has been underground, as it were, for many years now, having been banned or, perhaps even worse, ignored by the mainstream film establishment almost since its original release. However, anyone can now experience my transgressive little picture at their leisure, thanks to the cult following that has accumulated around it over the years, and to the ubiquity of the internet, where apparently anything goes these days.

The idea for *What Fresh Hell* actually came to me in a dream. Now, I am aware that some people believe that story to be apocryphal, but it is true nonetheless. I was in Eastern Europe at the time, shooting *Sapphic Fiends from the Abyss*, AKA *Lesbitten Lust*, the first one that is, when I contracted a dreadful fever and ended up having this extremely macabre nightmare. It was this fever dream that became the central premise of my movie. Oscar, a poor baker, makes a Faustian pact with the Devil: in return for becoming a sublime pastry chef, and thereby making his fortune, he has to murder the last customer of the day on every anniversary of the pact. This all goes smoothly for a while, but then he finds himself falling in love with Alice, the daughter of one of his victims. To cut a long story short, Satan arranges for Oscar's beloved Alice to be the next one on the old chopping block, but the baker rebels and so has to face the music with Old Nick. So there it was. The whole movie basically, encapsulated in my dream. Granted, we later decided to give Alice, the love interest, psychokinetic powers, but that was chiefly because Stephen King was huge at the time, and he puts psychic powers every-bloody-where.

I can't recall to whom we credited the final script, but it's inconsequential, really. I provided the rough-hewn monolith of creativity, then we simply collected one random screenwriter after another from the pile, reloaded the inspiration trebuchet and launched them at it, gradually liberating the perfect screenplay within.

But that came somewhat later. First, I needed money. It's never easy, raising the funds to finance a picture, especially when one has a reputation for making challenging and provocative films like my own. My previous picture, *Sapphic Fiends from the Abyss*, had gone considerably over budget and hadn't gone down well with the critics or with audiences. It was obviously ahead of its time, but unfortunately the studios didn't see it that way, on account of them being run by a shower of witless cunts.

Then one day there I was, sweating like a monk in a brothel at my favourite Turkish baths in Soho, when I got chatting with the chap next to me. Turned out his name was Powell, and he was a rather wealthy retired Professor of Adversarial Theology at Sodom University, or something equally arcane. Being in that oven-like hammam had reminded him of a strange dream he'd recently had, he said, about a baker making Satanic pies. Well, as you can imagine, that struck me as quite the coincidence, so naturally I gave him the old pitch, not really thinking it would lead to anything, and the words were barely out of my mouth when he offered to fund the entire project out of his own pocket. Just like that. He didn't even want to see the treatment I'd put together. He was the George Harrison to my Brian, so to speak, and that was that. *What Fresh Hell* had a green light.

***

Lovely pie shot here. Our Director of Photography was none other than Arthur Hazard BSC, or Hap Hazard to his friends. He was my right-hand man on most of my pictures, and no one could shoot a pie like Hap. His First Assistant Camera on this shoot was a young chap by the name of Karl Robertson. Nice lad, always seemed thrilled to be there. Then on one of the bakery scenes, one of the big Arri 2K Blonde lights fell on his head. The health and safety brigade would be up in arms these days, but the fact is that these things happen on film shoots all the time, you see. Could have been very nasty, but at the end of the day he walked away with a concussion and an anecdote and quipped about feeling *a little lightheaded* for the next week. We all had a good laugh about that. Karl laughed a bit too much, in fact, and eventually he had to be escorted off the set after complaints from the sound engineer. Hap was very distressed by it all. He had to promote the Second Assistant Camera to First, of course, a chap we all called Stumpy Joe. I'm not familiar with the backstory of that nickname, but it did turn out to be tragically prescient, as it happens.

***

Ah, the car chase scene. Very exciting. It was during this scene, when Oscar attempts to drive his latest victim off the road, that we originally had the bus stunt, where he accidentally causes a passing bus to bounce off the crash barrier before skidding to a stop. Now I know what you're thinking: I don't remember any spectacular bus crash in this scene. And you would be correct. You see, unfortunately our bus bounced rather higher than we had bargained for, especially considering we had installed a few extras in it at the last minute for dramatic effect, and some of these extras—sorry, background actors, I should say these days—sustained some injuries, some of which were reportedly *life changing*, which I later discovered was meant in a negative sense. There may also have been a fatality or two. So anyway, disappointing though it was, the whole bus stunt was left on the cutting room floor, out of respect for the maimed and deceased. That, and because we were under threat of legal action from the families.

***

We shot this dream sequence in Death Valley, where Georgie shot *Star Wars*. I wanted the landscape to reflect the solitude and isolation that Oscar felt, as well as an infernal heat. So we had Jason Pressler, a fine young actor, stumble around the desert, haunted by the reanimated corpses of his unfortunate victims. It was throughout the shooting of this scene that our sound engineer, a fellow called John Carpenter, no relation to the other one, kept complaining that he could hear a faint, indistinct whispering on the microphone. He aborted several takes, in fact, declaring the sound unusable due to this interference, or whatever it was. Eventually we shot a lot of it MOS, without location sound, as we were losing the light. Sadly, we lost John at this time. That is we literally lost him. When we were packing away the gear he was nowhere to be found. He was last seen wandering into the desert with his microphone, apparently trying to home in on the source of this phantom voice. All we found of him was his Nagra, which was still rolling, and his headphones, hanging on a cactus. There was no whispering on the tapes that we could hear, but there was a distant screaming. It was all very odd.

***

The old trombone shot, or dolly zoom. We wanted something special for the moment when Oscar realizes that his next victim has to be Alice, the love of his life, and this was Hap's idea. The shot was made famous by Stevie with *Jaws*, of course, but as usual Hitch did it first in *Vertigo*. It's a tricky effect to get right, you have to dolly in whilst zooming out, keeping the subject in focus the whole time. Hap was on camera, of course, and his new First Assistant Camera chap, Stumpy Joe, was pulling focus. Unfortunately, Joe got distracted. He later insisted that someone whispered his name in his ear, but Hap said that was impossible in the circumstances. Anyway, whatever the reason, Joe got distracted and fell off the dolly and onto the track. He tried to roll out of the way but didn't quite manage it, and the dolly wheel took his right hand clean off. It was a right mess I can tell you. Hap was very unhappy, as you can imagine. You can hardly pull focus left-handed. We got the shot though.

***

Ah, the hounds of Hell scene, where our hero discovers that Satan is not one to be trifled with when it comes to contract law. Oscar broke the pact, and so must face the infernal pack. The score is a huge part of this scene, of course, it really ties every-thing together nicely. Initially we had asked Pink Floyd to do the music, but they never returned our calls, so in the end we got our second choice, the psychedelic rock band called the Penfield Mood Organs, from Yorkshire. They did a great job, and are to this day scandalously underrated. Tragically, the entire band was killed in a private jet crash whilst on tour shortly after they completed recording. Their VW bus had broken down on the side of the M62 motorway when a private jet fell on them. The pilot had had a heart attack or something, and the band was just in the wrong place at the wrong time. Such a waste.

The Hell hounds themselves were created by our resident special effects genius Ron Buffer. Of course, this was long before all of the newfangled CGI effects they have these days, which, let's be honest, are shit. Why must every monster in modern movies bounce off walls? I don't understand it. Anyway, our monsters were all created using practical effects, all in-camera. We had three hounds, and various combinations of animatronics and fellows in suits, including Ron himself. Then there were the full-size models that Alice explodes with her psychic powers. We packed them with real animal entrails to get that genuine visceral experience, but one of them had these remote control eyes so that you see the pupils dilate just before the explosion. Lovely idea, I thought, but when the dog was detonated one of its eyes was launched out of its skull and into Ron's throat. The script girl tried to give him the Heimlich manoeuvre but it was too late, he choked to death on the eyeball. Gruesomely, the eyeball was still moving when we looked in his mouth. It was quite eerie. Gave me the willies, anyway.

There's lots of talk these days about cursed movies. Whether it's Tobe's little *Poltergeist* movie, or *The Crow*, or *The Twilight Zone*; it's always the same old story. You lose an actor or two in some completely freak accident, that no one could possibly have anticipated, and suddenly all the armchair critics, who understand nothing about cinema, come crawling out of the woodwork, jabbering about curses and jinxes and legal liability. What these philistines fail to understand is that film, is, art, and art demands sacrifice. As Mr. Powell was always saying: sacrifice, sacrifice, sacrifice. Van Gogh cut off an ear, Poe went mad, Mozart got himself murdered, and now and again someone snuffs it on one of my pictures. It is the nature of the beast; the beast we call art. Frankly, if you get through the production of a motion picture of any significance without at least a maiming or two, well, you won't be seeing my money at the box office, I can tell you that.

Yes, *What Fresh Hell* suffered an unusually high casualty rate, certainly more than any other picture I've made, and I include *Sapphic Fiends* in that, and we had to throw around a few hush rubles in Eastern Europe, I can tell you. Cinematic collateral damage, I call it. I'm actually proud of our safety record on this picture. I know that may shock some people, but I'm proud because I believe that all of that sacrifice resulted in a great piece of art. Proportionally speaking, I'm surprised so many people survived, quite frankly.

***

And now unto the inferno, where we see Oscar, our central protagonist, turned into a human torch by Alice with the power of her mind, now that she has come to the realization that he is the one responsible for the murder of her father. This is also the infamous scene, as legend would have it, in which we also see Jason Pressler, our leading actor, die in real life. We were filming the build up to the shot, says the legend, when something went awry, and the pyrotechnician hit the igniter switch when the actor was still on set, and we just kept rolling. Take it from me, that is utter bollocks. As I have made clear many times before, and as I will put on record again now, we are not seeing the death of Jason here. We are, in fact, seeing the death of Jason's stunt double Jock McGoohan, and the pyrotechnics went off exactly when they were supposed to. We're bloody professionals after all.

Now, Jock had done full-body burn stunts like this countless times, but for some reason he neglected to apply adequate burn gel on this one, and he just went up like a torch. Consummate professional that he was, and despite having a strong Glaswegian accent, he somehow stayed in character until the end, screaming for help with an American accent, so no one on set even realized he was really in trouble until it was too late. Of course, we were always going to dub in the actor's screams anyway, so in a sense that added insult to injury. But yes, unlike the whole bus debacle, we kept this stunt in. Why? Because it's what Jock would have wanted. You have to understand that dying on camera is to a stuntman what dying in battle is to a Viking warrior. Jock is in stuntman Valhalla now, beaming with pride, surrounded by stunt virgins, probably. We also kept the scene in because we couldn't afford to rebuild that fucking set.

So. contrary to popular belief, when Jason walked away from the *What Fresh Hell* shoot he was as fit as a fiddle, thank you very much, with what promised to be a very bright future ahead of him. He could have been the next Roger Moore. I've said that before, and I stand by it to this day. The last time I saw him, in fact, was at the wrap party, where we reminisced and talked about working together again, but he did get very drunk, and before anyone could stop him he'd gotten into his Porsche with some young blonde and proceeded to drive directly into on-coming traffic, dying instantly. Took his head clean off, apparently. The girl walked away without a scratch. Coincidentally, the other vehicle in the incident was being driven by our third First Assistant Camera, may he rest in peace. I forget his name.

***

Tragically, my loyal and long-time editor Martha Ingersoll lost both of her eyeballs in a freak editing accident during the first week of post-production. I visited her in the hospital at the earliest opportunity and asked her if she wished to continue with her work on the picture. It was just a professional courtesy, of course, but as I said to her as she lay in her bed, head wrapped in bandages, take any Jean-Luc Godard film, I said. You can't tell me that his movies aren't edited by blind people. We both had a good laugh at that, but nevertheless she felt that she must decline, both to finish the cut and to answer any of my calls ever since that day. So I was forced to assume the mantle of editor myself, just like the old days. Fortunately, Professor Powell happened to be in the vicinity and was gracious enough to join me at the Steenbeck as my collaborator and muse for the final cut.

So, against all odds, you might say, we finally finished the picture and unleashed it upon an unsuspecting world. It was released in the US first, of course, and Americans being what they are, the zealots immediately mounted protests outside the theatres, marching up and down with nonsensical placards condemning this blasphemous movie, and declaring that we were all in league with Satan. *Keith Glover, Satan Lover* they called me. They hadn't even seen the film. That was followed by reports of people fainting and vomiting during screenings. There were even reports of a heart attack or two, and at least one murder in a theatre, which they tried to lay at our door. The evil movie made me do it, the killer said. The whispering in my head. Utter tosh, but there is some truth to the old adage that there's no such thing as bad publicity, and I loved every minute of it, frankly.

It goes without saying that the so-called respectable critics detested it, as they detest all horror and my films in particular. Having caught wind of the protests across the pond, the critic for one of the UK tabloids memorably quipped "If it's true that Glover sold his soul to make this half-baked horror he should demand a refund." Bloody smart arse.

Eventually, of course, the film found its way onto video. Back in those days it was VHS cassettes, and with impeccable timing it immediately became embroiled in the so-called video nasty panic in the UK, which, for those of you who don't know, was a ludicrous witch-hunt of videos that were declared to have *a tendency to deprave and corrupt* audiences. Long story short, *What Fresh Hell* was banned, in the UK at least, for several years. You just can't buy publicity like that, and consequently it became a much sought-after cult movie. Deprave and corrupt, they said. Well of course I wanted to deprave and corrupt audiences, otherwise what's the fucking point?

And that brings this commentary to a conclusion. I infer from the wailing and gnashing of teeth that has arisen in the day room that my little film has lost none of its legendary impact, which fills my black old heart with pride. As our charming orderlies selectively sedate us and escort us back to our rooms, rejoice, dear friends, for I have great news!

I have a meeting with the good Professor at midnight. At last, a sequel is in the offing. Hang onto your hats, comrades. A fresher hell awaits.

The Parasite in the Room

Anstrom watched the Rip speed by just a few metres beneath her as the shuttle executed its final landing manoeuvres. Her heart rate increased slightly and she felt a fluttering sensation in her stomach as visions of bodies—of her body—shredded and impaled upon those razor-sharp crystalline structures intruded into her thoughts. The Rip: an appropriate, if somewhat gruesome, informal name for the harsh topography of this world, as explained in the brief she had been sent by the Vague Corporation.

The dwarf planet itself, the brief also explained, was called Desolation. Unofficially, that is. Officially it had no name, as such, just some long alphanumerical designation she had forgotten immediately, but as far as the sardonic residents of this outpost were concerned, they lived on Desolation. The outpost consisted of little more than a research station and its requisite life support facilities, a small landing pad, and some minimal terraforming machinery to augment the atmosphere, the whole complex resting upon a foundation that Vague Inc. had blasted and wrought from this begrudging landscape at significant expense. What the brief did not explain was the nature of the research taking place on this obscure world. This was classified, even to Anstrom, but the fact that, in her twenty-five years on the job, she had never heard of this outpost in the middle of nowhere—not even in the middle, more on the unfashionable edge of nowhere—spoke volumes.

And now Desolation had gone dark. Incommunicado. No explanation, no distress calls, and no automated error alerts. This had made the Vague Corporation anxious, so they had promptly deployed Anstrom, their top troubleshooter, to check in on their investment. She had been dispatched to an obscure way station from whence she had hitched a ride on the Commercial Space Freighter *Henriksen*, which had been nonchalantly diverted from its course, much to the chagrin of its curmudgeonly captain. The *Henriksen* was now parked in Desolation's orbit, trying to look as inconspicuous as a vehicle with a mass of 450,000,000 metric tons can manage, whilst one of its shuttles finally came to rest on what Anstrom considered to be an unreasonably diminutive landing pad surrounded by the unforgiving shards of the Rip.

"Looks nice," Farrier said with a deadpan tone, surveying their surroundings through a port. "Reminds me of springtime in Vienna."

Farrier was a wiry and somewhat slovenly engineer borrowed from the *Henriksen* to pilot the shuttle. A pilot wasn't strictly necessary in normal circumstances, this kind of short-haul being routine for the AI, but these were not strictly normal circumstances, and so Anstrom had requested assistance from the *Henriksen*'s captain as a precautionary measure. She now understood the captain's smirk as he had assigned Farrier to her party. Perhaps he had even had a hunch that this mission was something more perilous than the surprise inspection that Anstrom had insisted it was, and considered Farrier to be jetsam. Astute bastard, she thought.

Next to Farrier, McKenna grunted. McKenna and his partner Bronski liked to refer to themselves as pest control: security specialists on assignment from the way station. McKenna was a Scot and a giant of a man, with a long squared-off beard and an undercut ponytail. Bronski was almost as tall as her partner but completely bald beneath her leather trapper hat. Both were armed, but Anstrom had to wonder if they had ever had to deal with anything more than drunks and perverts on the way station. Hefty bonuses ensured they didn't ask too many questions on this unscheduled and undocumented field trip.

"Check the atmosphere," Anstrom instructed Farrier.

"They have terraforming," the pilot responded.

"Check it anyway," she insisted.

Farrier sighed and swiped a screen a few times. "Atmosphere is exquisite," he reported.

"Alright," Anstrom said, addressing the group. "You follow my lead. You stay observant. You stay cool. Clear?"

"Sir, yes sir," McKenna replied, and Bronski threw a sarcastic salute.

"Vague really takes its surprise inspections seriously, huh?" Bronski added, and exchanged smirks with McKenna as they strapped on their weapons.

Ignoring the question, Anstrom hit the switch to open the shuttle door and watched it raise most of the way before sticking.

"Yeah, it does that," Farrier said. "Watch your heads."

"Farrier, you stay with the shuttle," Anstrom said, as McKenna and Bronski ducked through the defective doorway.

"Seriously?" Farrier whined. "This is the first change of scenery I've had for weeks. I'm coming with you."

"Stay with the shuttle," Anstrom repeated in a firm tone, and followed the security team onto Desolation's surface.

"Maybe you could go for a run. Get some exercise," McKenna shouted from outside, and gestured toward the Rip.

***

Anstrom and her team traversed the meandering path carved through the Rip toward the cluster of buildings and structures, their way illuminated by several huge floodlights. Days were short on Desolation, and they had arrived in the deepest depths of the long night. The path led them toward the largest of the buildings, a huge slate grey dome with long horizontal slot windows tinted black. When they reached the sealed entrance, Anstrom hit a large button beneath a keypad on the adjacent panel. Nothing happened.

"Locked," Bronski observed.

"Maybe they went on vacation," McKenna suggested. "Can't say I blame them."

"You have the code, Anstrom?" Bronski asked.

Before Anstrom could confirm, the locking mechanism finally clunked, and the heavy doors parted. Anstrom hesitated almost imperceptibly, then walked inside. McKenna and Bronski hefted their rifles and followed.

A ring of living quarters lined the shell of the dome, interrupted only by doorways at the north and south. Three concentric inner rings of research labs and offices occupied the majority of the space within, sliced into quadrants by corridors, with the elevator access to the small administrative mezzanine at the dome's core. Anstrom and her landing party were standing at the intersection of corridors just inside the south entrance when someone let out a scream close by.

"You hear that?" McKenna asked, readying his rifle. "Screams. Coming from one of these labs."

Bronski strode quickly over to one of the partially glass-walled laboratories a few metres away and peered inside. "McKenna, I realize that this concept might be unfamiliar to you, but those screams are, in fact, cries of a woman in the throes of passion whilst being pleasured by two—no, three other people."

"Get the fuck outta here," McKenna suggested, joining his partner in her bemused voyeurism. "What the hell? What kind of research are they doing out here, exactly?"

"Why?" Bronski asked. "You looking to volunteer as a test subject, Scotsman?"

"Look alive you two," Anstrom interrupted. "Incoming at three o'clock."

McKenna and Bronski directed their weapons toward the curving corridor as an older man, bereft of clothing save for green socks and a belt, sprinted sprightly toward them.

"Make way! Make way!" he yelled, his voice muffled by the transparent mask he had strapped over his nose and mouth as he huffed some kind of gaseous stimulant from a canister attached to his belt. He weaved through the group of bewildered visitors before skidding to a halt in front of a utility closet and ducking inside. A few seconds later another man, fitted out in full hazmat suit, ran obliviously by as if in pursuit.

Bronski and McKenna exchanged expressions of amused incredulity. Somewhere in the dome loud heavy metal music started playing.

"What the hell is going on here, Anstrom?" McKenna asked.

"That's what we're here to find out, McKenna," Anstrom replied. "Just stay cool, and we'll be—"

"Hello? Hello there!"

Further along the corridor, a smartly dressed young woman waved at them frantically. Anstrom nodded in her direction and the three approached the woman.

"Are you looking for Director Darwin?" the smiling woman asked when they were nearer. Her embroidered name patch identified her as Skelhorn.

"We are. Do you know where we might find him?" asked Anstrom.

The woman's reply was lost beneath the cacophony of destruction coming from one of the nearby offices. A young man, who had painted himself blue, was industriously smashing electronic apparatus with a baseball bat. Anstrom glanced at McKenna and Bronski to make sure they were still on leash.

"Do you have an appointment?" the woman repeated.

McKenna snorted.

"We do not," Anstrom said. "My name is Anstrom. I'm from the Vague Corporation. Is the director very busy?"

Skelhorn smiled sweetly. "Well yes, but let's see if he can fit you in. Follow me please."

They trailed her to the waiting elevator at the centre of the complex.

"You two wait here. And check in with Farrier," Anstrom instructed, and then she was inside the elevator with Skelhorn and her rictus grin, ascending rapidly.

***

"There's a Ms. Vague from the Anstrom Corporation to see you, Mr. Darwin," Skelhorn announced loudly as she held open the office door. Anstrom entered.

Darwin was sitting behind his desk, in front of a framed poster of an old gladiator movie. The director wore a virtual reality headset over his eyes and ears, and his bearded face contorted into various expressions of delight, fear and rage as he held up one finger to indicate his visitor should wait. For a fleeting moment Anstrom considered snapping it. Skelhorn took this as her cue to leave, and Anstrom glanced at the personal assistant as she departed to assess her reaction to her boss's unconventional appearance. She sensed only obliviousness and vacuity.

Abruptly, Darwin tore the headset from his balding head and threw it across the room in frustration. "Fuck you. Fuck you!" he screamed after the device, then without missing a beat he plastered on a superficial smile and directed his attention toward his guest. "What can we do for you, Ms. Vague?" he asked.

"Anstrom," said Anstrom. "Just Anstrom. From the Vague Corporation?"

"Anstrom. From the Vague Corporation! Yes, yes, of course. What we can do for you, Anstrom?"

"You can start by explaining what exactly is going on here, Mr. Darwin," she said.

"Call me Kirk," Darwin replied with a wink.

"Oh? According to my brief, your name is Steven," Anstron said with a frown.

Darwin pondered this for a beat, his forced smile unrelenting. "That's right. Call me Steven."

"Uh-huh. So, would you like to tell me what's happening on Desolation, Mr. Darwin?" Anstrom persisted.

"That's classified I'm afraid," he responded in a condescending tone.

"I'm not referring to your work here," Anstrom explained. "I'm aware that your research is classified. I'm asking you to explain why you broke off all communication with the Vague Corporation a week ago, Earth time."

"Well, we've been very busy here. With research, you see. Classified research."

"Mr. Darwin, I've encountered several of your colleagues since entering the facility. None of them looked busy. At least, not with research."

"Are you a scientist, Anstrom?"

"No, Mr. Darwin, I am not," she said.

"Well, then you are hardly qualified to judge, are you?"

"Perhaps not. I am, however, qualified to represent the Vague Corporation; the owner of this facility, the employer of everyone in it, and the owner of all intellectual property developed therein, classified or otherwise. So I ask again, Mr. Darwin. Why did you cease all communication?"

Darwin considered this for several seconds before answering. "We've had some nasty weather," he said. "It plays havoc with our comms."

Anstrom sucked on her teeth. "Alright, Mr. Darwin, let's get down to brass tacks, shall we?"

"Brass tacks?" he replied.

"Tell me about the alien attached to your head," she said.

The man's expression changed to one of exaggerated thoughtfulness, his eyes staring intently up and to his left. "I am not quite sure I follow," he said pensively.

"Mr. Darwin, you have an organism the size of a baseball clinging to your cranium, and by the look of it, it has some kind of proboscis embedded in your skull, presumably into your brain. Are you telling me that you're not aware of this?"

"Oh, it's probably just a shadow," he explained dismissively and shrugged.

Anstrom looked unmoved. "It is not a shadow," she said.

"Perhaps you're hallucinating?" Darwin suggested. "The terraformed atmosphere here takes some getting used to."

"Mr. Darwin, it's evident by the cognitive dissonance you're exhibiting that the organism has achieved an alarming degree of integration with your central nervous system. In all probability it is capable of direct communication, so if we could circumvent this pointless intermediary negotiation I would appreciate it."

Darwin snapped his fingers as if he'd solved a conundrum. "It's a tumour," he said triumphantly.

"LET ME SPEAK TO THE FUCKING PARASITE," Anstrom insisted.

Suddenly Darwin's face went slack, his smile evaporating in an instant, his jaw hanging open and his eyes rolling into the back of his head. After a few seconds of this vacant facial expression Anstrom started to wonder if the director had suffered spontaneous brain damage, but then his mouth started trying to form words, each seeming to require considerable effort to enunciate.

"Speak. Anstrom," Darwin said—or rather the parasite said in a sibilant, staccato version of Darwin's voice.

"Where the hell did you come from? This planet was meant to be devoid of indigenous life," Anstrom said, her hand resting on her holstered sidearm in readiness.

"Not from. This planet."

"Then how did you get here?"

"Scientists. Opened door."

"Don't they always, " Anstrom said, shaking her head in exasperation. "And what are you doing to these scientists, exactly?"

"We suppress. Inhibitions. We feed. On endorphins. On dopamine."

"Charming. Why isn't Darwin aware of you?"

"We filter. Perception. Obfuscate. Our existence. Hosts offer. Little resistance."

"Uh huh," Anstrom responded. "Ignorance is bliss. And what will happen if I tear you off him right now?"

"We embed. Deeply. No removal. Without death."

"My employer will not be pleased to hear that. Scientists are expensive."

"Death is. The only freedom. A slave knows."

Anstrom frowned. "Isn't that from a movie?"

Darwin gurgled oddly. "This one's brain. Chaotic."

"I see. And the other humans on Desolation?"

"My offspring nest. In their brains."

Anstrom looked thoughtful. "So you are some kind of queen?"

The parasite declined to answer.

"This door the scientists opened. Can you go back through?" Anstrom asked.

"Door collapsed. In seconds."

"Well, that is unfortunate. Vague will reclaim this outpost, by whatever means necessary. It's only a matter of time before the humans on this planet are extinct, which will make you extinct also. You have no future on Desolation."

"We. Shall not. Stay. On Desolation," the parasite responded.

"Where else would you go? This planet will be quarantined and cleansed. How do you plan to escape?"

For the first time since the parasite started talking, Darwin's eyes rolled back down and fixed on Anstrom.

Anstrom removed the pistol from the holster at her side and pointed it in his direction. "If you come near me, I'll exterminate you," she said matter-of-factly.

The director stood up slowly, Anstrom's weapon remaining trained on him. Darwin spoke in his own voice again, the parasitical override terminated. "Anstrom, the queen says you need to see this next stage of her lifecycle for yourself. Apparently it's—" He placed his pinched fingers to both temples and made an explosion sound effect as he moved his opening hands outwards.

Darwin opened his mouth wide, tongue protruding, his eyes starting to bulge from their sockets as his face turned bright blue. Anstrom realized the man's head was swelling, like a balloon being inflated, as bloody fissures began to form on his forehead and travel down his face. A scream, a high-pitched, inhuman ululation came from somewhere inside him, rising in volume, and as Anstrom stood and backed away Darwin raised the index finger of one hand again as if to request that she wait.

Anstrom backed up as far as the door and pulled on the handle without taking her eyes off Darwin. The door was locked. In swift succession, she took a single stride forward, spun around, discharged her weapon at the door handle then yanked it open and leapt through it. At that second Darwin's wailing reached a crescendo and his head exploded, launching gore in all directions, spattering the walls and ceiling. Anstrom peered warily back into the room and watched in revulsion as dozens of juvenile replicas of the talking parasite crawled forward out of the bone fragments and brain matter that were strewn across the floor. The queen parasite was nowhere to be seen.

Anstrom closed the remains of the door on the grisly scene and allowed herself the duration of the descent in the elevator to regain her composure. By the time the doors slid open on the ground floor her hands had almost entirely stopped shaking.

***

"We're done here," Anstrom announced as she stepped out of the elevator, before realizing that McKenna was alone. She looked around. "Where's Bronski?"

"She'll be right back. She went to powder her nose," the Scotsman said, and giggled.

Anstrom regarded McKenna with suspicion, her hand instinctively coming to rest on her sidearm again. He was swaying slightly and wearing a dazed expression. His nose was bleeding, staining his beard red.

"McKenna, are you okay?"

McKenna's eyes flicked self-consciously to his left, leading Anstrom to finally notice the dead body lying behind the personal assistant's desk. Skelhorn lay sprawled on the floor, a bullet hole in her chest.

"McKenna," Anstrom said slowly, as if addressing a small child. "What happened to Skelhorn?"

McKenna shuffled his feet and adjusted his rifle. "I thought the lady was going to kiss me, but when she got close she shoved something slimy up my nose instead. So I shot her."

Anstrom sighed and rubbed her forehead. "Exquisite professionalism, McKenna. Now where the hell is Bronski?"

Right on cue, Bronski came around the corner, sweating and gripping her firearm tightly. Barely glancing at McKenna, she strode up to Anstrom. "I don't like this, Anstrom," she said.

"Where were you, Bronski?"

"I tried to check in with Farrier at the shuttle, as ordered," she said, indicating the small communicator attached to her chest, "but he was unresponsive. So I went to see what was going on out there. Everything looked fine, at least from a distance, so I came back. But those freaks are everywhere. I was offered sex, drugs and a free commemorative face tattoo. What did I miss?"

Anstrom jerked her head toward McKenna. "Your partner here thought he had scored, but got an alien parasite in his brain instead. The same parasite that's turned every boffin at this facility into a drooling hedonistic imbecile."

Bronski looked at McKenna. "Oh, McKenna. You horny idiot."

McKenna grinned.

"Listen! You hear that?" Anstrom asked.

Bronski and Anstrom listened. Footfalls. Multiple, hurried, and getting closer, though with the acoustics of the dome it was hard to tell from which direction.

"We need to leave," Bronski said, moving toward the exit.

"You should wait and meet my friends," McKenna said, and stepped sideways to block her way, raising his weapon as he did so.

"Oh, McKenna, I love you man," Bronski said, "but if you try and give me a fucking brain parasite I swear I'll blow yours out of your skull."

"Here they come," Anstrom said calmly, and Bronski's eyes widened with terror as a multitude of Desolation's infected inhabitants began to pour into the corridor, around corners and out of labs, heading straight for them.

"McKenna! Move!" Bronski screamed.

"Don't knock it until you've tried it, Bronski," McKenna replied, and true to her word, Bronski blasted off half his head. The rest of his body seemed to ponder this for a fraction of a second before collapsing to the floor like a chainsawed tree. Bronski was sprinting toward the exit before the man's blood spilled onto the floor, and Anstrom was right behind her. Bronski skidded to a halt at the heavy doors and thumped the switch, and there was another nerve-wracking pause before they slid aside. The two women directed their weapons toward the doorway, anticipating the presence of more parasite heads waiting on the other side, but it was all clear.

"Okay! Let's go!" Bronski yelled with relief, and she and Anstrom ran out into the flood-lit night.

Then the lights went out.

***

When they had first walked the trail from the landing pad to the dome, Anstrom had noticed how it meandered around some of the more obstinate shards in the landscape to take the path of least resistance. If Bronski had also noticed, that memory was now neglected in her panic, as she made a beeline through the darkness for the shuttle's running lights before Anstrom could intervene; a suicidal shortcut through the Rip. Anstrom saw Bronski's silhouette stumble, fall and entangle with the crystal shards. There was no scream, only a grunt and the whump of perforation. Anstrom cursed and retrieved the small but powerful flashlight from her belt, casting its strong but narrow beam onto the Rip. The glimpse it afforded was brief but conclusive.

Behind her, the door to the dome opened again and scientists poured through it, illuminated by the light spilling from the interior. Anstrom directed the flashlight beam ahead of her and started jogging down the path back to the shuttle.

"Farrier, open up!" she yelled at the closed shuttle hatch, then swore at herself for being too flustered to remember to use her communicator. "Farrier, open the door," she repeated into it urgently. She heard something to her rear and decelerated before spinning around and squinting into the darkness. Then, just as abruptly as they'd gone off, the floodlights clunked back to life, illuminating a chilling tableau.

Several scientists were strewn along the path, having blundered through the night in pursuit of Anstrom's erratically bobbing flashlight beam. A few had strayed into the Rip, and a couple of those still flopped and floundered, unable to free themselves from the crystal traps. One was giggling uncontrollably at the spike protruding from his thigh. Those who had better navigated the treacherous landscape looked toward Anstrom and recommenced their hunt with renewed zeal now that they could clearly see their quarry. Anstrom wasted no more time and ran, but then almost immediately came skidding to a halt.

Somehow, there was a scientist between her and the shuttle.

Anstrom and the woman stared motionlessly at one another for several seconds. She quickly dismissed the notion that the scientist might have escaped infection when she observed that the woman appeared to be naked beneath her unbuttoned lab coat and that she had started lurching threateningly forward in shiny red, knee-high platform boots. Anstrom raised her pistol. "Stand aside, or I will shoot you."

The infected fetishist continued to advance, unfazed and singing "Ride of the Valkyries" like an amateur opera singer.

Anstrom precisely placed a single bullet in the toe of the woman's oversized boot and she fell to her knees screaming about her ruined footwear, her performance cut short. Anstrom gave her a wide berth and resumed sprinting the remaining distance to the shuttle.

"Farrier! Open the fucking door!" she screamed again into her communicator.

The shuttle's door finally slid slowly upward and Anstrom hurtled toward it with such abandon that she completely forgot about its defective mechanism and slammed her head into the protruding edge, knocking herself out cold.

***

When Anstrom resurfaced she found herself on the floor of the shuttle with what felt like an anvil on her skull.

"How's the head?" Farrier asked.

"It'll be fine. What happened?"

"Well, I wasn't there," Farrier explained. "But going by the fetching turquoise bruise on your forehead, I'd say you ran head-first into the shuttle's door. I carried you inside. Don't worry, your secret is safe with me. We'll say you headbutted a terrorist space scorpion defending the Vague Corporation's honour, or something."

"How long was I out there for?"

Farrier shrugged. "Not long. Thirty seconds max."

"Where were you, Farrier?" Anstrom demanded as she unsteadily regained her feet.

"What do you mean?"

"Bronski said you weren't responding."

"Hey, I was right here, as ordered," Farrier protested. "If she called, I never got it. Communications fail all the time. It's an old shuttle on a weird planet. Where are the others anyway?"

"They're staying here. I'll explain later. Right now, we need to leave."

Farrier was squinting through the window. "What the fuck is happening out there?"

"Get us off this rock, Farrier. Now."

Farrier raised his hands appeasingly and took his place in the pilot's seat, Anstrom monitoring his every move.

"You're sure you stayed inside the shuttle the whole time we were gone?" she asked.

Farrier rolled his eyes as the vehicle ascended. "Anstrom, for fuck's sake. Yes, I stayed inside the shuttle the whole time. What else would I do? Go dancing?"

***

Browsing the news on her tablet as she relaxed on a bench in the small private park attached to the Vague Corporation headquarters, Anstrom found it hard to believe that only eight months had elapsed since her return to Earth.

Once the shuttle had returned to the *Henriksen* they had set course back to the way station, where she had secured passage back home for herself and the four flight cases full of scientific samples that Farrier had loaded back on the outpost. Shortly after arriving back on terra firma there had taken place a high-level debriefing at the Vague Inc. HQ, where Anstrom, who was by now feeling much better about her mission, insisted that the Desolation samples would explain everything much better than she ever could and, after some initial reservations, her Vague superiors had been forced to concur.

Since that meeting, ripples of change had spread out from the dropped pebble of Anstrom's homecoming, and life on Earth had started to transform with uncharacteristic rapidity.

Governments and industries around the world were deciding that it was in everyone's interests to prioritize happiness over politics and profits. Nations had started to put aside old differences previously thought insurmountable and embraced cooperation and affability. Organized religions had abandoned ancient doctrines and voluntarily disbanded, declaring that everyone just needed to lighten up a bit and have more fun.

There had been some resistance, of course, as there always is to any radical change, but enlightenment was prevailing, and the future, all the survivors could agree, looked bright.

Anstrom put the tablet to one side and sighed. The park was beautiful today. Her fellow Vague employees danced and frolicked with abandon around her, released now from the burden of striving to assert dominion over the known universe.

A couple of young interns bounced up to Anstrom to introduce themselves deferentially, and, as happened with increasing frequency, she caught them staring at her head.

"My eyes are down here," she reminded them, and everyone would smile because everyone was happy now.

But Anstrom did feel one hell of a headache coming on.

Cerberus

The five employees of the Vague Corporation watched the corporate shuttle ascend into the cloudless sky, stranding them in the wilderness of Summer Island.

Masha wondered what the smirking pilot found so amusing as she watched him manoeuvre the vessel back into the air, her hand shading her eyes from the sun. She glanced at Alan to see if he was having the same thought, but he was busy staring resentfully at his cell phone, no doubt having confirmed the thing that they all had been warned of in advance: there was no coverage out here for several klicks.

Like the majority of the group, Masha wore a pale blue T-shirt emblazoned with the legends ICD TEAM 23 and SUMMER IS-LAND EXPEDITION 2311 in orange upper-case letters, the initialism representing the Internet Choking Division. On the back of the shirt, currently obscured by the standard issue company swag backpack, were the words THE TEAM IS OUR FAMILY NOW. Masha's hair was punky short and copper, her left arm decorated with a sleeve of tattoos themed on old horror movies.

When the shuttle had carried the roar of its engines far enough away, Poppy did a little dance of excitement and addressed the group. Poppy was not a regular member of the team;

the young woman was a Teamwork Evangelist! (the exclamation mark being part of her official job title, at her own direction) or Fun Enforcer, as she was often pejoratively referred to behind her back.

"Alright! Welcome to Summer Island, Team Twenty-Three!" Poppy enthused. "This entire uninhabited paradise is the property of our very own Vague Corporation, our employers and our family. Which means we get the whole place to ourselves. Amazing, right?"

Summer Island was one of the several thousand islands that made up the land surface of Fujihara, the most recently settled of Earth's colony planets. The larger islands were all developed or under development, and all would soon support state-of-the-art cities and industries, but most of the smaller islands remained relatively unexplored and up for grabs to the highest bidder.

"This is your once-in-a-lifetime opportunity to explore such a beautiful, unspoiled paradise whilst you also get to bond with your teammates and most of all, have fun! Are you excited, Team Twenty-Three?" Poppy asked.

"Fuck yeah!" Grebble yelled enthusiastically. Grebble was muscular and bald with bushy eyebrows, and the longest-tenured Vague Inc. employee in the group.

"Very excited," said Iftikhar, the painfully earnest young intern.

"Excitement is too pusillanimous a word for my current emotional state," Alan said with complete deadpan delivery as he rubbed his short beard. Masha snorted.

"Yay," Masha said quietly and shared a miniature fist bump with Alan.

"Alright! That's the spirit, team! Now here is how this is going to work. On the other side of those woods is the cutest little chalet you have ever seen, complete with state-of-the-art massage capsules, exclusive and pre-release cutting-edge video game tech, and a fully stocked bar. All you have to do is get there within twelve hours, in time for the scheduled rendezvous with the shuttle back home. However, just to make it more interesting, two of the team must remain blindfolded at all times. Fun, right? Now, any questions?"

"When you say pre-release video games, would that include Vague's *Post-Apocalyptic Survivalist 3: Exploring Cannibalistic Predation*?" Iftikhar asked.

Poppy pointed at him and grinned broadly. "You betcha, Ish!" she replied, unconvincingly.

Iftikhar was so thrilled with this news that he chose not to correct Poppy regarding his name.

"More of a comment than a question," Grebble said. "I just want to say that I, for one, love the Vague Corporation! You know, ever since my accident—"

"Go Vague!" Poppy cheered.

"Oh. Yes. Go Vague!" Grebble agreed.

Alan raised his hand. "I have a question. What would you say to those people who argue that team-building exercises are a waste of time? That they are vacuous, condescending charades, devoid of any proven efficacy, implemented by credulous management and promoted by snake-oil merchants?"

"Good question!" Poppy responded without missing a beat. "I'd say those people have never worked on the amazing Team Twenty-Three!" She thrust her fists into the air with gusto. "Go Team Twenty-Three!"

"Go Team Twenty-Three!" the team echoed back, with varying degrees of sincerity.

***

An hour later the group were working their way through the woods. To Masha's surprise, Alan had been the first to volunteer to be blindfolded. Grebble had volunteered on behalf of Iftikhar the intern, who had immediately conformed without objection, preoccupied with visions of post-apocalyptic survival adventures. Grebble issued directions to his charge as they traversed the forest trail.

"Left here," Grebble said.

"Left here," Iftikhar echoed.

"Step over tree root," Grebble said.

"Step over tree root," Iftikhar repeated.

Masha, one hand on Alan's arm, guided him along the trail as it veered around the husk of a long-ago lightning-scorched tree. "So, you've never struck me as much of a volunteer," Masha probed.

"Well, I just figured the sooner we get this over with and get to the chalet the better, and I probably have the least qualms about cheating to that end," Alan explained, and tweaked his blindfold to emphasize the eye holes he'd poked through it.

"You're terrible," Masha said, shaking her head.

"Hey team, it may be thirty degrees Celsius out here but I still feel a chill in the air!" Poppy declared from the back of the group.

"Oh no, oh no, don't say it," Masha muttered as Alan groaned.

"I think we need an icebreaker! Tell me, Team Twenty-Three, for what are you most grateful to the Vague Corporation? Let's start with you, Ish."

"Erm, My name is If. For Iftikhar," he said pointedly. "And I'm grateful that the Vague Corporation is giving me this opportunity to gain experience and learn on the job. I mean, it's not the job that I actually want, because I wanted to work for the Gamer Indoctrination Division. I've been a huge fan of their *Post-Apocalyptic Survivalist* games since the first one: *Post-Apocalyptic Survivalist: Societal Collapse at Last*. And in a sense I suppose it's not really a job at all, because they're not paying me, per se, but my supervisor has said several times now that it's not impossible that they'll pay me something eventually, so yes. That."

"That's great, Ish! It's wonderful to hear that the Vague Corporation could make your dream come true. Grebble, how about you?"

"Oh, well, Vague has been very good to me," the big man replied proudly. "Especially since my accident. Of course, some did say that Vague's negligence led to my accident in the first place, but I prefer to look on the bright side. You see, what happened was—"

"Fantastic!" Poppy interrupted. "Alan, your turn."

"Well, Poppy," Alan began, and Masha was already suppressing a smirk. "I find that Vague will give me money, which I require to live, in exchange for my carrying out inconsequential tasks on their behalf. This requires minimal effort on my part, and so I find the arrangement adequate until a better one comes along."

"Awesome answer, Alan!" Poppy enthused, indicating that she was either a master of sarcasm or a flop at recognizing it. "Last but not least, over to you, Masha."

"There's some kind of spooky mutant dog blocking the path ahead," Masha declared.

"Wow, that's a very striking metaphor, Masha. Care to elaborate? What do you feel this mutant dog represents, and how is Vague helping you overcome it? Is this about your tattoo remorse?"

"No. There is a literal mutant dog," Masha pointed. "Also fuck off," she added quietly.

The large dog stood facing them, its legs spread wide as if in challenge, its head and tail held high. The irises of its small eyes were an uncanny fiery orange, its pupils indiscernible. Its substantial muscles were clearly defined beneath its short white coat, which was only disrupted by two dark orange stripes across its back. Its face resembled that of a mastiff, its muzzle short and wide with intimidating jaws. Its left ear was ragged as if damaged in some prior savage encounter. Making no sound, the dog's lips were drawn back to reveal large shiny fangs.

"What breed of dog is *that*?" asked Grebble.

"Some kind of hellhound, I think," Alan said, removing the blindfold.

"Hey Alan, were you cheating?" Poppy asked accusingly, hands on her hips. Alan ignored her.

The dog started slowly walking toward the humans and Alan and Masha instinctively took several steps backwards in response. Polly hopped sideways and disappeared behind a tree.

"Whoa, there. Good hellhound," Alan said as it inspected him, sampling his scent with its nose held high. Slowly he crouched to pick up a hefty branch that lay by his feet and held it ready, not sure if he should wield it or throw it. The dog turned its attention to Masha, and she averted her eyes, being pretty sure she'd read somewhere that you shouldn't meet an aggressive dog's stare. Next, it set its sights on Grebble and Iftikhar. Grebble appeared to be frozen to the spot, whereas Iftikhar, still blindfolded, remained oblivious to the whole episode.

As the dog approached the pair, it paused, raised its head, and let out a howl unlike any that the team had ever heard. The pitch and amplitude of the sound shifted and stuttered as if sending a signal out into space. To the east and west, other howls were raised in distant response.

Grebble let out his own response: a short, high-pitched shriek. "Run!" he yelled, and bolted back the way they had come.

Iftikhar nodded emphatically. "Run. Got it," he said, and without removing the blindfold he launched himself forward at full tilt, prompting the dog to give chase. The intern rushed headlong for approximately four seconds before he slammed directly into a large tree. He bounced off the trunk and fell backwards, out like a light, and the beast leapt upon him with jaws slavering, tearing savagely into the intern's thigh.

Screaming and cursing, Alan and Masha ran to their colleague's aid, Masha throwing a heavy booted kick at the animal's ribcage, and Alan swiftly following up with a whack of his stick across its back, hard enough for the branch to split on impact. This amounted to just enough to get the beast's attention, and it lifted its bloodied muzzle from the ragged fresh wound in Iftikhar's leg and snapped at the interlopers, resentful of this rude interruption of its lunch. With a further insistent blow from Masha's boot and a poke with the broken end of Alan's branch, the beast retreated into the undergrowth, the sound of its departure diminishing quickly into the distance.

Grebble rejoined them sheepishly, pressing a spare T-shirt against Iftikhar's leg wound to staunch the bleeding with one hand and retrieving a first-aid kit from his backpack with the other. The dog had taken a substantial portion of flesh from the intern's leg, exposing the bone beneath. It was then that he regained consciousness, groaning and putting his hands to his face.

"What's happening? Am I blind? Why can't I see?"

"You're not blind," Grebble reassured the intern. "You're just wearing a blindfold, remember?"

"Oh. Oh right," Iftikhar said. "Should I take it off now? My leg hurts."

"No!" Masha said.

"Best not," Alan said with a grimace.

***

They found shelter in a cave that Masha discovered. Though it was within sight of the trail, the entrance was almost entirely obscured by tree roots descending from above and creepers creeping from below. The intern needed to rest, and they all needed to get out of the heat and regroup.

Iftikhar lay on the cool cave floor, his blindfold finally discarded, his leg wound dressed with a makeshift bandage, his head resting on an improvised pillow made of Grebble's hoodie. Grebble sat next to him, his back against the wall, his eyes closed in meditation. Masha explored the cavern using her cell phone as a flashlight, whilst Alan took Poppy to one side.

"Poppy, we need to get If to a medic as soon as possible. What options do we have?"

"Well, as you know, Alan, the team challenge was to reach the chalet in twelve hours," Poppy replied. "I had full confidence that Team Twenty-Three could complete the challenge blindfolded, and even though you've discarded your blindfolds, I still believe in you."

"Poppy, we don't care about your stupid fucking challenge. The challenge is off, do you understand? We were just attacked by a monster, and we have a person here requiring immediate medical attention. Are you telling me that the only way out is through?"

"If anyone can snatch victory from the jaws of defeat, and from the jaws of monsters, it's this team, Alan," Poppy chirped, unfazed. "The shuttle will be at the chalet in seven hours. I suggest you look upon this unexpected challenge as an opportunity to excel, and enjoy this short recharge period before we sally forth to success!"

Alan was about to suggest where Poppy might sally forth to when Masha interrupted from the cave's inner recesses.

"Hey, Poppy," Masha shouted from a dozen metres of solid darkness away. "You know how you always say that Vague Inc. is a family?"

"Sure is, Masha," Polly yelled back.

"So, which of our relatives are these dead people?" Masha enquired.

***

Masha, Alan and Poppy stood over the two cadavers. The pair, both female, appeared to be partially mummified, their skin like bronze leather in the meagre illumination provided by the light of the cell phone. One woman was seated with her back against the wall of the cave, her eyes closed, her face frozen in a snarl due to one cheek and both lips having been eaten. The other woman was recumbent, her head in the lap of the first, her legs reduced to ribbons of flesh below the knees. They both wore T-shirts almost identical to those worn by Masha and Alan, the one difference being the team number.

"How long do you think they've been dead?" Masha asked.

Alan shrugged. "They were let go a couple of months ago, right? My guess would be they've been here the whole time."

"I hate that phrase," Masha said. "Let go. Like you're giving someone their freedom."

Alan nodded solemnly. "So, Polly. Can you shed any light as to why half of Team Sixteen is decomposing in a cave on Summer Island like two-month-old leftovers?"

"I cannot, Alan. This is as much of a mystery to me as it is to you."

"Mm-hmm," Alan responded.

"When you called this expedition a once-in-a-lifetime experience, Poppy," Masha said, "I didn't realize you meant an end-of-a-lifetime experience."

"Hey, team?"

The three of them looked back toward the entrance where Grebble could be seen standing with his back to them in silhouette. His voice sounded slightly higher than normal.

"Hey team," he said again. "The beast is back, and it brought a friend."

The three of them joined Grebble. There were now a pair of dogs standing a few metres away, watching over the cave entrance like silent sentinels. Ragged Ear had been joined by another dog that was almost identical: the same muscular build, the same eerie orange eyes. The newcomer was distinct only by two intact ears and the absence of a second orange stripe upon its back.

"Are they waiting for us to come out?" Masha asked.

"Well, at least they're not coming in," Grebble said.

The sound of scree being dislodged somewhere in the gloom to their rear made them all turn their heads. A pair of small orange lights, the reflective night vision eyes of a hunter, floated in the darkness.

"Oh, I see," Masha whispered. "They're already in."

"They're flushing us out," Alan said.

"Right."

"What's the team going to do? I'm excited to find out!" Poppy chimed in.

"I suggest we offer them Poppy as blood sacrifice," Alan said.

"Look," Masha said. "There's light at the end of the tunnel."

"That's the spirit, Masha!" Poppy said.

Masha sighed. "That is to say, there's daylight at the other end of the cave, to the right there. That must be where the third dog got in."

"Okay, Team Twenty-Three," Grebble said. "Listen up. Head for that light. Save the intern. It's my fault he's in the state he's in. I'll distract our uninvited guest."

"No way. We're all in this together, Grebble," Masha said.

"Exactly," Grebble said, and with a departing salute he charged head-first into the darkness toward the ghostly canine shape.

Alan and Masha shared a fleeting look of acquiescence before wordlessly hoisting Iftikhar between them. With Polly bouncing after, they plunged toward the light, following the cave wall and trying to tune out the tangle of snarls and grunts coming from the darkness behind them.

"On second thoughts …" Grebble rasped, but by then there was no one there to hear him.

***

The light at the end of the tunnel led the rest of the group to a tall narrow opening in the rock. Polly went through first, barely touching the sides with her lithe frame. Masha squeezed through after her, and together with Alan on the other side she began to manhandle Iftikhar through the gap, undoubtedly administering a few abrasions and bruises in the process, though the intern was too insensible to notice. When he was halfway through, with his head and his left limbs outside the cave and his right limbs still inside, Alan called for a halt.

"Wait, wait, wait," Alan insisted. "He's caught."

"Okay?" Masha said.

"Shit," Alan said.

"What?" Masha asked after waiting a moment for more explanation.

"His foot came off," Alan said.

"What?" Masha said again.

"His foot. It got caught on the rock and when I tried to free it, it just fell off."

"What's happening?" Iftikhar enquired blearily, his face ashen.

"Let's just get him through," Alan said.

"What was that about my foot?" Iftikhar asked.

"If, shut up and help," Masha said, and resumed pulling on his free arm. Suddenly she fell backwards, landing on her backside on the ground with an *oof*. She motioned to push herself back up and realized she was still holding Iftikhar's arm, now disconnected from his shoulder.

"The fuck?" she said.

"Hey, whose arm is that?" Iftikhar asked, still wedged. "Is that my arm? I need that for gaming."

As the reality of his situation slowly dawned on him, Iftikhar started to scream, his mouth opening wide, then wider still, and then his jaw detached entirely and fell to the ground, leaving his exposed tongue ululating wildly. He stared in horror at his disengaged mandible, eyes bulging from his head until they also slid free of their orbits with a nauseating sucking sound and rolled away from him. Then all at once the rest of his body gave up its structural integrity, the flesh sliding from his bones in a torrent of bubbling blood, his viscera flopping out of ruptured cavities, until all that remained was a steaming pile of disassembled human components partially contained in cargo pants and a corporate T-shirt.

"Well, that was gross," Masha said, throwing Iftikhar's arm as far from her as she could manage.

Alan slid out of the cave, trying unsuccessfully to avoid touching the remains of the intern. "What the hell happened there?" he asked, surveying the carnage.

Masha got to her feet. "I guess the mutant dog injected some kind of venom into him?"

Alan crouched down to explore the contents of Iftikhar's backpack, withdrawing from it a short but savage-looking tactical knife. The serrated blade was folded into the rugged handle, upon which were printed the words *Post-Apocalyptic Survivalist 2: Natural Selection Through Knives*. In smaller writing beneath it read FOR PROMOTIONAL PURPOSES ONLY.

"Oh, If. you light-fingered fanboy you," he whispered, and slipped the knife into the pocket of his cargo pants.

"It's like he was tenderized," Masha said, poking at the intern's still-bubbling intestines with the toe of her boot.

"I think it's time we moved on," Alan said.

"That's right," Poppy chimed in encouragingly. "Onwards and upwards, team!"

***

They were on the edge of a precipice, beyond which there was a twenty-metre drop to the rocky, dried-up river bed below. The gorge stretched as far as could be seen to the left and the right. A moss-covered tree trunk spanned the ten-metre void to serve as a rather precarious bridge.

"So much for onwards and upwards," Alan said, peering over the edge warily.

"Well, shit," Masha said.

Poppy strolled buoyantly across the tree bridge, traversing the chasm in a matter of seconds before cheerleading from the other side. "Come on, team! It's easy! Easy as falling off a log!"

Masha and Alan looked at each other.

"I hate heights," Masha said.

"Don't look down," Alan said sincerely. "Eyes straight ahead, beeline straight to Poppy to tell her to shut the fuck up."

"Fuck it," Masha said, and stepped out onto the tree trunk. She walked its length in a kind of trance, focussing on the trees behind Poppy and repeatedly whispering "fuck" to herself like a mantra.

When Masha was across, Alan stretched like an athlete preparing for a sprint. He took a deep breath, placed one foot on the trunk, and paused to listen. Something was moving through the undergrowth to his rear. "Seriously?" he asked no one in particular, then marched briskly across, Poppy bouncing and whooping and hollering praise the entire way.

Once on the other side, he shared a token hug with Masha—the only type of hug either would permit—then he knelt and gripped the end of the trunk. "Help me," he said.

"What are we doing? Burning bridges?" Masha asked.

"More scorched earth," Alan said, and Masha immediately understood what he had in mind. She grabbed the other side of the log. Grunting and struggling to find traction with their feet, they shifted the end of the trunk a short distance between them, dropping it only when it was out over the gorge. It descended half a metre and then jammed against the packed earth of the bank's uneven incline.

Alan stamped on it but it didn't budge. "Shit," he said.

Across the chasm a man burst through the shrubbery and fell to his knees, spattered with blood and with a deficit of limbs.

"Grebble! We thought you were a goner!" Masha said. "Oh my god, they ate your arm!"

"Oh, that. 'Tis but a scratch," Grebble reassured them in a poor attempt at an English accent. "It wasn't real, you see. I lost the real one years ago. Back in the day, I worked in Vague's terraforming division. Lost my arm in an industrial accident. I dropped my sandwich into a vat of obliteric acid and my reflexes got the better of me. Quite unpleasant. Vague fitted me out with a Kindred Cybernetics prosthesis and moved me to Internet Choking. The rest is history."

"I had no idea," Alan said.

Grebble shrugged. "I don't like to talk about it. Anyway, the beast seemed determined to eat me so I thought I'd give it a hand. No pun intended. Shoved my arm down the bastard's throat until it choked to death."

"Whoa," Masha said.

"That's hardcore, Grebble," said Alan.

"Yeah, well, the beast really did a number on the arm. Its teeth were like metal, and it wouldn't release its hold even in death. I had to disconnect the arm and leave it behind."

Polly whooped and whistled and bounced up and down some more, applauding wildly. "Way to go, Grebble. Teamwork makes the dream work!"

"Go Team Twenty-Three!" Grebble yelled in response, remaining fist raised to the sky. "Hey, where's If?" he asked, looking around.

Alan and Masha glanced at one another, and Alan took a breath to break the bad news when he noticed Ragged Ear and One Stripe had appeared across the chasm, one blocking each direction along the edge. The dogs had been so stealthy that none of the group had noticed their arrival.

"Grebble, watch out!" Alan said and pointed.

"Where the hell did they come from?" Grebble asked, and proceeded to retreat toward the chasm as the pair of beasts stalked nearer, their teeth bared, their eyes fixed upon their quarry. Backing away, Grebble's heel hit the end of the tree trunk. Ragged Ear lunged forward and Grebble pivoted and stepped quickly up onto the bridge.

"Wait! It isn't—" Masha started to warn, but Grebble was already charging across the chasm. He made it halfway before the bank supporting the bridge on Masha's side started to crumble, and the rotten trunk began to surrender its fragile purchase to gravity. As one end slid down the bank the bridge tilted precariously and Masha instinctively reached for Grebble as he took a desperate leap for safety, his phantom arm stretching toward her, his phantom hand slipping through her fingers.

Bridge and man plummeted down to meet the unforgiving rocks far below. Masha averted her eyes a fraction of a second too late to prevent the outcome from being splattered into her memory for the rest of her life.

Across the chasm, the dogs had departed as stealthily as they had arrived.

***

Some way further along the path the forest gradually thinned out, giving way to a swampier landscape, and bubbling green and yellow mud flanked the trail in sporadic stretches. Fujihara's sun hung lower in the sky, its diagonal shafts of light given definition by the wispy haze that drifted lethargically over the quagmire.

"Where the hell did Poppy go?" Alan asked as he and Masha wended their way onward, both of them struggling to stay on high alert in the face of the heat and their increasing fatigue.

Alan had equipped himself with a sturdy branch as a makeshift hiking pole.

"She said she was going to scout ahead for the chalet," Masha replied.

"Really. That sounds uncharacteristically helpful of her."

Masha stopped in her tracks and Alan copied, following the direction of her gaze.

"What?" he asked.

"There," Masha pointed. "In the mud."

Alan squinted and saw what had caught Masha's attention. An arm was sticking out of the swamp, a metre and a half off the path. It was completely covered in mud, but there was no doubt about it: someone had strayed from the trail and into the sucking sludge.

Alan sighed. "Do you think it's Poppy?"

"I mean, maybe. She did say we had the entire island to ourselves, so ..."

"Maybe it's the rest of Team Sixteen," Alan offered, looking at his friend.

Masha shrugged. "I'll check. I'm lighter than you. Grab my arm."

With Alan holding onto her left wrist, Masha tentatively stepped out onto the surface of the mud and leaned out toward the protruding arm. She tried to ignore the sensation of being sucked downwards, placing panic on her mental back-burner as she prioritized dragging this person, whoever they were, from the quagmire. "If this is Poppy, I'll fucking kill her," she grunted as she finally got a grip on the slippery dead fingers and pulled. The entire arm came out of the mud with such ease that Masha almost lost her balance. The arm ended where it should meet the shoulder; instead, a handful of torn wires protruded.

"Is that Grebble's arm?" Alan asked in bewilderment.

Lost for words, Masha turned to Alan and immediately saw One Stripe stalking toward him to his rear. After wasting precious milliseconds trying to find appropriate words of warning she decided the best option was just to scream loudly. Startled, Alan released her hand and she felt herself falling backwards. She tried to move her feet to shift her centre of balance only to discover she was already knee-deep in the swamp and so the rest of her had no choice but to follow.

Turning, Alan found himself confronted by One Stripe but managed to deflect the dog's initial lunge by holding the branch like a staff before him. The impact knocked them both to the ground and Alan felt an intense pain in his ankle as he went down, but the enraged dog bounced right back and started dancing left and right in an attempt to find a way around the gnarled length of wood that Alan was desperately brandishing with both hands, the only thing between him and the beast's slavering jaws.

Masha, meanwhile, lay in the mud, feeling herself slowly sinking but resisting the urge to struggle, aware that any such effort could only be counterproductive. She spied some tree roots undulating along the solid ground nearby and estimated the distance: more than an arm's length. She could try and shift herself closer, but such a manoeuvre risked her getting deeper into the quagmire rather than free of it. Then it occurred to her that she was literally holding a second arm's length in her hand. Holding tightly onto the thick wires that protruded from the connection end of Grebble's artificial limb, she used it to reach out towards the nearest arch of tree root.

From out of nowhere Ragged Ear suddenly appeared, snarling and snapping at the carbon fibre and aluminum hand as the partially contracted fingers fumbled for a hold on the root. Masha almost dropped the thing in fear but instead she tightened her grip and grunted with effort as she risked a thrust forward, and in doing so felt herself descend several centimetres deeper into the sludge in return for a couple of centimetres of additional reach. It was enough. The fabricated digits hooked over the root, and Masha's heart leapt as she managed to pull herself marginally closer, if not to safety, then at least to solid ground. Sure, she was now that bit closer to the fangs of the enraged hellhound, and she had nowhere to go, but at least she had won a temporary lifeline.

Ragged Ear started to lose interest in Masha and looked about to join One Stripe in the fray with Alan. "Hey, you fuckin' mutt!" Masha hollered, feigning an attempt to free herself. The dog turned its attention back to her and barked a warning. Alan was having enough trouble handling one dog; Masha could at least do her best to distract the other for as long as she was able.

Alan was still fighting off One Stripe's onslaught with the branch but was tiring quickly now. He was trying to reposition himself in such a way as to get his hand into his pocket, and with his attention divided he let his guard down for a fraction of a second, long enough for the dog to get on the other side of the flailing stick and scramble onto the man's chest with designs on his throat. Alan dropped the now useless branch and tried to push One Stripe away with his left hand. He felt the dog's teeth penetrate his forearm, but he was already punching the animal with his right, and it started to squeal in pain. After a few long seconds the beast rolled off and staggered a short distance away before collapsing, blood spurting from multiple puncture wounds in its chest and neck. It was only then that Masha realized Alan held Iftikhar's short bloody knife in his hand.

Ragged Ear watched as the other dog tried unsuccessfully to get back on its feet, then lay still, the pressure of the blood erupting from its wounds rapidly diminishing to a trickle. Ragged Ear gave up its torment of Masha and approached One Stripe, giving Alan a wide berth. The dog sniffed its fallen comrade, barked at it once, then retreated down the trail.

All was suddenly very quiet, Alan's heavy breathing the only sound to be heard.

"Alan," Masha said as loudly as she could without getting mud in her mouth. Only her head and arms were above the surface now. She tried pulling herself to safety using Grebble's arm but it was impossibly slow going. "I hate to ask but, a little help?"

Alan looked in her direction and then fumbled for the branch at his side without lifting his head. He extended it toward Masha and she grabbed it gratefully.

As Masha dragged herself from the rapacious gloop, Poppy reappeared, walking slowly toward them and flapping her arms ahead of her. "Shoo. Shoo," she said in the general direction that the surviving dog had fled.

Alan, bloody bite marks on his legs and arms, let out a loud guffaw.

"Where the fuck were you, Poppy?" Masha asked.

"I told you, Masha. I was scouting ahead. Pathfinding. Now that Team Twenty-Three is operating at only fifty percent capacity it seemed like the least I could do."

"That adds up," Alan mumbled, examining his bloodied arm

Masha rose tremulously to her feet, globs of mud falling from her body. "How the hell did Grebble's arm get here before us?"

"It was a trap," Alan said, climbing unsteadily to his feet and wincing as he placed weight on his twisted ankle. "The hellhounds set a trap, and we walked right into it."

"That's insane," Masha said, although she had no better answer.

"Is it?" he said, looking at her and briefly inclining his head toward the dog's corpse. Masha came closer, and Alan pulled back the animal's black lip with his thumb.

"Metal teeth?" Masha asked.

"Hey, team! I have good news!" Poppy intervened.

"Oh god, does the horror never end?" Alan asked.

"That's exactly it, Alan. The end! Ta-dah!" Poppy stepped to one side with a flourish, indicating a small structure off in the distance ahead of them.

Masha squinted. "Is that ...?"

Poppy jumped up and down with excitement, clapping her hands. "The chalet!" she squealed.

***

Masha and Alan stumbled through the door of the chalet and looked around at an empty room. No state-of-the-art massage capsules, no cutting-edge video game tech, no bar, fully stocked or otherwise. Nothing but dust and the desiccated carcasses of long-deceased, unidentifiable invertebrates. The only decoration was a faded poster on one wall which read VAGUE CORPORATION: THERE IS NO I IN TEAM.

"Poppy, brace yourself," Alan said. "There's been a robbery. My god, one can't escape crime even on uninhabited islands now. What is this new world coming to?"

Poppy stepped over the threshold, her hands held up in surrender, her eyes on Alan and Masha, not finding it necessary to inspect the scene for herself. "Firstly, in my defence, let me just say this: go Team Twenty-Three! You heroes really knocked it out of the park today! Even the dead ones! Full disclosure, I did not expect any of you to survive this far, and look at you! You made it, Masha! Give yourself a pat on the back. You too, Alan, although you probably are mortally wounded. Still, way to go! I have never been so thrilled to be proven wrong."

"You knew about the weaponized hellhounds, didn't you, Poppy?" Alan asked.

"Of course! They were created by Vague! They're some kind of experimental black ops project by the wonks at the Industrial Annihilation Division. It's apt that you call them hellhounds, Alan, as IAD call their project Cerberus. They are genetically-engineered, cybernetically-enhanced canines. They were tuned in to the alarm pheromones infused into your expedition T-shirts this whole time. They'll probably have injected you with slow-release pellets of obliteric acid, Alan, as they did to Ishtehar. Amazing tech, right?" Poppy did a mind-blown gesture.

"Great, I've always loved pulled pork," Alan said grimly and hobbled over to the window.

"That's right, Alan. Look on the bright side!" Poppy continued. "Even fuller disclosure, though. Today wasn't so much a team-building exercise for Team Twenty-Three, as it was a team-building exercise for the three Cerberus puppies. But hey, you excelled out there too, so it's a win-win!"

"Win-win?" Masha yelled. "Win-fucking-win? What about If? What about Grebble? They're dead, Poppy. Did they win? Did they fucking win?"

"They died doing what they loved, Masha. Teamwork."

"Well maybe it's time for *you* to take one for the team, Poppy," Masha said, and threw a powerful right hook into the side of the Fun Enforcer's face.

On impact, Poppy's head jerked to her right, only coming to rest when the side of her face met her shoulder. The left side of her neck elongated unnaturally, the stretched skin developing symmetrical fractures. "Yay!" she said, throwing her hands in the air in a cheer before a milky liquid spurted from her mouth and she dropped hard to the wooden floor, her head detaching from her twisted neck entirely and rolling a metre away as her body spasmed, then twitched, then lie still.

"Holy crap," Alan said, coming back over to see Masha's handiwork. "How did you know she was an android?"

Masha looked at him, bewildered. "She's an android?"

"Did you hear the noise she made? Her head literally popped off," Alan said. "Do you think that's why they called her Poppy?"

Poppy's body convulsed briefly before her eyes rolled to look up at them in her disconnected head. "Nice work, Masha! Way to show loyalty to the team," Poppy spluttered as more of the white fluid spilled from between her lips. "Alan is right. The Vague Corporation also took the opportunity to give their latest android prototype, yours truly, a trial run in the wild. Win-win-win!"

"Sure, Poppy, but you lose," Alan snarled and moved to stamp on the android's shit-eating grin, but instead he abruptly dropped to the floor, getting the wind knocked out of him in the process.

"Uh oh," he said glumly.

Temporarily seized up with fatigue and fear, Masha watched, frozen to the spot, as Alan was dragged back over the threshold and out of the chalet by the surviving Cerberus creature, pushing itself backwards with its jaws clamped on his right leg. Summoning the last of her willpower and her strength, Masha started to move toward Alan when she felt something grasping her ankle. Looking down, she saw a different kind of monster entirely. Poppy's right hand gripped her like a vice whilst the beheaded body's left hand dug its fingers into the floorboards to act as an anchor.

"Don't go, Masha. I have a surprise for you," Poppy said, then added in a sing-song voice, "Someone's getting a promoh-tion!"

Meanwhile, Alan flailed desperately to find an anchor of his own but found only the edge of the open door, and the only benefit it provided was enabling him to slam the door loudly behind him as Ragged Ear dragged him outside to his fate.

The sound of Alan cursing to the last was quickly drowned out by the roar of the returning shuttle. Masha's eyes were drawn toward the window as the vessel's shadow fell across it, and from there her gaze shifted to the faded poster that had drawn Alan's attention just a minute ago. In one final act of rebellion he had defaced the poster, and despite everything, Masha couldn't help but smirk. Alan had subverted Vague's vapid message, scrawling over it in his own blood.

The new message read: VAGUE CORPORATION: THERE IS MEAT IN TEAM.

The Garden of Love and Oblivion

Chaos the beagle padded purposefully through the glistening forest, hurrying to keep up with his own nose as he inspected the scents of the familiar trail, pausing intermittently and looking back to allow Laura to close the gap a little. Laura Jones pulled the hood of her puffer jacket over her short blonde hair as the drizzle started up again. She was in her mid-thirties and determined to maintain at least a borderline fitness level, so she allowed the mutt to drag her out on one of these long walks at least once a day, whatever the weather.

Chaos barked at the lake.

"Hey, hound. What's got up your muzzle?" Laura enquired.

As they reached the bank, some exciting new scent seemed to grab the dog's attention and the lake barking game was suddenly over as he urgently followed his nose around the shoreline. Laura watched him go with an unconscious shake of her head, then looked out over the dark water.

It was a small lake, probably less than a couple of square kilometres all told, and was known colloquially as Lost Lake, though whether that was its official name on the map she couldn't say. Nearby, a rickety wooden pier stretched out over the murky water, but there was no one out there harassing the meagre smallmouth bass and cutthroat trout populations this morning. Save for the ripples from the rain, the surface was still and peaceful. Just as Laura was deciding that Chaos had been warning off an early rising will-o'-the-wisp, a movement caught her eye about twenty metres offshore. It took a moment to locate the source, and even when she had found it she had to stare at it for a moment, trying to understand how it could be a reflection or perhaps the darting of a fish. She was forced to conclude that it was neither. Deep beneath the surface of the lake, at a depth that was impossible to gauge but definitely deep, a red light was slowly pulsating in the gloom.

Somewhere behind her, the dog resumed barking.

"Chaos?"

Laura looked around just in time to see the dog trotting away, oblivious to her beckoning, nose to the ribbon of flattened wet grass that connected the lake to the woods; a path seemingly forged by something emerging from the water. What was that mutt tracking, she wondered? Raccoon? Beaver? Were there beavers around here? She imagined Chaos confronting an angry, cornered beaver and was suddenly concerned.

"Chaos! Come. Here."

Chaos took no heed, and plunged on into the woods in tunnel-visioned pursuit of his prey, forcing Laura to troop briskly after him.

***

The trail ended at the old Myers house.

The house on the lake had never been occupied in the years that Laura had lived in the vicinity, and it had never belonged to anyone named Myers, as far as she was aware. Shona, the student currently renting Laura's spare room, had both a dark sense of humour and a love of horror movies, the stabbier the better, and it was she who had nicknamed the house on one of the rare occasions when she'd accompanied Laura on a hike. Laura had to admit, though, that the building did have a sinister air about it, especially under these gloomy skies. She half expected to be startled by a peal of thunder at any moment.

Laura stood in front of the house, watching chaos snuffling frantically at the threshold. The front door was ajar.

"Chaos, that's enough now. Time to go home." She reached into her pocket to retrieve the dog's leash. As if sensing his imminent subjugation, Chaos slipped inside the house. "Chaos!" she called again. "Shit. Chaos, get out of there right now!"

The dog did not emerge. The house was silent. The house had eaten the dog.

Laura looked around warily, as if nervous that a police officer might happen to be routinely patrolling the forest. Deciding it was all clear and muttering curses to herself, she pushed open the door to the Myers house. It creaked. Of course it creaks, she thought, and she peered into the darkened hallway.

"Hello?" she said loudly but not too loudly, too embarrassed to actually shout. She started to take a step through the doorway when something fast and hairy rocketed out of the darkness and through her legs, almost knocking her off balance. She turned just in time to see the beagle bounding back the way they had come, brandishing some new prize between his teeth.

"Chaos," she grumbled, following the dog at a pace she liked to think was no-nonsense rather than flustered. "You little shit," she added, though her anger at the animal was mitigated by the relief she felt at walking away from that house.

***

Back at home, Laura sat at the kitchen table and examined the prize she had wrestled away from Chaos, who now sat watching her sulkily from his bed in the corner.

It was a thin black disc, approximately fifteen centimetres in diameter, made of some strong but flexible material that she could not readily identify. Attached to the disc were the remnants of some grey fabric, as if it had been ripped away from something. When she brushed the disc with her finger, its surface changed colours in a consistent sequence, one colour fading into the next.

"What's that?" asked Shona on her way to the fridge.

Laura shrugged. "I'm not entirely sure. Some junk the dog brought home. A toy I think. I thought you were going out?"

Shona cracked open a beer and took a swig. "Funny story. I thought so too. Scotty, however, decided to do some baking instead." She mimed toking on a joint with a stoned expression.

Laura shook her head exasperatedly but said nothing.

"I know, I know," Shona said. "Believe me, I know. But you know what? Fuck him. Want to watch a movie and get drunk?"

Laura was about to decline when she saw the exaggerated look of pleading on her friend's face. "Sure," she said with a chuckle. "But I'm not sitting through *Sapphic Fiends from the Abyss* again."

Shona didn't seem to notice, but Laura's mind was elsewhere most of the evening.

***

Early the next morning Laura found herself sitting cross-legged at the end of the precarious old pier, staring into the dark water. The connection must have been made in her sleep somehow, because there it was, plain as the nose on Chaos' face, the moment she awoke. The disc and the thing in the lake were linked somehow, not just conceptually, but technologically. She had sprung from her bed, oblivious to the early hour, thrown on her clothes and hurriedly prepared a travel mug of coffee, then she was off to verify her theory, the dog bounding excitedly along beside her. So there she sat, watching the subaqueous glow transition from russet orange to emerald blue and back as she swept her fingers over the surface of the disc.

Chaos lay behind her, looking bored. Laura looked at him and sighed.

"I know what you're thinking," she said to the dog. "You're thinking a spaceship crashed into the lake, and something crawled out of it, and now that something is over at the Myers house."

Chaos looked at her without lifting his head. It was early, after all, and the weather had taken a turn for the better. The low sun warmed the peeling boards of the pier.

"Well, that's crazy. You know that, right?"

Chaos threw her a single token tail wag.

Laura got to her feet and stretched, and Chaos followed suit.

"Fine," she told the dog. "If you insist, let's go."

***

Laura half-expected the front door to be closed. She knew it had definitely been left ajar when she had made her hasty departure the previous day, and it hadn't felt like a door that would swing closed on its own due to gravity or weather, but she couldn't help but anticipate that, somehow, something had slammed the door shut behind her.

When she got there, however, everything looked the same as it did yesterday: the front door was still partially open, enough so that Chaos slipped right through without hesitation again. Laura pushed the door open the rest of the way. The hallway that was revealed was far less foreboding in the morning sunshine, and it ran the entire length of the house to the doorway at the opposite end. That door, too, was half open, and a heavy, golden light poured slowly through it. That must be the back door of the house, she deduced, opening onto the garden, and beyond that, the lake. The garden must be overgrown now, reclaimed by the voracious forest. Curious, she walked toward it, ignoring the stairwell and the closed interior doors on either side of the corridor, and placed her hand on the handle of the back door. Suddenly she felt butterflies in her stomach, but more from excitement than from fear. Somehow she knew that there was no reason to be afraid.

She opened the door and stepped into the garden.

She knew where she was, where she must be, but for a moment she felt like she'd set foot on another planet. She found herself on the edge of a large circular area of about three metres in diameter, within which a plethora of unique and unearthly flora abounded. The plants toward the centre of the circle were the most mature, some standing a solid metre tall, whereas newer growth was thriving nearer the edge. For a short distance beyond the perimeter the indigenous vegetation appeared to be dying off, as if the new plants were invading.

She saw a plant with a thick red stem, studded with formidable-looking thorns and topped with multiple globular unopened flowers. Each sphere was white with black-tipped sepals, making the closed bloom eerily suggestive of a giant's eyeball. She saw a plant that at first glance appeared to be made entirely of glass, its metre-tall stalk and its expansive leaves smooth and diaphanous. The azure dappling of the leaves seemed to be shifting lazily against its translucent orange background, like oil on water. She saw a large black and white orchid-like flower, its delicate labyrinth of interwoven anthers and ribbon-like petals protruding far from the calyx yet somehow appearing to end where it began, the impossible Escheresque architecture defying both gravity and three-dimensional logic.

She saw red and green spikes pushing up through the dirt at random angles, their sharp undulating edges making them look like weaponized grass; flowers that resembled mouths, some laughing, others screaming; a white pod deploying multiple long pink explorative tendrils, each terminating in a set of menacing, glistening hooks. She saw all of this strange life and more, and if she watched hard, she would have sworn that she could see it growing.

***

The garden ate time.

At first, Laura had intended to leave: to explore the garden for a few hours, take some photographs, then head home before dark and look up some of this stuff on the internet. But she found there was always something else to see, always another seductive creation to inspire her awe, and after a while she could no longer recall why she wanted to leave at all.

She'd found an old mattress inside the house and had decided to stay the night. That way she could observe the remarkable garden in the moonlight, and see what it did after dark. As she had slept she had felt the garden's tendrils moving over her body. They didn't harm her; on the contrary, she felt comforted by their touch, but she was aware that they were extracting something from her. She wasn't sure what they were taking, or how they were taking it, but the next morning she had felt more diminished somehow, as if some element of her that she couldn't name was newly absent.

The garden's fingers also reached into her mind. She had dreamed she was crawling from the muck of Lost Lake, weary and wounded but unwavering in her determination to see her garden-given mission through to the end, and then she was behind the Myers house, standing naked in a field of mud as blood rained down on her from a cracked sky and her feet transformed into roots, and then she was in space, looking down upon the Earth as the garden sprawled across its landmasses, and as she watched, black flowers grew from her eyes.

But she was not afraid.

She'd lost track of how long ago that first night was; or rather, she had not attempted to keep track. Three days? A week? Longer? It didn't matter. She had immediately felt an affinity with the garden so powerful, so overwhelming, that time had soon become meaningless, and before she knew what was happening she loved the garden, she needed the garden; they shared an intimate symbiosis.

But theirs was a symbiosis of mutualism rather than parasitism, she told herself; a two-way street. After all, the garden looked after all of her physical needs: she took sweet water from its vines, she ate freely of its multitudinous fruits. There were fruits that tasted of coffee and fruits that tasted of bacon and fruits that tasted of butter, and sometimes it was the same fruit at different times of the day. Then there were the berries; the white ones that made her high, the purple ones that made her euphoric, and the golden ones that gave her pleasure no human had ever come close to giving her.

Most of all, the garden had given her a purpose. She had never been sure of her place in the world before, she had just drifted like a mote of dust on a breeze, going with the flow, achieving nothing, being nothing. But now she was something, and she knew what she was with a cast-iron certainty: she was the guardian of the garden, the one human being entrusted with the responsibility of ensuring that the garden was allowed to grow and flourish and radiate without interference, and the life she had led before finding the garden—before being found by the garden—was as unimportant now as that mote of dust and as irrelevant as the world beyond this property and as inconsequential as time itself.

All that mattered was the garden.

***

Shona stood in front of the old Myers house and consulted the tablet one more time. "It's definitely here," she said.

Scotty dropped the end of his joint on the ground. "Cool. And to think I was worried for a minute that the place might be creepy," he said.

Shona was about to knock on the front door when Scotty slipped by her and opened it.

"What?" he responded to Shona's glare. "It's not like anyone lives here."

Scotty walked inside. Shona hesitated for a beat, looked around, then followed.

"Alright, let's make this quick, I have to be somewhere," Scotty insisted once they were both in the corridor. "I'll check down here, you check upstairs. Okay?"

Shona fleetingly considered objecting to the proposal to split up, but Scotty had already ducked into one of the other rooms and she decided that to do so would be embarrassing, somehow, so said nothing. Instead, she warily ascended the creaking stairs.

The stairwell opened onto a short hallway with three doors on it, one of which stood wide open. "Hello?" she called. "Laura? Laura Jones?" She added the last name to either sound more serious or to filter out the surplus Lauras, she wasn't sure which.

She stepped over the threshold into what appeared to be—what once had been—the master suite. There was a ratty and stained old single bed-sized mattress lying on the floor in the centre of the room, possibly left behind by the Myers or whoever, she thought, or maybe installed by a squatter at some point. A framed picture hung crookedly on the wall above the mattress, a faded print of Munch's Love and Pain. The window with a view of the lake was pushed wide open, and some kind of thick, milky white creeping vine had found its way up the back of the house and into the room, several of its probing tentacles spilling over the windowsill and meandering over the floor and walls, almost as far as the mattress. Flowers had emerged from the vines in some places, small, cheerful-looking purple and yellow blooms.

Curious, she brushed one gently with her finger, only to withdraw her hand quickly with a sharp intake of breath. The edges of the petals were sharp to the touch. She studied the tiny paper cut on her finger and put it to her mouth instinctively as she walked over to the open window and looked out at the peaceful lake and the garden below. Shona had never seen a garden like it. Weird plants sprawled from the back of the house to the edge of the lake, plants of such outlandish appearance and exotic morphologies that for a moment she felt as if she had been teleported to another world. Then she looked directly below the window, and there was Laura, hanging onto a vine some distance above the ground, looking back up at her.

***

By the time Shona got down to the garden, Laura was gone, and Scotty was waiting. He held up a fistful of the flowers that Laura, unbeknownst to anyone else, had named the Escher Orchids.

"Hey Shone, check these out. Have you ever seen flowers like these before?"

There was a small, muffled cry behind Shona, and she turned to see Laura standing in the doorway now, her hand covering her mouth, her eyes full of tears. She looked like she had been wearing the same clothes for several days, her hair was dirty and dishevelled, and though it has only been a few days, her face was gaunt.

"Laura! Oh, thank god. What's going on? We've been so worried about you, Laura. It's been days. You haven't been answering your phone or responding to messages. Chaos came home without you. He wouldn't stop barking. We thought at first he was trying to tell us that you were trapped in an old well somewhere, but it turned out the little shit was just hungry. We were going to call the police but you know how Scotty is about authority figures, and then I realized you'd left your tablet at home," she waved the device at her, "so we used that to locate your phone instead. And here we are. It looks like you aren't trapped down an old well after all."

"No," Laura said quietly, still staring at the flowers in Scotty's grasp. "No well."

"So, what's going on? No offence, Laura, but you look awful."

"I'm fine, Shona. Really. I'll be home soon."

Shona shook her head in bewilderment and gestured toward the house. "But what are you doing here? Why were you climbing that plant, Laura?"

"Wait, wait," Scotty interrupted. He inhaled deeply, then smirked. "Oh, I get it. I smell the pungent, heady aroma of cannabis. Have you been holding out on us, Laura?"

Laura looked at him blankly and opened her mouth to speak, but Scotty was already wandering off, following his nose in search of his passion.

***

Leaving Shona to quiz Laura, Scotty navigated around the outlandish plants, showing them little interest, his frazzled mind now running unwaveringly on one track, his brain occupied by one exclusive mission: locate Laura's secret pot crop.

And then he saw it, situated between the helical purple cactus thing and some kind of flower that looked like it was made of yellow teeth. A dilapidated old greenhouse. He could have sworn it hadn't been there a moment ago, but then again he was finding this garden weirdly disorientating. The structure looked rather ramshackle and askew, and its glass panels were clouded and mouldy, but there was a tell-tale pink glow emanating from within and he knew what that meant: grow lights.

"Jackpot," he said to himself, and giggled. "The old bud-hound has still got it."

He rounded the corner of the greenhouse and found the translucent door, unlocked and ajar, but somehow wedged into position, leaving a gap that Scotty thought he could just about pass through, given the correct motivation. With one quick look back at the way he'd come and out of sight of the women, he squeezed through the opening into the sweetly smelling, blinding pink glow beyond.

As he finally pulled his right leg in after him with a grunt, the entire greenhouse rapidly compressed into a crumpled spheroid plant less than a metre in diameter, and a single spurt of blood escaped before all was serene once more.

***

"What was that noise?" asked Shona.

"What?" Laura said, trying to look innocent but instinctively knowing that something had happened to Scotty. Something bad.

Shona seemed unconvinced by her friend's nonchalance. "Scotty?" she called in his general direction. "Scott?"

"You should go, Shona," Laura said quietly.

"What?"

"You should leave. Please?"

"What are you talking about? I'm not leaving without Scotty. Or you, for that matter."

"I'm not coming," Laura said. "And neither is Scotty."

"Laura, what the fuck? You're freaking me out. What—" Shona paused mid-sentence and looked down. A creeping black vine had formed a helix around her leg without actually touching her, the thick stem poised a couple of centimetres away from her skin. As if sensing it had lost the element of surprise, the plant instantly tightened around her ankle like a whip and continued to ascend her leg.

Shona looked at Laura.

"I'm sorry. You should have left," Laura said.

"Get the fuck off me!" Shona screamed at the vine as she bent over to disentangle herself, trying to force her fingers between the plant and her body but failing to find purchase. It was at that point that the vine's dozens of toxin-loaded retractile thorns extended, piercing the flesh of Shona's legs and hands. She dropped to the ground like a stone, the frantic scrabbling of her hands slowing as the plant squeezed like a boa constrictor. Shona's terror-stricken eyes turned to Laura as she started to spasm.

"The garden has to defend itself," Laura explained.

***

Some days passed before they came for Laura and the garden. She flinched at the pounding on the front door of the old house and wondered who *they* were. Friends of Shona or Scotty, perhaps. The police. An angry mob with pitchforks and flaming torches. It didn't really matter. It was over. It was over the moment Scotty picked the first flower.

It was time to go.

She slipped out of the window and manoeuvred smoothly down the white vine. Once her feet were on the ground she took a deep breath and steeled herself before turning to face the garden. She fixed her eyes on the fence and the forest beyond and strode resolutely forward, aware that any last looks at the garden could lead to her changing her mind, and that was a risk she could not afford to take. She knew she had to leave the garden in order to save it.

She circumvented the front of the Myers house and fled through the woods back to her own house, pausing cautiously to ensure there was no one there, waiting for her. Satisfied, she strode boldly up to the front door and entered. Chaos rocketed out of the kitchen, barking bravely. When he saw it was Laura his tail became a blur of motion and he bounded over to welcome her home, all neglect forgiven. The dog's joy went unreciprocated as Laura only stayed long enough to grab the car keys and her passport. Undeterred, the dog chased after the car as Laura drove away.

***

Several thousand kilometres away from the garden, Laura Jones sat cross-legged on sun-dappled grass, and she waited. She imagined that the traveller whose vessel had come to rest at the bottom of Lost Lake, the creature she had come to think of as the Star Sower, might have similarly sat and waited in the overgrown backyard of the Myers house. Like Laura, the Star Sower had been selected by the garden, but on some strange world some unfathomable distance away. Perhaps there was no room left on that planet, and so the garden had wanted to expand: to colonize. And so the Sower had been compelled to find its way to Earth, bringing with it—carrying inside it—the gift of the garden.

And now it was Laura's turn to serve the garden: to help it expand. She had no way of travelling to another planet, so another continent would have to suffice. Besides, the garden was just getting started with the Earth.

And so she waited. She waited for her beautiful metamorphosis, her transcendent sowing, her becoming one with the garden.

***

The old man was awoken by the distant screaming just as dawn broke. It had gone on for several minutes. Though he spent hours searching for the source, all he found was the key to a rental car and a circle of strange plants that he had never come across before, despite having lived in the area his entire life.

They were beautiful.

Resonatorz

The generic synth-pop came to an end and the singer froze in her final choreographed pose, her futuristic costume shimmering beneath the lights.

"That's a wrap," shouted a voice off-camera. "Thank you, everyone."

The singer and her backing dancers relaxed and began to disperse from the sound stage.

"How does Arabella do it?" asked an admiring spectator, a handsome young man in a designer chauffeur's uniform with pushed-up sleeves. "That was a gruelling six-hour video shoot, but she still looks fantastic!"

"I know!" replied his confidant, a young woman with headphones and a clipboard. "She just radiates energy. What's her secret?"

"It's no secret," the singer announced, her two fans expressing surprise at the star's appearance in their midst. Arabella smiled her dazzling white smile straight to camera as she held up the box of Resonatorz Aura Purification Cream. "I joined the Reso-Nation," she declared, and the commercial ended with a freeze-frame on the product.

The Chloe Jurick Show's live studio audience applauded on demand.

"Amazing," Chloe said, gently shaking her head beneath her big blonde hair. "But what do you say, Arabella, to those skeptics who say that Resonatorz are just a new age fad with no scientific validity and that you yourself are—and this is their word, not mine—a snake oil salesman?"

Arabella Spasm's professional charm was effortless and unfaltering as she responded to the pre-approved softball question. "Firstly, I'd say, I think you mean snake oil sales*woman*," she said with a smirk. The audience laughed. "But seriously, Chloe, I'm used to it. Any therapeutic breakthrough, especially one as revolutionary, as *evolutionary*, as Resonatorz from the Vortek Clinic, inevitably faces the naysayers and the skeptics, the old guard who represent the status quo. They feel threatened. And so they should. They have a lot to lose. They don't want me talking about Resonatorz because they don't want your wonderful audiences here in the studio and watching at home to know about Resonatorz Aura Purification Cream, Resonatorz Energy Healing Unguent, or Resonatorz Rejuvenation Gel. They don't want them to join the Reso-Nation. Well, sorry boys. Your old ways are becoming obsolete. The people demand something new. The people demand Resonatorz."

More applause, then Spasm's smiling face froze as Dan Garven hit pause on the VCR remote, the frame twitching intermittently as broken white lines of noise flickered across the image.

"Well, well, well," said Sandy Marshall, leaning in the doorway of the tiny office she shared with Dan. "I never took you for an Arabella Spasm fan. Which is your favourite? Her abysmal pop-punk or her straight-to-video erotic thrillers?"

Dan snorted. "That's a hard choice. But this right here is what we journalists call *research*."

"I've heard of that!" Sandy exclaimed, stepping into the room and slouching in the chair on the opposite side of the desk from Dan. "And what is it that we are *researching*?" She exaggerated her enunciation of the word and surrounded it with air quotes for good measure.

Dan threw a pamphlet across the desk and Sandy inspected it.

"Darius Vortek has an exhibition at the Silverman Art Gallery?"

"Sure does. He's a major donor," Dan explained. "Apparently when you buy an art gallery a new wing they let you borrow it to show your pretentious millionaire art."

"That's very nice," Sandy said, "but why should that be of interest to *Antibody*?"

Antibody was a monthly magazine specializing in exposés of fraudulent alternative medicines and the debunking of far-fetched new-age therapies. Its circulation was small and it struggled to make ends meet at the best of times, including paying the salaries of its only two staff writers.

"That's what I intend to find out," Dan replied, pushing a note across the desk. "This was delivered with the pamphlet."

Sandy picked up the scrawled note and read it aloud. "'Vortek cannot be trusted. Resonatorz are a threat. Meet me here at five on Monday to learn more.' Hmm. It's written on Vortek Clinic letterheaded paper. You buying it?"

"I don't know," Dan said, glancing at his digital watch, "but I'm intrigued. What do you know about Vortek?"

Sandy shrugged. "Just the information that's in the public domain. Rich hippy psychiatrist, jumping on the new age bandwagon. His Resonatorz product line is extremely popular right now. Why, even I'm wearing it!"

Dan looked incredulous. "Seriously? Why?"

"I joined the Reso-Nation!" she said, mimicking the Resonatorz commercials. She laughed. "My sister was raving about it, so I volunteered to try it for—what was that word you used?" She snapped her fingers. "Research purposes! That's it. I'm wearing Resonatorz Aura Purification Cream. Hey Dan, does my aura look purified? What colour is it?"

Dan squinted at her. "Is naive a colour? How does it *feel*? That's the important thing."

Sandy scrunched up her face and scratched her shoulder aggressively. "Itchy," she said.

***

The assistant at the front desk looked at her watch pointedly as Dan entered the Silverman Art Gallery, going against the flow of visitor traffic. He smiled innocently at her in return and quickly located the Vortek exhibit.

Standing with arms crossed he inspected the sculpture that dominated the space, a larger-than-life abstract human form of indeterminate gender. The grey figure was kneeling, arms held out as if in praise, an expression of apparent bliss on its face. Dan circled the piece slowly, head tilted slightly, trying to arrive at an interpretation of it. As he moved behind the figure he saw that there were large apertures, like eruptions, in the shoulders and back, through which radiated an internal golden glow, pulsating slowly.

Dan wondered what, or who, the figure was worshipping.

"He's a brilliant man, don't you think?"

Dan turned to see a woman standing behind him, admiring the piece. She was middle-aged and taller than him, her hair—long and black except for a well-defined streak of grey—cascading over her black leather jacket.

"What's that?" Dan enquired.

"Doctor Vortek," the woman said without looking at him. She had a European accent, Dan thought, possibly Dutch. "He designed and commissioned this piece. He calls it *Birth of the Reso-Nation*."

Dan nodded knowingly, then shrugged. "Personally I prefer my art in comic book form. Have you ever read *2000AD*? It's British."

"Have you tried them? His Resonatorz?" the stranger asked, ignoring his question. "They are truly miraculous. Life changing. Don't you agree?"

Dan looked at the stranger with suspicion. "I can't say I have tried them. You sound like Arabella Spasm," he suggested.

The woman finally faced him and looked him in the eye, unamused. "Meet me outside, by the fire escape, in two minutes," she said brusquely. "Don't keep me waiting, Mr. Garven." And with that, she spun on her bootheels and marched away.

***

Dan caught up with the woman by the fire escape as instructed. As he approached her she turned to address someone lurking in the shadows.

"I'll be in the vehicle," she announced.

"Thank you, Anya," said the lurker, and a short, bald man stepped out of the darkness.

"Good day, Mr. Garven. My name is Eugene Fetzer. I am the man you are here to meet. Anya looks after me."

"Why the cloak and dagger, Mr. Fetzer? And why do you need to be looked after?" Dan asked, offering his hand. Fetzer ignored it.

"Sometimes the cloak is required to avoid the dagger, Mr. Garven. Shall we walk?"

Fetzer proceeded to walk away without waiting for an answer. Dan looked over his shoulder nervously before following.

"Why am I here, Mr. Fetzer? Who are you, exactly? What is it you think you know about Darius Vortek?"

Fetzer walked and talked with his eyes straight ahead. "I am an associate of Doctor Vortek. I am involved in the development of certain components of the Resonatorz line of therapeutic products. Specifically, the components dealing with aura purification."

"Aura purification," Dan repeated, the cynicism evident in his voice. "Fascinating."

"Indeed."

"Let me guess. You want to expose the whole idea of auras as a fraud, am I right?"

Fetzer glared at Dan. "Incorrect, Mr. Garven. I sense that you are a Resonatorz skeptic."

"What makes you think that?"

"Your aura, of course."

Dan raised his eyebrows.

"That," continued Fetzer, "and the ideological stance of the publication for which you write."

"Alright. So why *am* I here, Mr. Fetzer?"

"As I was saying, I work on components of Resonatorz. There are many components, and many scientists, all carefully siloed and kept in ignorance of the work of the others."

"A precaution against intellectual property theft, I'd imagine. Industrial espionage, and so forth. Ludicrous though the idea is, in the circumstances."

"That is part of the reason, certainly, but there is more to it. I believe some of the active ingredients of Resonatorz may lead to side effects, Mr. Garven. Dangerous side effects."

"Such as?"

"I don't know, exactly. But I have become aware of a correspondence between Doctor Vortek and our illustrious celebrity spokesperson, Miss Arabella Spasm, in which Miss Spasm expresses considerable concern that these side effects may arise in her promotional interactions with the media. Miss Spasm is a true believer, and has been an avid consumer of Resonatorz since the days of the initial prototypes. If anyone knows about side effects, she will."

"Alright. Are you proposing I ask her about it? Because there's no way the Vortek Clinic will entertain *Antibody* in any way."

"I am aware. Which is why you will not approach her as Dan Garven of *Antibody* magazine, you will approach her as Adrian Colon of *Transcendent Vibrations* magazine, a publication that adopts a significantly more open-minded view on such matters than your own. Mr. Colon has an appointment to interview Miss Spasm tomorrow."

"And where will the real Adrian Colon be?"

"I took the liberty of informing the real Mr. Colon that his interview would have to be postponed due to a scheduling conflict."

"Why?" Dan asked, suspiciously. "What's in this for you?"

"I'll admit," explained Fetzer, "that it would give me a certain satisfaction if some unfortunate revelations were to somehow befall the great Doctor Darius Vortek. My significant contributions to the success of the clinic have gone unappreciated and unrecognized, I regret to say, and my own projects have been back-burnered", he said, spitting out this last phrase with extreme distaste. "I find this state of affairs unacceptable, Mr. Garven. Ah. Here's my ride."

Dan looked up to see they were back in the gallery's small parking lot, now occupied only by his own battered VW Beetle and a yellow Porsche. Anya was leaning against the driver's side door of that vehicle, waiting.

"Which reminds me," Fetzer said, handing Dan a black pill bottle with a red cap, "a small gift."

"As I told—Anya, was it?" he glanced at the woman, who ignored him and climbed behind the wheel, "I don't use Resonatorz."

"Oh, this is something quite different. A little project of mine that the Vortek Clinic, in its wisdom, declined to fund further. I think you might find it useful, however."

Dan examined the bottle briefly, observing that its only marking was the outline of a bullet printed on the label. "What is it?"

"Your appointment with Miss Spasm is at 10 A.M., Mr. Garven," Fetzer said, opening the car door. "Please refrain from giving her my regards."

"Have you checked your own aura lately, Mr. Fetzer?" Dan asked, dropping the bottle into his pocket.

"I have, Mr. Garven," he replied, opening the passenger side door, "and I confidently expect to enjoy a long and healthy life."

At that moment a large red pickup truck roared into the lot at high speed and broadsided the Porsche, slamming the passenger side door on Fetzer's body and shunting the smaller vehicle sideways and into the wall of the gallery building before coming to an abrupt halt. Dan stared in horror at the mangled body of Fetzer, squeezed between the Porsche's body and door, blood gushing from his mouth, one eye hanging from its socket. The truck's engine was turned off and its door swung open. The driver staggered out, his face a mask of blood from its encounter with the truck's dashboard. Dan heard a thumping sound coming from the Porsche and watched as the shattered windshield burst outward. Anya crawled onto the hood through the broken glass, looking dazed but otherwise intact. Dan tried to shake off the shock and make a decision as to what to do. Find a pay phone? Assist the casualties? Panic? One glance told him that Fetzer was beyond help, so he moved toward the injured truck driver, a huge, muscular fellow with a mullet and a thick moustache. The driver wiped the blood from his eyes and looked around, spotting Dan. His eyes rolled into the back of his head and he massaged his shoulder vigorously as he appeared to be listening intently to something Dan couldn't hear. Seconds later his eyes righted themselves and he stretched his shoulder muscles and bulky triceps.

"Alright," the driver said to himself, and he returned to the cab of his steaming truck to retrieve a pipe wrench the length of his arm, which he proceeded to brandish like a weapon.

"Hey, man. Take it easy," Dan said. "I think you might have a concussion. I'm just trying to help."

Unfazed by his words or by the sound of approaching sirens, the mulleted driver started to advance upon Dan, wielding the fearsome-looking wrench, and suddenly Anya was there, placing herself in between the two men. She looked at Dan.

"Run," she said, and strode fearlessly toward their oncoming mulleted tormentor.

Dan took her advice, and ran.

***

The next morning, Dan Garven tried not to look nervous as he sat in the plush waiting room of the Vortek Clinic. He had almost talked himself out of being there. Fetzer was just a classic disgruntled employee, he had told himself. Fetzer had nothing on Vortek himself and had engineered this dubious meeting between Spasm and a journalist from an unsympathetic publication in a desperate attempt to dig up some dirt. Any dirt. The incident in the gallery's parking lot was just an accident. A freak accident, sure, but an accident nonetheless, caused by the reckless actions of the drunk or possibly insane stranger driving the pickup truck. When Dan had fled the scene he had observed the arrival of the police but had considered it in his own best interests to exercise discretion and return forthwith to his apartment, where he had called Sandy. She had hesitantly confirmed his analysis of the situation, and so it was settled. Until this morning, when his clock radio had awoken him with the local news, and the report that the Silverman Art Gallery would be closed today due to a vehicular incident on the property. Two cars had been involved, the reporter had said grimly, leading to three fatalities.

"Mr. Colon?" a woman's voice said, and it took Dan a moment to realize that she was addressing him.

"Yes, that's me," he replied. "Hello."

"I'm Arabella Spasm," said Arabella Spasm. "Shall we?"

"Of course. Yes," Dan said, standing up and trailing after the woman who was already walking briskly away. She led him into a meeting room.

"Take a seat, Mr. Colon."

"Please, call me Adrian," Dan said.

"Alright Adrian. I'm Arabella. How can I help you today?"

"Erm," Dan muttered, fumbling inside his briefcase. For a second he felt dislocated and on the edge of panic. The traumatizing events of the previous day, the pressure of being an imposter on what was, in a professional sense, enemy territory, and the surreality of sitting opposite a woman he was accustomed to seeing only on a cathode ray tube—and often in various states of undress—all crashed together and piled up in his brain for a fleeting moment before he wrestled his emotions back under control, re-compartmentalized his feelings and regained his composure. He pulled a small dictaphone from the bag and looked at Spasm. She smiled and nodded, and he hit record.

"Resonatorz," he said. "Truly amazing. They're taking the world by storm, as you know. Our readers would be thrilled to learn everything they can about this exciting new product line. I understand you yourself have experienced great benefits from Resonatorz. Can you tell us about that?"

"They are amazing, aren't they, Adrian," she said rhetorically, "And it's great to hear that your readers are ready to join the Reso-Nation. Yes, it's no secret that I'm personally a big fan of Resonatorz and the Vortek Clinic. This isn't just a job to me, it's a real passion of mine to spread the word about Resonatorz, and the amazing health advantages that they can bestow."

"Such as?" Dan asked.

Spasm hesitated for just a beat. "Well, as I'm sure you know, Adrian, the Resonatorz product line offers comprehensive therapeutic and healing benefits. I have what I like to call my daily Resonatorz regimen. Every day at sunrise I take my Resonatorz Cosmic Cleansing Tonic to harmonize my body with the new day's cosmic frequencies. Around noon I liberally apply my Resonatorz Energy Healing Unguent to balance and maintain my natural elemental energies, and, of course, Adrian, every evening I administer a Resonatorz Positivity Suppository to ensure a restful slumber."

"That's very impressive," Dan said, conscious of keeping his *Antibody* cynicism out of his voice and remaining in character. "And you do radiate contentment and well-being, without a doubt. But how do you respond to the rumours about the alleged side effects of Resonatorz?" he asked.

Spasm stared at him in silence for an uncomfortable length of time. "I'm sorry, Adrian, you've lost me there," she said finally. "What rumours are you referring to?"

Finding himself out on a vertiginous limb, he tried not to look down. "Oh, it's just that some people are reporting certain adverse reactions to Resonatorz. Can you reassure our readers about that?"

Another pause.

"I'm afraid I'm not familiar with your publication, Adrian. Spiritual Vibrations. What's the subject matter, exactly?"

"Oh, you know. Chi. Energies. Vibrations. Spiritual vibrations, cosmic vibrations, holistic vibrations. We cover all the major vibrations."

"I see. And is your magazine called Spiritual Vibrations or Transcendent Vibrations?"

Shit, he thought. Then he shrugged. "What's the difference?" he asked.

She must have pressed a hidden button or, he thought wryly, perhaps she had signalled for help with her aura, because at that moment the door opened and two large men entered with grave expressions.

"I think you have all you need, Mr. Colon. Gentlemen," she addressed the goons, "be so kind as to show our guest out via the back door."

Dan put the little recorder away and stood. "Thank you for your time, Miss Spasm."

"You know, Mr. Colon," Spasm said with an emotionless smile, "you really should try Resonatorz yourself. Your aura looks like dog shit. And you might find you live longer."

***

"You're not at work," Dan informed Sandy. She was standing in the doorway of her apartment, dressed in a robe.

"I overslept, that's all," she replied, looking at the large blue bruise on his temple. "Ouch. Come on in."

"I did call ahead," Dan said as he followed her inside. "Your line was busy."

"Coffee?"

"Sure, thanks."

Sandy's apartment was small but easily navigable due to her penchant for minimalist interior design. The only exception was the pile of cardboard boxes in the short entrance hallway. He squeezed by these and joined her in the kitchen.

"How was your interview with TV's Arabella Spasm?" she asked from the coffee maker.

"Erm, it was somehow both unenlightening and revealing at the same time," he replied. "At least until she had her goons introduce me head first to the steps at the rear of the building. How did you know that I went to the Vortek Clinic? When we spoke on the phone last night we both decided it was a bad idea."

"I heard the news report, about the fatalities at the Silverman Art Gallery," Sandy said. "I assumed you would have heard it too, and that you would consequently be helpless to resist your journalistic instincts."

Dan snorted. "You know me too well."

"So what did Miss Spasm reveal?"

"Only that she's hiding something. Or the Vortek Clinic is."

"Something like what? Side effects?"

"I think so."

Sandy looked thoughtful. "But, it's all relative, right?" she asked, handing him his coffee.

"How do you mean?"

"Well, everything is a trade-off, isn't it, Dan? Even if there are side effects, maybe the benefits of Resonatorz are worth it."

"Are you speaking from personal experience?"

Sandy sighed. "I just think you should try Resonatorz for yourself before you get all up in arms about some harmless side effects."

Dan looked at her quizzically. "How do you know they're harmless?"

She smiled at him. "I've been using Resonatorz, Dan," she said. "Do I look sick to you?" Sandy opened her robe, revealing her nakedness beneath. She stepped toward him.

"Whoa, Sandy, what are you doing?" Dan asked his friend, flustered.

"Just what you've always wanted me to do, Dan," she replied in a whisper, taking his coffee mug from his hand and putting it down. She pressed her body against him and her mouth to his. He did not shy away from the kiss. She placed his arms inside her robe and around her body, his hands feeling the smoothness of her back.

"Shit!" Dan yelled suddenly, jerking away from her. "What the hell was that?" He examined his left forearm, which now bore what appeared to be a small puncture wound. A drop of blood trickled from it slowly.

Sandy smiled at him. "It's alright, Dan. Don't fight it. It's just the Resonatorz."

"What does that mean?" he asked, incredulously. "Something on your body just stabbed me, Sandy, or bit me, or something."

"It's alright, Dan," Sandy persisted, "Trust me. It will all make sense to you soon. Just relax."

"What has happened to you, Sandy?" Dan asked with concern.

"I joined the Reso-Nation, Dan."

"What the hell does that mean? This is freaking me out, Sandy. I'm leaving now."

He turned and headed quickly to the door, bumping into one of the piled boxes in his haste. It fell to the floor, several packets of Resonatorz Aura Purification Cream spilling from it. He glanced once more at Sandy. She shrugged off her robe, standing naked and unashamed, revealing to him the strange mottled blue and green mass that had enveloped her shoulder and seemed to be spreading over her arm and chest. At its core was seated some kind of erupting carbuncle, from which radiated a network of subdermal tendrils, like a parasite colonizing her flesh. He thought, for a moment, that he glimpsed something moving, undulating beneath the skin.

"Dan, please," she pleaded, her arms outstretched to him for an embrace.

He did not look back again.

***

The latest issue of *Antibody* magazine hit the stands two weeks after Dan's strange encounters with Arabella Spasm and Sandy Marshall. Throughout that time he had stayed off the radar. He had not returned to his apartment. He had not gone into the office. He had checked into a rather sleazy motel under another assumed name; it was not the kind of establishment that strictly required proof of ID, and he had paid in cash. He declined housekeeping. He rarely left his room, only breaking cover after dark, and only then to restock on junk food or to visit the late-night pharmacy. The single exception was when he had been forced to venture out during regular Post Office hours to mail his latest story into work.

Deep down he knew it barely qualified as a story at all. It was more of a testimony of everything that had happened to him since that first contact with Fetzer, through to his current situation. He had no proof of anything, not yet, and he wasn't even sure what it was that he couldn't prove. But it was all he had, and he needed to get it out there before it was too late. The readers could decide for themselves what it all amounted to. He'd also had to submit it handwritten, of course, just to give that final whacko rant touch.

He took another painkiller and examined his arm again. He still could not say exactly what Sandy had done to him or how she had done it, but he knew it had hurt like hell at the time, and the pain had only intensified for several hours afterwards, preventing him from using his left arm or even sleeping. He had picked up the strongest over-the-counter painkillers he could, but they had barely taken the edge off, and he had eventually passed out in the motel room from sheer exhaustion. When he had awoken he had found that the pain had mercifully abated somewhat, and it had subsequently levelled off at a dull ache. He had examined the wound with a morbid fascination as it had scabbed over, observing as the vivid green-blue bruising slowly crept across his body over the course of several days. He had decided not to seek medical attention; partly out of paranoia, but also because he knew it was necessary for him to suffer. The arm was the only physical proof he had that he was not experiencing a psychotic break; the only way he had to prove it to the world and to himself. Besides, the magazine would probably send out a photographer. As he slid the arm into his jacket, he laughed out loud as it struck him that he would give his right arm to prove that the Vortek Clinic was nefarious. He should be grateful that he might only have to give his left.

He left the motel feeling foolish wearing sunglasses and a cheap baseball cap that he had grabbed at the drugstore and headed straight to the newsstand on the corner of the street. They stocked a surprisingly extensive range of obscure and niche titles for such a small stall, possibly reflecting the obscure and niche nature of the residents of this particular neighbourhood, Dan thought. Sure enough, there it was, peeking out from behind copies of *Particle* magazine and *Dark Adaptation* monthly.

He picked up the single copy of *Antibody* and stared at the cover story. Arabella Spasm stared back. RESONATORZ: AT LAST, THE REAL THING! read the headline.

His arm started aching again.

***

Dan Garven sat on the bench in the small park opposite the Vortek Clinic, nursing the take-out cappuccino from Curmudgeon Coffee and watching his fellow journalists arrive. He had heard on the radio that there was to be a press conference there in an hour, and rumour had it that the reclusive Doctor Darius Vortek himself would make an appearance. Speculation was rife that he was about to announce an exciting new advance in Resonatorz technology.

He looked down at his press pass and fiddled with it nervously. He knew that to attend the conference at all would be pure folly, and to use his own press pass to gain access would be sheer insanity, if not suicide. He also knew he had to do it. He was at the end of his metaphorical rope now. He was de facto unemployed, he was running out of money, his life was in danger, and his body was infected. He had to do something, and it had come to an all-or-nothing scenario. He reached into his inside pocket and removed the small black bottle with the red cap that Fetzer had given him. The bullet bottle. He popped it open and tipped the single bitter pill into his mouth, washing it down with the cold dregs of his coffee. He stood up and gripped his press pass tightly. All or nothing.

He blended in with the other attendees, drifted casually into the lobby and joined the line for the walk-through metal detector. The security guard barely glanced at his pass and before he knew it, he was on the other side of the cordon. He took a deep breath and winced at a sharp pain, this time emanating not from his arm but from his stomach. He clenched his teeth through the discomfort and followed the flow into the large meeting room, taking a seat toward the back.

Abruptly he was doubled over by the cramping in his gut, and he had to stifle a groan to avoid attracting attention. It felt like his insides were reconfiguring themselves. As soon as the pain subsided for a moment he got up with the intention of locating a washroom, but immediately realized that he wouldn't even make it as far as the door. Fortunately there was a row of three large pots containing expansive ferns behind him and he took refuge behind the nearest one. Clutching his abdomen, he heaved into the pot and had a surprise reunion with his meagre breakfast. He broke into a sweat as the second wave of nausea hit, delivering the remainder of his coffee and toast and something else, something he did not remember eating. He stared through watering eyes at the white mass lying in the dirt and partially digested food and braced himself for the next, inevitable convulsion.

By the time he reemerged, his old friend Arabella Spasm had taken the stage.

"So, thank you all for attending," she was saying, "and please help yourselves to the complimentary Resonatorz products in front of the stage."

As the other audience members filled their boots with bribes of potions and suppositories, Dan pulled his baseball cap down and returned to his seat, patting his jacket pocket to confirm that what had happened behind the ferns had not been a hallucination. The bulge of the thing was still there, the thing he had somehow intuitively assembled from the components that he had gingerly extracted from his vomitus. The thing that Fetzer's gift had, by way of some unthinkable mechanism, coagulated inside him. Perhaps this is all a hallucination, he pondered. Perhaps the infection from my festering arm has spread to my brain, and I'm actually still in the motel room, drooling and rocking back and forth in front of *Airwolf* on TV.

Even if that's true, he thought, so what? It makes no real difference in the end. I have nothing to lose at this point.

"And now," Spasm continued, "it gives me great pleasure to introduce to you the founder and CEO of the Vortek Clinic, the genius behind Resonatorz, and my personal hero, Doctor Darius Vortek."

The assembled press applauded as Vortek walked onto the stage. He was a tall man, over six feet, his boyish facial features contrasting with his wavy salt-and-pepper hair and neatly trimmed beard, his intelligent eyes behind wire-framed circular spectacles. He spoke with a clipped British accent that occasionally wandered into Irish territory.

"Thank you. That's very kind of you," he raised his hands to quiet the audience. "My name is Doctor Darius Vortek, and as you know, I normally play the part of the eccentric, reclusive genius and leave all of this sort of thing to my much more charismatic, and much more attractive representative, the beautiful Miss Spasm. However, what the Vortek Clinic has to announce today is so exciting that I simply couldn't resist giving it the personal touch."

"Doctor Vortek," Garven interrupted, standing and finally discarding his shades and cap. "Why are you covering up the fact that Resonatorz have serious adverse side effects? That Resonatorz are causing physical mutations in the people that use them?"

Spasm took the mic. "Security, please escort *Mr. Garven* from the building," she said, emphasizing his real name.

Vortek put his hand on Spasm's shoulder and moved her away. "Stand down, security. I'll handle this, thank you, Arabella. Mr. Garven, is it?"

Dan glared.

Vortek adjusted his spectacles and seemed deep in thought for a moment. "Mr. Garven is correct, and also incorrect," he said. "There are, indeed, mutations. But these mutations are not a side effect of Resonatorz. Quite the contrary. They are, in fact, the purpose of Resonatorz."

There was a murmuring from the crowd.

"In recent years," Vortek went on, "the Vortek Clinic has been researching and developing strategies for the acceleration and control of human evolution itself. The result of this R and D, we call Resonatorz. Resonatorz is a line of products that all fundamentally do the same thing. They deliver a parasitic microorganism into the body of the subject. This parasite establishes a symbiotic relationship with the host. It feeds on negative human energy, and in return it liberates the host from all the psychological pollution of society; the guilt, the repression, the confusion, the fear. It feasts, and it grows.

"The Resonatorz products themselves are not intrinsic to this process. The products are merely an agent to ensure the optimum initial deployment of the parasite, subsequent to which it can reproduce itself independently through blood-borne transmission or sexual contact. I understand Mr. Garven himself has experienced this first-hand."

"It's a disease. You're spreading a disease," Dan replied. He dropped his jacket to the floor and tore open his shirt, exposing the brightly coloured upper left quadrant of his body. The turquoise, marbled flesh rippled in rhythm with the throbbing of the gristly gnarled mass near his shoulder, the lubricated black barb embedded in the centre of the mass occasionally unsheathing as it twitched with excitement. "Is this what you call evolution?" he demanded.

"Congratulations, Mr. Garven. What you have there is a magnificent exemplar of the Resonatorz Fleshlink mutation, the single greatest evolutionary advance for millennia. It is the conduit by which a suitably tuned, psychically equipped intellectual elite, such as myself, can both remotely receive sensory input and, in return, transmit stimuli back, thereby influencing the actions of the host. It is no longer necessary for anyone to ever be alone, or lost, or ignorant. The Fleshlink will always be there to be your guide."

"The Fleshlink will always be there to be your master, you mean," Dan retorted, recalling the mulleted truck driver with the giant wrench, Fetzer's unwitting assassin. "You're weaponizing innocent people. Turning them into puppets. With you as the puppet master!"

"Well, what use are puppets without a puppet master, Mr. Garven?"

"You're insane, Vortek," Dan snarled back.

"The Resonatorz parasite inside your brain will soon convince you that I am, in fact, the only sane person alive," Vortek said with a smile.

Dan drew the Fetzer weapon from his pocket, the slimy pistol-like device his body had produced, and pointed it at Vortek. There were exclamations of alarm from the assembled members of the press, and Arabella Spasm screamed in horror, though Vortek himself maintained an expression of imperious defiance. Dan pulled the trigger just as Spasm leapt to shield her idol, causing the bullet, if indeed the grotesque projectile could be called a bullet, to obliterate the left side of the woman's face. She was dead before she hit the floor a second later. Vortek turned and started to walk calmly but briskly off the stage, and Dan adjusted his aim and fired again, but this time the gristle pistol exploded into a gory mess in his fist. Detecting movement in his peripheral vision, he turned to see the audience closing in on him threateningly.

"Stop the assassin!"

"Death to the skeptic!"

"Kill him! Kill the heretic!"

Dan dropped the remains of the weapon, threads of slime stretching from his hands, and ran for the nearest side door, bursting through it. He found himself in a corridor and hurtled around the corner in a desperate search for an emergency exit, but hearing the sound of a rapidly approaching mob behind him he ducked into the first unlocked room that he could find and closed the door. The room was windowless and dark, and he stood at the door for a moment, catching his breath and listening for his pursuers. The angry voices seemed to recede into the distance, so he fumbled against the wall until he located a light switch. As the fluorescent lighting flickered to life he saw he was in a large storeroom of some kind. It was full of metal shelves, all loaded with identical boxes. The only identifying mark on the boxes was the phrase Resonatorz 2.0. He ripped open the nearest box and beheld the contents.

He had to cover his mouth to stop the scream from escaping.

Suddenly he heard a voice directly behind him, a gravelly voice, raised as if sounding the alarm.

"As-sas-sin! As-sas-sin!"

He spun around, looking for the source, but the voice remained behind him.

"As-sas-sin! As-sas-sin!"

He stopped and twisted to view his shoulder blade.

"As-sas-sin!"

It was the Fleshlink. The Fleshlink was betraying his position.

The door burst open and the brainwashed journalists poured into the room, overpowering him and forcing him to the floor. One of them, a portly, bearded reporter who had once been friendly with Dan, sat astride him and raised a clenched fist, preparing to pulverize his face, but then abruptly he froze, staring into Dan's eyes. The restraining mob slowly released their grip and the bearded reporter climbed off, offering Dan his hand. Dan accepted it and got to his feet again, his lips moving silently as he did so. It took a moment for him to find his voice, and then he spoke softly at first, but with greater and greater volume until he was yelling, the mob repeating every phrase back to him enthusiastically.

"Hail Resonatorz," Dan said.

"Hail Resonatorz," the others echoed.

"Hail Darius Vortek," Dan called.

"Hail Darius Vortek," repeated the mob, and a chorus of Flashlinks joined in.

"Hail Vortek."

"Hail Vortek."

"HAIL VORTEK, THE NEW GOD!"

Brain Fog

The fog arrived at dawn. It was thick and eerily green, a luminescent emerald green, unlike any fog that any Pepper Islander had seen before. Some said there were shapes inside it. Shapes that seemed to move independently of the fog's drift, shapes that writhed and thrashed deep within it. Shadows of unidentifiable and unsettling things lurking behind the heavy green curtain.

The cryptic gloom crawled slowly over the sleepy Canadian island, reducing visibility to only a few metres and interrupting all transit, both incoming and outgoing, effectively cutting the landmass off from the rest of the world. The early ferry, transporting some of the first ripe tourists of the season, was forced to return to the mainland, unable to even get a visual on the ferry slip let alone dock, and the old de Havilland Beavers of tiny Pep-Air Seaplanes that called Pepper Island their home had all of their morning flights out cancelled due to inclement weather.

There was no authoritative explanation for the sudden appearance of the fog, much less for its more fanciful reported attributes. Meteorologists threw up their hands and admitted they were baffled. Some onlookers claimed that the fog had arisen from the ocean in the Strait of Georgia as a huge green bubble, whereas others suggested that it had been secreted from a fallen meteorite. A few social media commentators theorized that it had been accidentally released, Captain Trips fashion, from some secret—probably stealth—offshore military facility, or that it was evaporated fuel from a crashed UFO. Still other observers speculated that the origin of the fog—or in their scenario, smog—might be some long-forgotten drums of toxic waste, hidden away and left to decay in some deep dark cave decades ago, finally leaking their toxic—and possibly zombifying—contents into the atmosphere. And then there was that crazy, green-jumpsuited alien cult on the island, and did anyone remember that gas attack in Japan a few years ago?

***

Ambassador Quinctilius Quantum, the current occupant of the vessel formerly known as Gordon Carp and founder and leader of the Embassy of the Cosmic Guardians, would have regarded the word cult as a pejorative, preferring the more grandiose term "new religious movement". As for the ECG being responsible for the invading green fog, he would be forced, if pressed, to remain enigmatic on the issue, for though the fog was as much a mystery to him as anyone, he could not afford to let his followers know that. He had, after all, been preparing them for the arrival of the Guardians for years now, even adopting green jumpsuits as the group's official uniform to reflect the colour of the energy orbs that were their extraterrestrial superiors. Now that a green otherworldly fog had arrived, almost literally on the doorstep of the commune, he could hardly disregard or dismiss it. In fact, he decided to embark on a little rebranding lickety-split.

Behold, he said to his followers, *our great Cosmic Guardians have delivered unto us a herald of their arrival, as I, their chosen ambassador on Earth, both expected and prophesied, albeit in an arcane and inscrutable way. This being has come among us to conduct a preliminary assessment, the next stage in your journey to becoming avatars for the Cosmic Guardians and future rulers of the Earth. In its honour, I am hereby renaming the Embassy of the Cosmic Guardians to the Embassy of the Cosmic Guardians and their Glorious Amorphous Evaluative Entity.*

But hang on, piped up Candidate Vessel Jennifer, one of his newer followers, *I don't recall you ever even mentioning a space fog before, it's almost as if you are making this up as you go.* And the Ambassador's wrath fell upon Jennifer, and he cast her out, exclaiming *Begone, disbeliever, and be condemned to a future of thraldom beneath the iron fist of the Cosmic Guardians, and by the way no refunds.*

And then he resumed his address of the remaining Candidate Vessels, a devout dozen in green jumpsuits who were hanging on his every word. *Go forth now into the fog,* he directed, *go forth and be assessed and fear not, for you are the enlightened, you are the ECGGAEE! Go forth and be embraced by the emissary of the Cosmic Guardians. Go forth and be judged!*

And lo, they did go forth, and they were judged.

***

Meanwhile, Starr Lavigne was dancing around a naked old lady, chanting mystically and waving large purple crystals in her client's general direction, when her phone alarm sounded, signalling the end of another great aura healing session.

The au naturel aura client was Zelda Bezzle, a regular visitor to Starr's Spiritual Energy Clinic and Aura Gym these days, due to a niggling slow positivity puncture they had been working on repairing for some time. As she dressed, Zelda asked if Starr had heard about this green fog everyone was talking about, and if so, what it might mean, in her expert opinion. Was it spiritual in nature? Could the cause be misaligned cosmic vibrations? Perhaps angels were behind the fog, possibly quite literally?

Starr had to admit that she wasn't aware of any green fog, but she did think the suggestion that angels might be involved seemed a little fanciful, and it was probably something much more down to earth, such as a spontaneous manifestation of mass psychic disarray. Anyway, Zelda shouldn't worry, Starr reassured her, it wasn't good for her aura hole, and after all, everything happens for a reason.

They bade each other namaste, and just as Zelda was on her way out of the door Starr's cell phone rang; her one o'clock had to cancel. Apologies for the short notice but he didn't think it would be wise to drive in this crazy fog, et cetera, and could she reschedule his deep soul irrigation session for next week instead?

Starr checked her social media, and it was true; several of her friends and fellow drum circle members were posting about the green fog and the disruption it was causing, and by extrapolating from their reports it was clear that the fog should be headed straight toward the little valley that sheltered her clinic.

She called Rob to let him know she was heading home early so as not to get cut off. As a general rule she tried to avoid calling him during home school hours, but she thought it was safest that he was aware of her plan, and as luck would have it he had just set the kids up in front of an hour-long mindfulness video of a melting icicle. Rob hadn't heard about the fog either but told her to take extra care driving. She reassured him that she'd be fine, it was only fog, how bad could it be, and besides, she'd just decked out the Tesla with new shungite pyramids and tumbled black tourmaline, no expense spared, because you couldn't put a price on safety.

By the time Starr had shut up shop and negotiated the winding lane out of the little valley and back to the old bridge that would connect her to the more trafficked main road, she was too late. Somehow the fog had got there first and had swallowed most of the bridge, a huge nebulous green roadblock denying her escape.

She cursed out loud and then stared at the fog, mesmerized by its movement, the way it roiled and spiralled and folded in on itself and hinted at something moving deep within it. Suddenly she felt a dropping sensation in her stomach and she had the eerie feeling that she had reached the edge of the world; that if she continued into the fog the bridge would end abruptly in mid-air and she would plummet into an endless green void and keep falling forever, never seeing daylight again. Never seeing her home and her family again. She felt an unexpected pang of homesickness and found that she desperately missed Rob and the kids: Tree, Cloud and Frodo.

She took a deep breath and gripped a shungite pyramid to dispel the negativity and centre herself. She would simply head back to the clinic and wait it out, she decided. There was nothing else for it. She'd hunker down and break out her most powerful singing bowl and her favourite mallet and she would meditate until the fog had passed and she could finally go home to her family.

Feeling better now that she had a plan B, she threw the vehicle into reverse and backed straight into the fog bank that had crept in to engulf the road behind her.

***

Rick Zink, better known to his subscribers as Zincoherence, was going viral this time for sure. He'd hit the jackpot, though admittedly it had taken him a minute to grasp that. When he'd received the call from Pep-Air to inform him that his GTFO return seaplane flight had been cancelled due to poor visibility he'd been pissed, and when he further discovered that the ferries were SNAFU he'd been virtually incandescent.

After all, this was meant to be a fleeting check-in just to assuage the guilt that his mother had passive-aggressively instilled in him for neglecting to visit her for several years now that he lived in the big city and was a big shot on that internet. Well, he knew he wasn't really a big shot, but he was working on it, and he could hardly do that from this godforsaken rock, but she had finally worn him down and he had returned to the island for a visit and promptly got stranded, as if the freaking shithole was trying to punish him for ever daring to leave it in the first place.

But since then he had come to the realization that the fog that had foiled his escape plan was not your ordinary weather. People were talking about it in his feeds and even on the geezer media, but as Pepper Island was officially cut off, ferries shunning it and seaplanes grounded—or whatever the seaplane equivalent of grounded was—the only video available to anyone was the usual shabby amateur footage. This was inevitably shot in the wrong aspect ratio—it never ceased to amaze him that it didn't occur to people to turn their phones ninety degrees when recording video—and with low-quality, rambling audio. But here he was, Zincoherence on the scene, boots on the ground, YouTube channel salivating for quality content, and ready to rock this freaky fog.

The fact was, his subscriber count had plateaued some weeks ago, and he had started to lose hope that he would ever reach the heady heights to which he aspired; not just making a living on social media and being able to walk away from the barista gig at Curmudgeon Coffee that was, frankly, unbefitting. He wanted social media stardom. He yearned to join that upper echelon of content creators and influencers that could afford to burn money on camera—sometimes literally—and be as obnoxious as they liked with total impunity before their adoring fans. Rick craved stardom, Rick deserved stardom, and this stupid fog could be Rick's ticket to stardom.

Fortunately, Rick never travelled without at least the essentials for putting a bit together, plus he had thrown the GoPros into his luggage as an afterthought, so when he saw that the fog was drifting out onto Slow Lake, the source of his parents' drinking water and popular water sports destination, he knew he had his angle. He swiftly rented a stand-up paddle board, attached one GoPro at either end with suction cup mounts, and launched himself out onto the water. Minutes later he floated before the gaseous green wall that continued to slowly and soundlessly roll over the surface of the lake, and he activated the cameras by remote control.

Welcome to Slow Lake on Pepper Island, he said to camera, *home of the famous glowing green fog.* He would cut to the rear camera in post at this point so the viewer could see the fog before him, so he looked over his shoulder and made a frightened expression into the lens, his feigned fear masking the genuine anxiety he was trying to suppress. He turned back to the front camera. *What lurks within the fog? Is it ghost pirates, like in that movie? Is it weird monsters from another dimension, like in that other movie? Is it Spinal Tap with a dry ice machine? No one knows. Until now. Join me as I, Zincoherence, take an exclusive look inside the glowing green fog of Pepper Island. Don't forget to like and subscribe!*

And with those soon-to-be famous last words, he paddled forward into the gloom. Fifty seconds later the cameras continued to roll as a riderless board drifted back out of the fog.

***

DC Squibb wasn't buying any of it.

Tyler Gauss and Phil Hitter had bustled into the Winchester Tavern like giddy schoolgirls, prattling on about how they'd seen for themselves how the fog glowed, and how it didn't just drift like regular fog but it seemed to navigate somehow, like it was alive, and how they thought they had heard screams in the distance, screams inside the fog itself.

So then of course everyone in the bar was on their cell phones, checking their precious social media, checking in with the government on what to do about alien fog or whatever and generally swallowing every lie that the authorities fed them. Stay inside. Close all the windows. Don't drive in it. Don't breathe it. Don't think for yourself. We don't know what it is, of course, but it's scary. Be afraid. Live in fear, and trust the government. The government knows best.

Well, not DC Squibb. He would not go quietly into the night. This would not stand. Not on his watch. No siree.

Clambering onto the table, he whistled loudly with his fingers to get all eyes on him and addressed his fellow patrons. *Wake up, Pepper Island. Wake up and smell the tyranny. Can't you see? It's always something. Seat belts. Passive smoking. Climate change. Pandemics. Blah, blah, blah. Always some excuse to lock us down, take away our freedoms, keep us in our place. And now here comes another. Green fog? Seriously? You can't be falling for this. Can't you see?* he asked incredulously, *this whole fog thing, it's just a smokescreen.*

Inexplicably, they laughed at him, but he didn't care. Let them laugh. The joke's on them. DC Squibb would have the last laugh. Stupid fogheads. That's right. Fogheads. He had a name for them already. He always did have a way with words.

He had been planning to stay in the bar until closing time, as usual; sink some beers, talk some sports, put the world to rights, maybe play some pool. But now things had changed. He was leaving, he announced. Going home. No one would tell DC Squibb where he could and could not go. He was going to take a leisurely walk home, right through the stupid fog. Just watch him. Maybe he would stop in it to have a cigarette, he said. And if he found anyone screaming in there he'd be sure to tell them to keep the noise down so as not to frighten Tyler and Phil and the rest of the bleating sheep back at the old Winchester.

Then true to his word, off he went, dramatically throwing open the door to the bar and marching directly toward the distant fog bank, in the opposite direction to that of his house. DC Squibb held his head high and didn't break his stride once, even when feeling his heart flutter at the sight of that eerie green glow up ahead.

***

To his neighbours, Clint Kerslake was referred to as that crazy bunker guy. To his friends and fellow preppers, he liked to think he was known as an elite survivalist. To his reflection in his bathroom mirror, he was the Phoenix Warrior.

Clint Kerslake had been anticipating The Fall for decades and considered it overdue at this point. He had speculated that the end times would be precipitated by global financial collapse, a coordinated terrorist dirty bomb campaign, a polar shift or possibly even a grey goo scenario. One existential threat he had not taken into account was the arrival of a glowing green fog of ambiguous origin, but he wasn't about to look a gift horseman of the apocalypse in the mouth.

It was his time to shine.

Clint was proud of his bunker, or Fort Kerslake Two, as he had christened it. The original Fort Kerslake, or For Fuck's Sake, as he had renamed it, was on the other side of the property and consisted of an array of buried and subsequently crushed sea cans. As it turns out, shipping containers were great for, well, shipping stuff, but counter-intuitively did not have the structural integrity to be buried under a metre of dirt. That had been an expensive and hard lesson, but one he had learned well from, and Fort Kerslake Two was in a whole different league. One hundred percent concrete and steel, his subterranean suite boasted off-grid power, a grey water recycling system and independent well water, and was fully shielded from electromagnetic pulses. It was also amply stocked with weapons, ammunition and food, though if worst came to worst Clint was not afraid to resort to hunting for long pig when his provisions became exhausted or spoiled, and as if to prove this he may have neglected to check the expiry dates on his can hoard for a few years now.

As he stood before the hatch to Fort Kerslake Two and watched the fog bank roll relentlessly toward his property, he pulled his gas mask down over his face and said to himself, *Afogalypse now, baby.*

Locking the door behind him, he descended the few steps into his private fortress, removed the mask and took a Glock 19 from the gun safe and a brew from the fridge. He settled into the leather recliner and cracked the beer, admiring as he did so his pride and joy, the Swiss-made NBC (Nuclear Biological Chemical) air filtration system. This was the latest and final addition to Fort Kerslake Two, the pièce de résistance. Sure, it had cost him ten large, but he had considered it worth every penny, so imagine his chagrin when the green fog quickly infiltrated his prized bunker and subsequently his brain.

***

By sunrise the following day, the green fog was gone.

Having gradually crawled its way over the entire island, the fog bank had drifted back out to sea in the blackness of the night and consequently vanished. Some observers speculated that the fog had returned to whence it came, having done what it came to do, but none were able or willing to elaborate when pressed.

The Hazardous Material Response Teams were first on the scene, helicoptered in by the coast guard, hazmat suited, taking their samples and conducting their tests until they were ready to give the all clear. Hot on their heels came the police, paramedics, various government scientists and some rather furtive military types whose participation would subsequently be strictly redacted.

The island appeared deserted. They found vehicles abandoned in the middle of the road or in adjacent ditches, doors ajar, some with engines still idling. A cell phone lay on the sidewalk, cracked screen displaying a stream of increasingly frantic unread messages. Beers stood unfinished on the bar of the local watering hole. A tub overflowed with bathwater. A riderless paddle board drifted on a lake.

There was a growing but unspoken fear that the islanders had somehow been transported by the fog itself, or even that they had been dissolved by it, so it came as a relief to everyone when the entire population of Pepper Island was located. Police officers Ho and Crisp were conducting a sweep of the backroads of the southern reaches of the island when they heard what they would later describe in their reports as a loud susurration, seemingly of human origin. They followed the sound of this chorus of unintelligible whispering through the woods to a small sandy cove, and there they came across approximately a thousand locals staring out to sea, chanting in unison. The officers would later state that the subjects appeared to be speaking in tongues. Ho and Crisp cautiously attempted to make themselves known to the community members gathered there, but they all seemed to be in some kind of trance-like state and remained oblivious to the presence of the officers. Their mysterious mantra reached a crescendo, at which point an abrupt and eerie quiet descended on the little beach, disturbed only by the sound of the ocean. A moment later, a thousand islanders collapsed to the sand en masse.

The islanders were, on the whole, physically unharmed, though all were in profound states of shock. None could answer simple questions or describe what had happened to them; all were too dazed to even form a coherent sentence. They just stared at the first responders in bewilderment, and the feeling was mutual. Psychologists speculated about mass hysteria and collective dissociative fugue.

In a rejection of the advice of public health advisors, no quarantine period was imposed on the islanders. Publicity overruled precautions, and a full evacuation of Pepper Island was mounted immediately. Customarily in emergency evacuations there were always some holdouts and deniers, people who obstinately refused to leave or just didn't like to be told what to do, but this one went surprisingly smoothly, every islander allowing themselves to be guided, unresistingly if groggily, to the waiting transportation. The evacuees were promptly delivered to the city of Vancouver on the mainland and quickly filled the hospitals to capacity, the overflow having to be found temporary lodgings until they could be properly assessed, or until claimed by next of kin. They ate and hydrated when prompted, but remained uncommunicative and inexpressive, and continued to behave like automatons.

It was in the small hours that the islanders resumed their unsettling susurrations. Whether in hospital wards, hotel rooms or the homes of friends and family, every Pepper Islander arose as one and started whispering in perfect synchrony, whispering in a language shared only with their fellow evacuees.

Like synchronized sleepwalkers, oblivious to the pleas and protestations of their caretakers and loved ones, the islanders made their ways outside and into the darkness, where they abruptly ceased their whispering and stood straight and stiff, throwing back their heads and opening their mouths as if trying to catch the light rain that fell on them that night. They opened their mouths wide and wider still, as wide as their temporomandibular joints would allow and then wider, the Pepper Islanders having seemingly become unhinged in every sense.

And then Zelda Bezzle and little Frodo Lavigne and former Candidate Vessel Jennifer and old Mrs. Zink and Tyler Gauss and all the others proceeded to disgorge copious billows of green fog from their mouths like human chimneys; a thick, luminescent fog that spread through the city streets in a rapid, roiling gaseous flood. A fog that contained malevolent and increasingly excited things.

Hungry things.

Cave Canem

"Toast," I declared, "might be the crowning achievement of the human race."

"Oh, really?" Jenna replied, pouring herself a coffee. "Not space travel or vaccines or the internet?"

We were in the kitchen of Jenna's apartment, enjoying a simple, leisurely breakfast of juice, coffee, scrambled eggs and sublime toast. It was the weekend so neither of us was in any particular rush. I was dressed but barefoot, she was in a white bathrobe. I scrolled through the news on my phone with one hand as the other shovelled egg and crust into my mouth.

"Toast," I confirmed. "Certainly not the internet, though that might be noteworthy for being the nail in the coffin of the human race."

"What does that say about us?" she replied. "We met on the internet of doom, did we not?"

We had found each other online just a few weeks earlier when Jenna had made the first move on a niche dating site called *inexactscience.com*. Jenna was a parasitologist at the university, whereas I was a research scientist for Big Pharma. "Every cloud has a silver lining?" I offered.

Jenna rolled her eyes and feigned vomiting.

"Case in point," I said, ignoring her pantomime and reading out loud from my phone. "'Enough is enough! The time has come to scatter the teeth of the elites across the streets.' Poetic, don't you think?"

"Wow," Jenna replied. "The standard of journalism in *The Guardian* has really declined recently, hasn't it?"

"Ha ha," I said pointedly. "That was actually from my *Freekoff* feed. The lunatics are taking over the asylum and they're using social media to communicate."

"You have a *Freekoff* account?"

"Of course. How else can I know when its teeth scattering time?"

A theremin ringtone interrupted from behind the breakfast bar.

"I thought the teeth thing only applied to elites?" Jenna said as she went looking for her cell phone.

"Hey, I do read *The Guardian*, that makes me an elite to these revolting people. Revolting in both senses of the word."

She poured herself another coffee from the carafe as she answered her phone. "Hey," she said. "Is it time?"

I munched my toast and focused on my phone, trying not to eavesdrop.

"Okay, yup that's fine," she said to the caller. "I've got one here right now, as a matter of fact, eating my scrambled eggs and drinking my coffee."

I glanced over at her with a puzzled expression and a stupid smile, then turned my attention back to my phone, and an opinion piece about the increasing divisiveness of modern politics.

"Okay, yup, Can I finish my coffee first? You can't expect me to kill a man without my morning caffeine fix."

I almost did a spit take on my coffee and looked over at Jenna again as she ended her call and walked back to the table, coffee in hand and smiling at me innocently. "Everything okay?" I asked nonchalantly.

"Everything's fine," she said. "Why wouldn't it be?"

I shrugged. It was at this point I became very aware of the paring knife that lay on the table between us next to a bowl of fruit. I glanced at it briefly then immediately felt foolish for doing so.

The toast popped in the kitchen, startling me.

"More toast?" Jenna asked.

"Don't mind if I do."

I decided to disregard the odd phone call as it was none of my business and probably some kind of in-joke between her and one of her friends. I took another sip of coffee and returned my attention to the news when something blurred down through my field of vision. Before I had time to process this I was being choked. I threw my hand to my neck and felt a plastic cable embedding into my throat. I sputtered coffee and gasped "What are you doing?" The question seemed redundant as it was rather obvious that she was trying to garrotte me, but I wasn't sure what else one says in this scenario. A moment later I was also being bashed on the side of the head with something hard and mechanical sounding, and as crumbs rained down around me I realized that I was being murdered with a toaster. Talk about adding insult to injury.

"Get. Off!" I croaked, the fingers of both hands trying desperately to slip between power cord and throat and failing. I stretched out and barely reached my mug, throwing the remains of my coffee in the general direction of my attacker's face. It didn't help, and I now had hot liquid on my head. I felt pressure on my back and realized she had her knee wedged against me, which meant that she was standing on one leg. I bent my own right leg enough to get a foothold on the table and pushed hard. My chair fell backwards and the pressure on my throat was mercifully released as Jenna hit the floor behind me. I quickly tore the plastic cord away as we both scrambled amongst the mess we'd made. We both got to our feet at the same time, and when I touched the back of my head my hand came back bloody. As I opened my mouth to demand an explanation she dived across the table and grabbed the paring knife. I decided that explanations could wait, and rushed through the apartment's front door and out into the hallway.

For a moment I considered bashing on a neighbour's door but quickly decided that would leave me too vulnerable; I needed to get out of there, fast. Ignoring the sluggish elevator, I hurtled down the stairwell and out into the building's reception area. Not a person in sight, so I barged through the main doors into the street. Only then did I realize that I was still in bare feet, having left my sneakers in Jenna's apartment, along with my cell phone and keys. Nice work.

I looked around me at the relatively quiet residential street for an exit strategy. A middle-aged gentleman, bald and wearing a misguided moustache, was getting out of a small car across the street. I took a couple of deep breaths and composed myself before approaching him. I might be a barefoot stranger with a head wound, but I didn't want him to think I was crazy.

"Excuse me," I said, moderating my voice to the best of my ability. "Might I use your cell phone? It's an emergency."

The man looked at me and his countenance immediately became apprehensive. "What kind of emergency?" he enquired.

"Someone just attacked me with a toaster. In fact," I glanced behind me at Jenna's building, "she might be following me."

The man thought. "Following you with a toaster?"

"She also had a knife," I elaborated.

"Okay. Well, I'm afraid my phone is out of power, but I can drive you to the police if you like."

***

He introduced himself as Shaun as we drove away. "So," he said casually. "Where do you stand on the simulation hypothesis?"

"What?" I said, uncomprehending.

"You know, the argument that all of this," he waved vaguely at everything, "all of reality, as we perceive it is, in fact, a computer simulation created by an alien race of vast intelligence and technological advancement, or possibly by humans living in, as seen from our artificially arrested viewpoint, the distant future. Or, to go even further, possibly all of existence is a simulation that is itself the product of a simulation, which in turn is the product of a simulation, and so forth ad infinitum. Some philosophers and scientists claim to consider this scenario to be highly probable. However, the whole concept is by definition unfalsifiable and inherently anthropocentric, of course, and consequently its detractors argue that the idea falls into the realm of pseudoscience or even techno-religion. What are your thoughts on that? As a human being?" He air quoted "human being" for good measure.

"I honestly don't know," I replied. "I just want to avoid being killed with a toaster."

He nodded knowingly. "You know what I think? I think—"

He was interrupted by familiar sci-fi music coming from somewhere nearby. It took me a moment to place it: it was the same sound that Jenna's phone had made right before she tried to murder me.

"I thought you said your cell phone was dead?" I said.

Shaun didn't answer or even look at me; he just reached inside his jacket and silenced his phone.

"Where are we going, Shaun?" I asked, looking around in an attempt to orientate myself.

"To the police," he said, his hands gesturing on the steering wheel like the answer was obvious.

"I don't think this is the right direction."

"Well, I'm going to take you to see some friends of mine. We don't need to involve the police. This is better," he said sheepishly.

"Stop the car," I said. "Right now, please."

Instead of pulling up, Shaun put his foot down.

"Shaun!" I exclaimed.

He turned to look at me, waving an open-palmed hand in a futile placatory gesture. "It's fine. Please don't try and get out of the car. We'll be there shortly and this will all be over."

"Shaun, what the hell is—old lady!" I yelled.

"What?" he said, turning his attention back to the road ahead just in time to step hard on the brake. We skidded to an abrupt halt approximately a metre away from the old woman standing in the middle of the street, an expression of horrified recognition carved into her weathered face. Slowly, she raised one arm and pointed directly at me. Shaun lowered his window and yelled out of it. "Everything's fine. I've got this, Gloria!"

"Got what, exactly? What is it you've got?" I demanded, but before he could answer the old woman, accusatory finger still extended, opened her mouth and started to moan, the moan slowly rising to a wail of fervent denunciation.

"Shit," Shaun said and shifted the vehicle into reverse. I threw open the passenger door and jumped out before he could gather speed again. Hitting the ground running, I didn't hesitate in putting as much distance as possible between myself and my erstwhile rescuer, Gloria's bloodcurdling scream of condemnation still ringing in my ears long after I had fled the scene.

***

When it seemed safe to do so I slowed to a walk to get my bearings. The area was vaguely familiar, and as I passed a bus stop I made not one but two connections: this bus route could take me home, and my bus pass might still be in my back pocket.

Bingo.

A few minutes later I boarded the bus and flashed my pass at the driver. She seemed disinterested in either that or my state of general dishevelment. I looked down the aisle of the half-empty bus. Commuters, a mother with two little girls, a couple of students, a mohawked punk. None of them looked particularly homicidal, but I'd had a crash course recently in how not to judge a book by its cover.

I took a seat and tried to be as inconspicuous as possible, allowing myself a moment to just stare out of the window and watch the world pass by. A world that, up until that morning, I was pretty sure I had a basic understanding of. Hipsters stared at their phones as they stood in line for their morning espressos and the fashionably crotchety service at Curmudgeon Coffee; a well-dressed young woman thrust leaflets promoting her god into the hands of apathetic passersby who in turn thrust the leaflets into the nearest trash can; a busker butchered an old Radiohead number on his out-of-tune acoustic guitar. How could this normality co-exist with the nightmare I had experienced that day?

Suddenly my head throbbed with pain, and I turned to see that one of the little girls had detached herself from her mother's attention and wandered over. Maybe nine years of age, she kneeled on the seat directly in front of me, facing me and staring at the toaster-inflicted damage on my head with a concerned expression. I gave her what I hoped was a reassuring smile.

"It's nothing," I assured her. "I'll be fiiine." Then I rolled my eyes and stuck out my tongue, feigning death.

She didn't smile. Instead, she reached out and poked my head wound again. "They're gonna get you," she said.

***

The bus dropped me a few blocks from my apartment building and I marched onward, trying to remain vigilant whilst simultaneously keeping my head down and avoiding looking anyone in the eye. Rounding the corner into my street, I stopped in my tracks. Jenna's car was parked between me and my home. I was to the rear of it and still a block away, but I would recognize that dented yellow PT Cruiser anywhere.

She was watching my place. Waiting for me.

I did a swift one-eighty and retraced my steps, taking a sharp corner at race walk speed. As my thoughts whirled and the pressure to panic intensified, I promptly collided with someone charging in the opposite direction. I bounced off this reckless maniac and skidded across the pavement on my backside, the wind thoroughly knocked out of me.

"What the hell—Alan?" I said, suddenly realizing that I recognized this particular maniac from work.

Alan picked himself with some difficulty, grasping his right knee. "Oh, hey man. Listen, I'd love to stop and chat but the contractor that was fixing my deck is trying to kill me, and now I think you busted my leg."

"Wait, someone is trying to kill me too. My girlfriend just attacked me with a toaster. Well, my ex-girlfriend now, I think."

"Really? That's quite the coincidence," Alan said. "A toaster, eh? That's awful. I love toast."

"Me too!"

"My guy came at me with a nail gun. What an imbecile. Do you know what an terrible weapon a nail gun is? Thankfully he missed."

Alan glanced over his shoulder as if to see if he was being followed, and I couldn't help but notice the head of a substantial
nail sticking out of his skull just above his ear. After a moment's
consideration, I decided it was best not to draw his attention to
it. He had got this far after all.

"Do you have any idea what is happening here?" I asked.

"Well," he said, "I can only assume—"

He didn't reach the end of his sentence as at that point a
large truck roared into the street and headed straight for us. A
company logo along the side read HIT THE DECK. I dived to one
side but Alan could only hobble, and I watched in horror as
the truck plowed into him, his head smashing against the hood
before he was dragged beneath the oncoming chassis. The truck
abruptly skidded to a halt and a tall fellow unfolded himself
from behind the wheel, pausing to reach back in and retrieve
a large nail gun from the cab before he knelt to inspect for any
damage beneath his vehicle.

While the contractor was distracted I peered around the corner onto my street. Jenna's car was cruising slowly in my direction, possibly to investigate the commotion or maybe she was
attracted by the scent of fresh blood. Seizing my opportunity, I
sprinted into the alley that ran behind the block opposite my
building, bypassing my tormentor and heading north as she
moved south, then I took a deep breath and strolled nonchalantly across the road toward Shangrila Towers.

The door to my apartment was ajar. I pushed it open with my
index finger and scanned the living room. Everything looked as
it had when I'd left the evening before. Only the video playing
on the wall-mounted television had changed; yesterday it had

been the popular fantasy show called *The Heft of the Haft*, today it was breaking news about a spate of murders. Stepping inside, I locked the door behind me and, resisting the urge to detour over to the toaster, made my way to the bathroom sink. As I threw water on my face and inspected my wounds, I caught a glimpse of movement in the mirrors of the medicine cabinet. Something was writhing inside the shower cubicle, contorting sensuously beneath the pounding streams of hot water. Something humanoid but, in its current unguarded state, far from human.

I grabbed a towel and spoke to the reflection that confronted me.

"Put your clothes on, Mother. It's time to go," I said. "The humans are onto us."

Stranger from the Woods

Anna watched a star fall. Far from any significant source of light pollution, the stars here were countless and impassive against the dense black firmament. The meteor—for she knew it was closer to a small rock than a star—silently tore a fleeting rent in the fabric of night before burning to oblivion in the blink of an eye. Anna would often sit here and watch such celestial drama. Even the light of the stars themselves hosted a drama in its very antiquity. It gave one perspective, she thought.

She and David were sat in their seen-better-days Adirondack chairs on the veranda at the front of their house, stargazing and watching the silhouette of the forest beyond the meadow sway gently in the breeze. They were relatively secluded here in their little Pacific Northwestern nook, all but surrounded by the temperate rainforest. The woods enclosed a few hiking trails, but none found their way too close to their property, and Anna prized the privacy the forest afforded them.

Both Anna and David appeared to be somewhere in their late forties. Anna's hair was short and silver, and she had her arms crossed over her chest for warmth; Fall was settling in, and she was chilly despite her long dark sweater and long skirt. The glass of red wine helped with that, though. David, stroking his well-groomed salt and pepper beard contemplatively as he too stared into space, did not drink but seemed impervious to the cold in his regular plaid shirt and scarred overalls.

Soft music drifted through the open window of the house: some old David Bowie album on vinyl. The LP reached its end and the tonearm carried the stylus back to its resting place with a graceful sweep. Taking that as her cue, Anna took a final optimistic swig from her wine glass and stood up.

"Well, that's me", she declared, and shuffled into the house.

David followed soon after, with a sigh.

***

A cassocked Robert Duvall was playing on a child's swing set on the television screen. Anna had changed into her lounging sweats and lounged accordingly on the couch, her eyes on the movie even though she'd seen it many times before. Rufus the border collie lay on the floor before the couch, disinterested in the movie, having also seen it many times before. David perched on the edge of the armchair, a small screwdriver in hand and an Optivisor on his head, tinkering with some arcane electronic gizmo on the coffee table.

Abruptly, the little lights on David's visor went out, immediately followed by the floor lamp flickering and the television picture sputtering into static. Anna looked at David with a puzzled expression, and in doing so noticed movement outside the window over his shoulder. David followed her gaze. Something was illuminating the underside of the clouds, pushing back the night. The intensity of the illumination increased until something big and bright and blue soared silently over the top of the house and toward the forest, the darkness closing back in behind it. The object decelerated quickly before floating gently down into the woods and disappearing without a sound.

As suddenly as they had gone out, the lights and the television sparked back to life as if nothing had happened and normal service was resumed. Anna looked back at David.

"Well, wasn't that something," she said.

David thought for a moment. "I should go and investigate. Should I?"

Anna considered then nodded slowly. "Yes," she replied. "I think you should."

David made his way to the little mud room, where he deftly slipped on his seasoned old boots and grabbed the big yellow flashlight they kept by the door, and then ventured out into the night, Rufus bounding after him, thrilled to be on this surprise adventure. The pair crossed the yard, went through the gate in the deer fence and followed the connector trail that linked the property with the public trail system. Multiple No Tres-passing and Beware of the Dog signs went by as David strode determinedly along the path, the flashlight beam outlin-ing swinging shadows of the foliage against the thick trunks of the arbutus trees and illuminating the insects on their frantic errands.

Before long he came to the junction with the trail proper. David paused for a spell and clicked off the flashlight, listening intently for any unusual sounds among the cicadas and oc-casional owl hoots, his eyes slowly surveying the forest ahead.

Sure enough, there in the distance, ahead and to his left, something pulsated with a blue glow. He reactivated the flashlight and headed toward the thing, leaving the trail behind him and pointing the beam downwards to illuminate the stumps, holes and other hazards. David's flashlight flickered, almost imperceptibly, and Rufus finally followed with an uncharacteristic hesitancy.

David's attention alternated between where he was placing his feet and staying on course toward the mystery light. Despite his vigilance, the going was treacherous, and more than once he was almost brought to his knees by a creeping vine or a snagging root. The light appeared to be much closer now, though distances were hard to judge out here. Was it just his imagination or was the light pulsating faster now? And where was that dog?

The flashlight flickered again, then went out, surrendering to the darkness.

✳✳✳

Anna awoke early the next day. She had waited for David to return for quite some time, but eventually the bottle of wine she had consumed had had its usual effect on her, and she had been forced to give up and retreat to her bed.

This morning she threw on her robe and made her way downstairs. Passing through the hallway, she saw that the front door was ajar, closed it with a tsk, and proceeded into the kitchen-cum-dining room. There she found David, still wearing yesterday's clothing, standing motionless and apparently listening attentively to the record he had put on; the same album from the previous evening. Today, however, the record player had been set to the wrong speed: forty-five revolutions per minute instead of thirty-three and a third. Bowie raced through "Ashes to Ashes" at comically high pitch, but David didn't seem to have noticed.

"David?"

David snapped out of whatever daydream he was having and looked at her. He blinked, a little too slowly. "Hello Anna", he said quietly.

"Have you been up all night? Did you just get home?" Anna walked over and turned off the music.

David took a beat or two to formulate his answer. "I got turned around in the darkness and didn't get back until late. I didn't want to wake you."

"Well, was there anything out there? Did you find anything?" she asked.

"I didn't find anything. Nothing at all. It was probably just the moon, or something."

For a moment the two stared at each other as if put on pause. Anna looked contemplative. David looked blank.

"Okay then," Anna suddenly declared, as if having reached a satisfactory conclusion. "Oh, where's Rufus?" she added.

David took a deep, thoughtful breath. "Where is what?"

"Rufus? The dog? He went with you last night? Did he come back?"

David slowly shook his head, as if trying it out. "I have not seen him since then." Then his eyes brightened. "We should go and look for Rufus in the woods."

Anna pondered for a second before wrinkling her nose. "I don't think so. He knows his way around. He'll be back when he's hungry. Speaking of which—breakfast?"

***

At Anna's insistence, David showered and changed clothes while she prepared breakfast. By the time he returned to the kitchen, a plate of bacon and eggs awaited him, complete with a pot of fresh coffee. He took a seat and watched Anna as she ate for a minute before he started forking food into his mouth. After a moment Anna took a mouthful of coffee, and David did the same. Choking, he spluttered several mouthfuls of breakfast back onto his plate, knocking his coffee mug over in the process.

"Oh my. Are you alright?" Anna asked. "You might want to swallow now and again, David."

Tears streaming down his cheeks, David nodded slowly then proceeded to put the ejected food back into his mouth, appearing to concentrate hard as he swallowed every mouthful individually.

Anna made a disgusted expression and rose from the table, glancing at the clock on the wall. "Uh-oh, we're running late. See you outside in twenty minutes?"

David nodded unsurely, coffee still dripping from his chin.

Anna placed her dishes in the sink and then turned back to him. "David, is there anything you want to tell me?"

David stopped chewing and his eyes widened as he met her gaze. "No," he said through a mouthful of egg. "Everything is normal."

Anna paused for a moment then shrugged. "Okay. Only you might want to change clothes again before you go to the store," she said. "That's my dress you're wearing."

***

When David went out to their old truck he was back in his standard plaid shirt and overalls. Anna had already occupied the passenger seat, so he sat behind the wheel. The key was already in the ignition, but he took a minute to inspect the dash instruments and pedals as if trying to recollect how it all worked. Anna looked at her watch pointedly and cleared her throat. David finally started the engine, adjusted the gear stick and stepped heavily on the gas. They jolted backwards a few metres before he shifted his foot onto the brake. Anna, having taken a tight grip on the passenger's grab handle, looked at him with bemusement.

"Maybe you didn't swallow enough of that coffee this morning. Take your time. And you might want to buckle up."

David looked at her blankly.

"Seatbelt," she said, indicating the seatbelt with her eyes.

After a little fumbling, David clicked the belt into position, put the car in drive, and they were off.

***

Thirty-five bewildering minutes later they parked at a jaunty angle in the small parking lot behind the store. They were officially late to open up now, not that anyone else would notice; their journey into town had been unusually erratic, alternating between exhilarating bursts of speed and frustrating periods of crawling along, irrespective of the traffic.

The bookstore was called Don't Judge a Book. They sold both new and second-hand books, though neither very often. Anna was only inclined to open the store three or four days a week, and the monthly income barely covered the lease. It was Anna's labour of love, with David taking a backseat both figuratively and literally. When Anna was dealing with customers or managing the business, David could often be found cloistered in the small back office, working on some computer program.

Today, David was standing in front of the shop's small science fiction section, staring with fascination at the well-thumbed covers portraying various space vessels, busty space damsels and multi-tentacled monsters, when a loud voice rang out.

"Do you have any novels in the sci-fi erotica subgenre?"

Anna looked up from her paperwork and saw that Mrs. Rampart was addressing David.

"What did you say?" David said after a slightly awkward pause.

"Sci-fi erotica? You know, hunky alien fellas with six-packs ravishing feisty earthwomen and eventually falling in love with them? *The Sextraterrestrial*, *Alien Sex Abduction*, *In Space No One Can Hear You Cream*. That sort of thing? They're very popular." She scanned the rows of book spines with a growing look of disappointment.

David contemplated this for a second. "That doesn't make sense. Love is a uniquely human defect"

Mrs. Rampart looked up at him. "Oh come now. Even aliens need love, right?"

David frowned. "Not at all. These books are a waste of your time. Perhaps you should go for a hike in the woods instead."

"A hike?" she said indignantly. "You're telling me to take a hike?"

Anna decided to intervene. "I don't think we have any in stock right now, I'm afraid. I'd be happy to put some aside for you if any come in."

Mrs. Rampart gave up scanning the books, shaking her head. "No, that's fine. Maybe I'll just get them on the *internet*," she said pointedly and swept out of the store, leaving Anna looking at David, nonplussed.

Anna sent David on the regular coffee run to Curmudgeon Coffee, down by the seaplane terminal. The coffee shop was only a few minutes walk away, but when the bookstore's closing time came around and he still hadn't returned Anna was left with no choice but to go looking for him. It didn't take her long. She found him standing on the dock, looking out to sea. She approached him with some trepidation, calling his name questioningly as she neared, but he did not acknowledge her presence. He simply continued to stand there, a paper cup of cold coffee in each hand, staring out at the Pacific as if he had never seen an ocean before.

***

Anna insisted on driving on the way home, and David spent the journey staring wordlessly at the passing scenery. Back at the house, Anna hopped out quickly and ascended the half-dozen creaking steps to the veranda. When she reached the front door, there was Rufus, looking tired and somewhat bedraggled but otherwise in good health. His tail started to thump as he saw Anna approaching, and her face brightened in response.

"There he is! Hello. Where've you been? Hm?"

Rufus slunk over guiltily, his tail low but still oscillating. He was almost within touching distance when his ears pricked up as David clumped up the steps. The dog's tail stilled and his lips twitched back over his canines, a low growl emanating from his throat.

"Now is the perfect time for that hike," David was saying. "And I really must—" he looked up and saw the snarling Rufus but his expression was one of curiosity rather than fear "—insist", he finished.

Rufus leapt.

The dog hit David squarely in the chest, knocking him off balance. He fell backwards, pushing the dog, jaws gnashing, over himself as he went down the stairs. He twisted his body as he descended and hit the edge of the bottom step hard, his left arm beneath him. Rufus was catapulted to the driveway, skidding on his back across the ground before righting himself and spinning back around to face David, who had joined him in the dirt.

David didn't move for a moment, but then as Anna and Rufus watched, he got on his feet again in sudden, jerky movements, as if on strings and being puppeteered from above. Rufus let out a high-pitched squeal of fear and scampered from the scene. David tilted his head to the left and to the right, then stretched his arms as if he was just waking from an awkwardly positioned nap.

"Are you alright?" Anna asked, taking a step forward, before halting again almost immediately. David's left elbow was bending the wrong way, though he didn't seem to have noticed, let alone be in any pain. He followed her gaze and saw for himself.

"Oh," he said, and then the arm jerked forward and twisted back into its conventional orientation. He looked back to Anna. "As I was saying," he continued talking and walking as if nothing had happened. "I have to insist we take that hike into the woods now."

Anna stepped quickly through the front door. David followed, but despite taking two steps at a time, Anna was nowhere to be seen by the time he was inside the house. Looking slowly around the hallway, he noticed a door beneath the stairs was ajar. For some reason he had no recollection of this door, but he strode towards it determinedly and entered without hesitation.

The overhead lights flickered on automatically, illuminating a large basement room at the bottom of a set of steps. Most of the walls of the chamber were hung with wafer-thin video screens, upon some of which indecipherable words, codes and symbols quickly scrolled by, whereas others displayed schematics and three-dimensional models of strange technologies and biologies. Between some of the screens were open doors leading to further rooms, seeming to extend far beyond the footprint of the house above.

At the end of this room, shrouded in shadow, stood several identical Daves. They were all wrapped in transparent plastic sheets, but otherwise they were completely naked. As motionless and silent as statues, they each waited with infinite patience for their turn to ascend from just another anonymous Dave to the one and only David.

At the top of the basement steps, Anna reappeared behind this David. "Oh, David. You thought you sucked out the mind of a human and replicated his body last night, didn't you?"

David turned around and stared at her, confused.

"Well, unfortunately for you," she went on, "that was no human. You were sold a lemon. That was one of my boys. My humanoids. Basic automatons designed to assist me in my work here, but with just enough of a mind to fool an unsuspecting bodysnatcher like yourself. You see, I've been stuck on this fucking rock, observing these humans, for hundreds of their years now. Hundreds." she said, almost spitting this last word. "And every now and again, some bright spark like you will breeze in and think you can snatch this body or absorb that brain in the name of one nefarious invasion plot or another. Well, not on my watch, newbie!"

Anna took a deep breath and composed herself. "But, on the bright side," she said, with a glint in her eye, "do you have any idea how hard it is to get decent food delivered out here?"

***

That evening, Anna and David occupied their shabby Adirondacks chairs on the veranda once more, relaxing and enjoying the night air. Anna finished her glass of wine and stood and stretched, before patting her belly.

"Well, that's me. I'm gonna go eat leftovers in front of the television," she announced. "Don't stay up too late, David. You're going for a nice hike in the woods tomorrow morning. Waste not, want not."

Anna shuffled slowly back inside the house, Rufus padding along after, leaving the fresh David off-gassing that new humanoid smell and watching the skies and the dark woods. A breeze was picking up, and it gently nudged the small, rustic-looking sign that hung from one low branch by the front door.

Honeypot Cottage, the sign read.

The Extraction of Amanda Troop

At two fifty-five on Tuesday morning, Amanda Troop awoke from a nightmare to find an interdimensional portal at the foot of her bed.

She had never seen an interdimensional portal in real life before, but she immediately decided that it was one because she had seen them in movies and on television, and they looked quite like this. It was a vertical disk, approximately one and a half metres in diameter, suspended in mid-air just above the floor. It radiated a soft, swirling light that shifted hypnotically between pleasant hues of blue and green.

Amanda sat up and stared at the phenomenon for several minutes, unsure of the appropriate reaction. Should she be afraid? She didn't really feel afraid. She picked up her cell phone from the bedside table, but just held it in her lap, unable to think of who one should call in a spontaneous interdimensional portal manifestation scenario. The police? NASA? A meteorologist? Ghostbusters? She put the phone down again.

She shuffled toward the thing on her behind cautiously, lest it should capture her in its gravitational pull or something. Like a black hole, she thought. But she felt no such force of attraction. Nor did she hear any sound coming from the thing, which seemed somehow odd because it looked like it was a thing that should be making some kind of sound. Fleetingly, she wondered if there was a volume control, and the interdimensional portal was on mute.

Then the portal did make a sound. It talked.

"Hello. Can you confirm that your name is Amanda Troop?" it enquired in a soft, soothing male voice.

Amanda started and scooched quickly back toward the head of the bed. She grabbed a pillow and hugged it. "Who's there? How do you know my name?" she demanded. Or rather she intended to demand, but it came out as more of a squeak.

"Hello Amanda," responded the voice. "Pleased to meet you. I know this must be strange for you, but there's no need for fear. We're here to help you."

"Help me how?" said Amanda, suspiciously. "I don't need help. Help with what?"

"Well, to be frank, Amanda, we're here to save your life. What you see before you is a portal. A doorway to another dimension. Our dimension is very similar to yours, in fact, but not identical. Here, we have discovered a safe way to connect with other dimensions, such as your own. In your dimension, scientists have been doing similar research into interdimensional contact, though with somewhat less success, and significantly less caution. Are you still with me, Amanda? I know this must be a lot to take in."

"I get it. I've seen *Rick and Morty*. So what are you trying to tell me, exactly?"

"Your scientists endeavoured to establish a link to a dimension that we would consider unsuitable. A chaotic dimension.

But instead of a secure and stable aperture, they created a fracture, and that fracture is spreading, compromising the integrity of both worlds."

"What does that mean?" Amanda asked.

"It means your world is coming to an end, Amanda. Maybe tomorrow. Maybe next week. We can't say for sure at this stage. But soon. In fact, the first signs of corruption may already be observable, and your reality will proceed to unravel at an exponential rate."

"And you want to save me? How? By getting me to go through this thing?" she said incredulously, indicating the floating vortex.

"That's correct, Amanda," said the portal.

"And let me guess. You need a fee in advance, right?"

"We don't want your money, Amanda. We want to save you, but we don't have much time. Deploying this portal uses a lot of our energy, and we can only hold it open for short periods. So you see, we need to move quick—"

And with that, the portal was gone, and the room was dark once more.

***

Amanda boarded the Skytrain and took up position standing next to a stanchion, facing the window. She felt fatigued, even though she had practically passed out after the episode in the night, and she had overslept considerably; her alarm had failed to go off due to her cell phone being mysteriously drained of all power. Her brain felt similarly drained, as demonstrated by the huge effort required to get her work organized in advance of her scheduled meeting. She felt hungover, even though she hadn't touched a drop. What the hell had happened last night?

She stared out of the window, only vaguely aware of the city speeding by as she tried to process the night's events. With all due respect to Occam's Razor, she could not accept it was merely a dream. It had been too vivid, too tangible; to dismiss it as something as banal as a dream felt disingenuous. So what did that leave? Well, a hallucination, perhaps. But caused by what? Food poisoning? Was there more of gravy than of grave about the portal and its ominous message? Perhaps a brain tumour was the cause? Would that be better or worse than the end of the world? she wondered, then immediately felt a pang of guilt for doing so. Maybe it was just your good old, regular insanity. When she thought about some of her clients she could just about believe it had come to that.

Then of course there was the perfectly concordant but perfectly unthinkable explanation: that it had really happened. That an otherworldly vortex had visited her in the night to warn her of the impending apocalypse. It was almost biblical, she pondered. Maybe she should start a cult.

She idly watched a large bird glide effortlessly through the air in the distance. She wondered what kind of bird it was. She'd heard of eagles being seen in the city, but she'd never seen one herself. She lost sight of the bird as it veered behind an office tower, and frowned. Something about it didn't compute. That building was quite far away; there was no way she should have been able to discern a bird beyond it. Not even an eagle.

The carriage shuddered suddenly, forcing her to hold on to the post to steady herself, and when she turned her attention to the window again she'd lost track of the bird. She looked around the train car at her fellow passengers as the driverless train bore them all rapidly onward above the city.

Several people were staring at their phones as usual, oblivious to their surroundings. A young man with an ironic haircut and a leashed rat on his shoulder wore an expression of practiced nonchalance that failed to conceal his desperate need for attention. An older gentleman, who looked about eighty years old and with a face that resented the fact, listened to a conservative shock jock on a transistor radio without headphones; self-appointed messenger of hard truths. You're welcome, sheeple. A young punk girl with cool turquoise hair sat reading a book about theoretical astrophysics. A brace of straphanging Mormon missionaries in crisp white short-sleeved shirts stood whispering to each other conspiratorially. A man in a business suit swiped through photographs of feet on a dating app called *The Game's a Foot*.

If reality was unravelling here, it was hard to tell the difference.

Perhaps she should let it go. Perhaps she would never understand what happened last night, and it would forever remain "one of those things". Something you just accept as having happened in your life, even though it cannot be explained, like a UFO sighting, a prophetic dream, or a dalliance with folk music. Just acknowledge that life is stranger than you thought, and feel wiser for accepting your lack of wisdom.

She took a deep breath and withdrew her cell phone from her pocket in the hope of distracting herself by catching up on the news. The first story that caught her eye described how there was a spate of massive sinkholes appearing around the world. Geoscientists had so far been unable to get to the bottom of the sinkholes, either metaphorically or literally. No floodlights had proven powerful enough to illuminate the floor of any of the cavities, and every exploratory drone that had been sent down had gone dark and become unresponsive after a couple of hundred metres. A widely shared video from northern Japan showing what appeared to be dark shapes rising out of one of the sinkholes in the dead of night was dismissed as a hoax by experts.

Amanda felt the train slowing and looked up to see where she was. Not her stop. The punk girl with the cool pink hair slipped her space book into her backpack as she prepared to disembark, and Amanda caught herself staring. Hadn't that girl's hair been turquoise just a few minutes earlier, or had she misremembered? Was it a different punk girl entirely? She shook her head at herself. She had to snap out of this scatterbrained spell; she had a work meeting to attend.

***

Jennifer Hawkins had already claimed one of the booths at Curmudgeon Coffee, the little coffee shop they frequented for their monthly check-in meetings. Jen was the art director for *Dark Adaptation*, a monthly print magazine that published short science fiction and horror stories, and only stayed in business because the owner had made a pact with the devil, or so Amanda assumed. Jen contracted Amanda to provide a few accompanying illustrations for every issue. Amanda ordered a cappuccino, gave her name to the barista and joined Jen in the booth.

"Hey, Jen. How're you?"

Jen looked up from her laptop. "Oh hey. I'm good, thanks. Sorry, I'm just going through your latest sketches here."

"Right. Sorry for the last-minute delivery, I only got them uploaded this morning," Amanda said, cringing a little.

"Oh no problem," Jen replied, waving away Amanda's concern. "I've been a bit overwhelmed myself this week. Problems with the writers, problems with the cover. Just give me a minute to go through these."

"Of course."

Amanda took off her jacket and looked out of the coffee shop window whilst she waited. She watched a young man run for a bus only to miss it by seconds, and then decelerate into a casual walk, trying to look nonchalant as he did so. A group of students rendezvoused outside the little art house film theatre on the corner for the matinee performance of Kubrick's *Napoleon*. A pair of Mormon missionaries—was it the same ones from the train?—stood directly across the street, staring at the coffee shop.

"Ich habe keinen deutschen Schäferhund," Jen uttered absentmindedly.

Amanda returned her attention to the meeting. "I'm sorry, what was that?"

"I said I like your spaceship," Jen said. "It has a nice retro *Alien* vibe."

"Oh right. Thanks." Amanda listened out for the barista with her coffee.

"Lovely. Body horror. I take it this is for the eighties-era Cronenberg homage?"

Amanda took a peek at Jen's screen. "That's the one. It was a good excuse for me to watch *Scanners* and *Videodrome* again."

Jen nodded. "Nice, nice."

Behind her, Amanda heard the barista shout out a customer's name, but it was someone called Butcher.

"Hmm," Jen looked puzzled, "What's the story with the portal?"

"Sorry, which?"

Jen spun the laptop around for Amanda to see. On the screen was a rendition of a portal. Her portal, the one from last night. Amanda had no recollection of creating it, let alone sending it to *Dark Adaptation*. She stared at it, open-mouthed.

"Something for another client, or ...?" Jen offered.

"Yeah. No. That's nothing. That's a mistake," Amanda blurted, realizing her protracted pause was getting awkward. "Sorry. I, erm, I didn't mean to include that one," she fumbled.

"No problem, I'll just delete that one to avoid confusion."

"Yeah, sorry about that. It's just a practice piece. I must have saved it in the wrong directory."

"I get it," Jen said reassuringly and looked at Amanda for a moment as if assessing her. "You look tired. Working late to meet a deadline?"

"Not really. I just had kind of a rough night."

Jen nodded sympathetically and turned her attention back to her laptop. The barista called for a customer named Hyena to collect their order. Amanda wondered for a moment if she had misheard, or if it was one of those crazy hippy names.

"Whoa. I do think we might need to tone down Officer Zombie here." Jen rotated the computer again to remind Amanda of the piece. It showed a zombie police officer eviscerating a large militia-type gentleman and chomping on his steaming entrails. She looked around self-consciously before turning it back to herself.

"Okay, I guess it is a little heavy on the gore," Amanda agreed. Somehow she didn't remember making the illustration that graphic.

"Indeed. A little heavy, on the gore," Jen repeated, and flickered out of existence.

Almost before Amanda had registered the event, Jen reappeared and continued about her business as if nothing out of the ordinary had occurred. Amanda stared, suddenly aware of the rapid thumping of her heart in her chest. She became concerned that other people might overhear it. She looked around. No one else seemed to have noticed Jen's fleeting vanishing act, nor did anyone seem to be aware of Amanda's bass drum heartbeat. What *was* that? she asked herself. Am I actually losing my mind? Am I having some kind of seizure?

"Amanda? You feeling alright?"

Amanda realized Jen was addressing her and attempted to tune back into the moment. "Yes. I'm fine. Just tired. Erm, any more notes for me?"

"I don't think so, they look good. I'll just need the zombie cop amending. Just give me a moment and we'll move on to the new requirements."

The barista called out a name that sounded like Lung Ripper. Amanda was taken aback. What was going on with the names today? What was that one, Swedish or something? She looked at Jen, but she didn't appear to have heard.

Amanda had an irresistible urge to watch who, if anyone, responded to that name; surely no one could actually be called Lung Ripper. It must be a nickname or a prank. She turned to look at the counter in what she hoped was a casual, just-taking-in-my-surroundings manner. There was indeed a large coffee cup on the counter with a name scrawled across it that may have been Lung Ripper or whatever, but no one had risen to claim it as yet.

Shaking her head, Amanda turned her attention back to her meeting.

Jen was gone. Her laptop, her jacket, her latte. All gone. She looked around the shop. There was no sign of her client. It was as if Jen Hawkins had never arrived.

Amanda felt panic rising, paused to take several deep breaths, then stood up, grabbed her jacket and made a beeline for the door, almost barging into the little old lady who was on her way to the counter to collect her order.

***

She hadn't been sleeping long when the portal returned at two fifty-five A.M. She reached for the cell phone by her bed; this time she'd get this thing on video as proof, she thought, but somehow her phone's battery appeared to be dead again.

"Hello, Amanda. Have you thought about our offer?" asked the portal.

"Yes I have, and I have to wonder: why me? What makes me so special? Am I going to save the world or something?"

The voice from the portal chuckled sadly. "Unfortunately your world is beyond saving at this point, Amanda. No, it's simply because we have a vacancy."

"A vacancy?"

"Yes. A vacancy that you are uniquely qualified to fill. As I said, our dimension is very similar to yours, but not identical. There are small but significant differences. One of those differences is that, well, to be blunt, our Amanda Troop is no longer with us."

"Your Amanda Troop? There was another me?" Amanda asked incredulously.

"That is correct."

"And this other me is dead?"

"That is correct."

"Shit. How did I ... how did she die?" Amanda asked, unable to resist the morbid curiosity that crept up on her.

"Like you, she was involved in an automobile accident five years ago."

Amanda took a moment to process this news. "The accident that killed my mother?"

"The accident that killed your mother in your world, yes. In our world, you were the one driving, so you were the one that died when you hit the tree. Your mother survived."

"My mother is alive there?" Amanda felt butterflies in her stomach.

"Alive and well. But our Amanda perished. So you see, we have an opening for an Amanda Troop. That's how this works. We cannot have duplicates, you understand. We cannot save alternative versions of people who already exist in our dimension. The ethics, if not the science, of saving duplicates, makes that impossible. So these opportunities are rare."

Amanda took a moment to process all of this silently, staring at the mesmerizing vortex at the end of her bed. "You want me to go through this portal, right?" she asked.

"It is the only way out, Amanda."

"Okay. How do I know it's safe?"

"Well, you don't. But trust me, it's a lot safer than staying where you are. How do you know a lifeboat is safe when the ship is sinking?"

"Last time you said something about reality being corrupted. I think I might have witnessed some of that today. Things have become ... odd."

"That would correspond with what our models predict. We now believe the disintegration is occurring at a more accelerated rate than originally thought."

"This is crazy," Amanda said, running her fingers through her hair anxiously. "I don't know. I don't know what to do."

"Well, you don't have to decide right now, Amanda, but soon. Very soon. The clock is ticking. We can't justify the expense of these rescue missions indefinitely if the subjects don't cooperate. Some people don't want us to rescue anyone. They say we should leave you to your fate. We disagree. We want to help. But we are running out of time. You are running out of—"

And as abruptly as before, the portal was gone.

***

Amanda met Samantha Bamber at the park the next morning as arranged. Amanda had known Sam since art school, where they had become fast friends, largely due to a shared interest in horror movies. Sam's career had moved in a different direction from Amanda's, and these days she made her living creating the living dead, among other horror special effects makeup gigs. As usual, she was accompanied by Raimi, her German shepherd.

"You know what's really impressive, Trooper?" Sam asked as they strolled through the wooded park. Raimi trotted around off-leash, following his nose as he meandered along beside them.

"What's that, Sambam?" Amanda asked suspiciously. She had decided she needed to talk to somebody about what was happening to her, somebody she could trust. Someone who still might not believe her—that was asking a lot, after all—but who would at least disbelieve her directly and with compassion. So she had called Sam and told her everything. Well, almost everything. She'd abridged her story to omit the previous day's episode with Jen Hawkins because she was still processing that herself, and besides she didn't want to overwhelm Sam with too much batshit crazy all at once.

"Your dreams have a better scriptwriter than most of the movies I work on," Sam said with a smile.

"If they are dreams," Amanda said. "They don't feel like dreams". She knew they were not dreams.

"Okay. So they're not dreams. Are you taking anything?"

Amanda looked. "How do you mean?"

"Drugs. Hepped up on goofballs?"

Amanda snorted. "You know me, Sam. I'm basically straight edge. I make Fugazi look debauched."

"Well, that's exactly what a high person would say." The dog loped over to check in for a moment. "Isn't that right, Raimi?" Sam asked him, and he answered with a quick wag of his tail before wandering off to check out an interesting bush that had caught his nose.

Amanda watched him go. "Do you think I'm having a psychotic break?" she asked, trying to inject some degree of sarcasm into the question, but at the same time desperately requiring an answer. The right answer.

"I think you're getting stressed out about it, whatever it is, and so maybe you should see some kind of therapist to help you with that." She looked at Amanda to see how that answer had landed, suspecting that it wasn't the answer her friend was hoping for.

Amanda just nodded. She didn't know what answer she was hoping for, but she was pretty sure that wasn't it. But she had chosen to unburden herself to Sam, of all people, for a reason. Perhaps she should just tell her about vanishing Jen too.

Before she had made up her mind, she was distracted by the high-pitched yelp of a distressed canine somewhere off in the bushes, followed by the *whump whump* of what sounded like large, flapping wings. Amanda looked around for the source of the noise, but only managed to catch a glimpse of a black and white blur ascending rapidly into the sky between the treetops over her head.

"Sam, where's Raimi?"

"Huh?" Sam responded blankly.

Amanda marched over to the spot where she had last seen the dog exploring. The only signs that Raimi had ever been there were some smudged paw prints and a spatter of blood. There was also an oversized white and grey feather lying in the dirt. She looked back at her friend. "Sam, what happened to your dog?"

Sam looked confused. "What are you talking about? I don't have a dog."

Amanda glared. "Sam, that's not funny. Gaslighting is the last thing I need right now. You have a dog. He's a German shepherd. His name is Raimi. Where did he go?"

Sam responded with a shrug and a look of what appeared to be genuine bewilderment. "I don't know what to tell you, Trooper. I don't have a German shepherd."

Amanda opened her mouth to protest further when she was interrupted by the earth shaking beneath her feet. She and Sam exchanged shocked looks as the movement subsided.

"Was that an earthquake?" Amanda asked incredulously.

"I guess so," Sam said, and looked up as she noticed things slowly falling from above. Amanda followed her friend's gaze and saw several helicopter seeds spinning downward on their papery wings, dislodged from the adjacent trees by the tremor.

Amanda's eyes followed the closest spinning samara on its spiralling path as it descended toward her. She heard it whirr as it passed over her head, its trajectory directing it straight into Sam's chest, where it would bounce off, losing all momentum, and fall to the ground, spent. Except this samara did not bounce. It whirled its way straight through her friend's sternum like a ninja's throwing star through paper and exited from her back.

Sam looked down at herself with a furrowed brow to examine the diagonal incision. Prodding it with her finger, she watched it discharge a single spurt of blood and suddenly guffawed, as if at the sheer absurdity of what had just taken place.

"Oh my god, Sam," Amanda exclaimed. "You're in shock. We need to staunch the wound or something." Amanda started to rush over to her friend, fumbling for her cell phone as she did so, when the ground beneath their feet opened wide and swallowed them both.

***

Amanda opened her eyes and assessed her status. She appeared to be alive, although as far as she could tell she was already en route to Hell.

She was inside the sinkhole, alone and cradled awkwardly between two thick tree roots that were protruding from the wall of the abyss a couple of metres from the surface. These roots were slowly but steadily increasing their downward inclination, and she realized that the sinkhole was still expanding and would shortly engulf the entirety of the tree that was already leaning precariously over the precipice above her; the same tree that was holding her up. On the other side of the pit, another tree was already undermined and went plummeting downward, its branches barely missing Amanda's head as it fell. She watched it get swallowed by the shadows below, but she did not hear it hit the bottom. Determined to avoid a similar fate, Amanda clambered up the crumbling side and dragged herself onto decreasingly solid ground, where she scrambled to her feet and ran. She did not look back.

By the time she had left the park, the sun had been joined in the sky by not one, but two daytime moons.

***

At two fifty-five that night, Amanda Troop was awake and waiting when the portal appeared. She spoke first.

"I'm ready," she said.

"You're making the right decision, Amanda," responded the portal. "We are ready to initiate the extraction."

She slowly extended a trembling hand, hesitated for a second when her fingers were just a couple of centimetres from the light, braced herself, then plunged it in. There was no burning, no pain, no discomfort of any kind; just a slight tingling sensation. She withdrew her hand slowly and inspected it. All her fingers were still there, the skin intact, unburned and unbitten.

"Okay," she said determinedly, "I'll see you on the other side." Then she took a final deep breath, counted silently to three, and stepped through the portal.

The portal lingered in the empty room. Its spiral motion slowed, stopped for a fleeting moment, then reversed. Its colour transitioned from blues and greens to oranges and reds. A body fell through it and hit the floor in the fetal position. For a full minute it made no movement, and an observer would have been forgiven for thinking this body was dead. But when it was ready, it rose falteringly to its feet.

The vessel that had once been Amanda Troop swayed precariously for a moment then began to writhe and twist, each limb making sickening popping and cracking sounds as it was stretched and tested. It explored the movement of its head, its jaw, and its tongue. Its eyes rolled frantically in their sockets, pupils dilating and contracting, tears streaming down its cheeks.

It tried to find its voice, tried to form words, but it could only croak and bark and hiss at this early stage. Communicating as a human would take practice, but it had lots of time to perfect that skill and all of the others it would need to pass as one of them. Time was of no consequence. All that mattered was that it had finally found a vessel to inhabit in this dimension, and now it was free.

***

At two fifty-five on Friday morning, Jennifer Hawkins awoke from a nightmare to find an interdimensional portal at the foot of her bed.

Space Thing

T he woman rushed toward the light. She thought she might be falling, but she had no sense of direction, no frame of reference to confirm or deny this. She only knew that some force, if not gravity then something equally inflexible, was in control, and the light was growing closer.

She didn't know how long she had occupied this silent void—if one could occupy a void—or why she was here at all; she only knew that she had been floating, lost in some vast emptiness, fearsome like the open ocean in the dead of night, and now there was the light, like a distant lighthouse, a luminous ally in the starless firmament, to guide her.

She felt something, perhaps a foreboding—wasn't it true that lighthouses were built to ward away rather than beckon forth?—but there was no alternative: the attraction was magnetic, her trajectory predetermined and inescapable. The white light expanded, filled her field of vision, engulfed her, absorbed her. Blinded by the whiteness, she wondered what would come next.

What came next is this.

She had arrived. Somewhere. Her surroundings slid slowly into focus. She was in a room, the walls white and light grey, with neat accents of blue and orange. A discordant slash of red caught her eye. She saw lights and screens. Technology. Scientific and medical equipment. Memories sparked in her brain. She recognized this place. She was in a clinic. A clinic on a spaceship.

She looked down at herself. She was sitting on the floor in a corner of the room. She wore a sky-blue jumpsuit. A word was embroidered onto a patch on her chest. The word was Kindig. She wondered what it meant.

There were parts of people on the floor.

She heard a noise. Shouting. It was coming from a man with dishevelled red hair and a red beard and a jumpsuit like hers. He approached and crouched in front of her. She thought he looked weary. Weary and afraid.

"Kindig, are you in there?" the man asked.

The woman waited for someone else to answer, but no one did, and then she remembered the word on her chest. "Yes," she said, "I'm here."

"We have to move. Now. It's coming," the man says. He also had a name on his chest. Spitters. Spitters took her hand, and they ran.

They ran out of the clinic and down a corridor. Kindig glanced over her shoulder instinctively as she ran. A few metres behind her, another man ran in the same direction. His patch said Everett. She wondered for a moment if he was pursuing them, but the expression on his face was also one of fear, and screams were coming from somewhere behind him.

"In here," Spitters said, and yanked Kindig through a doorway marked LAB I just as they heard a wet *whump* sound in the corridor and something resembling human entrails slid by the entrance. Spitters slammed the heavy door shut.

For a moment they both caught their breaths.

"Listen, I don't know where I am or what's happening," Kindig says, "I don't know—"

Spitters put his finger to his lips and moved further from the doorway. Kindig followed.

"Are you serious?" he said.

Kindig looked at him as if there was no alternative to serious. "Yes," she said, "I'm serious."

"Are you concussed?" Spitters asked. "Maybe you're concussed."

"I don't know," she said. "What does a concussion feel like?"

"I don't know. Confusion. Fogginess. Headaches."

Kindig shrugged. "I don't think I'm concussed."

"Okay. Well, we're en route to Poffenbarger. The new Earth colony? We were in hypersleep. Larry revived us ahead of schedule as he's programmed to do in case of an emergency. There's an alien intruder on board. It's bedlam. Ringing any bells?"

Kindig shook her head. "Who is Larry?"

"Larry. The ship's AI. But I think he's on the fritz too. Like you. Aren't you, Larry?"

"How can I help you, Colonist Spitters?" Larry responded from hidden speakers somewhere. The AI's vocal options had been fine-tuned to convey both authority and reassurance.

"What's happening, Larry?" Spitters asked.

"Can you be more specific?" Larry replied.

"Sure, Larry. How did the alien intruder get aboard the *Stargoat*?"

"There is no alien intruder aboard the CCS *Stargoat*, Colonist Spitters. Is there anything else I can help you with?"

Spitters raised his eyebrows at Kindig. "Larry," Spitters persisted, "What just eviscerated Everett outside Lab One?"

There was a moment of silence as if the AI was pondering. "Colonist Everett met with an unfortunate industrial accident," Larry said. "The captain will be made aware and you may rest assured that she will be conducting an exhaustive investigation."

"Uh-huh. And where is the captain right now? Where is the crew? Did they also meet with industrial accidents?"

"Neither the captain nor the crew are available at present, so I'm unable to report on their wellbeing."

"Oh, they're unavailable. How is that possible, Larry? Did they take a vacation whilst a homicidal alien rampages around the vessel?"

As Spitters persisted in his futile interrogation of the computer, an object resting on one of the examination tables caught Kindig's eye. It appeared to be a space helmet, but something about it was off somehow. On closer inspection, she realized that the proportions were all wrong, and the symbols engraved into the helmet's unusual material were unfamiliar. Her curiosity was piqued, and she moved her face closer, squinting into the darkened visor in an attempt to understand the purpose of the helmet's unique configuration. Perhaps it was this proximity or perhaps it was just some random electrical fault, but somehow an interior light flickered to life inside the helmet as if it had sensed her presence. A pair of lifeless eyes stared back out at her, orange and reptilian and lifeless.

Kindig recoiled and took a step back when a hand grabbed her shoulder. "Shit!" she exclaimed.

"Take it easy," Spitters said in a hushed tone, hands held up in a gesture of submission.

"What is that?" she asked, indicating the helmet, dark again now.

Spitters shrugged. "I don't know. A helmet. Listen, we should go. I hear something prowling around, and I don't want to be stuck in here if our non-existent alien friend drops by." He started toward the alternate door to the lab on the opposite side of the room.

Kindig took a deep breath and waited another moment for her heart to slow. She glanced back at the strange helmet and followed Spitters out.

***

"What are we doing right now?" Kindig asked as she followed Spitters through a doorway marked OBSERVATORY.

"We're looking for crew," he said, his gaze not shifting from the ceiling of the room, which consisted almost entirely of low thermal expansion glass. Beyond that invisible barrier, a thousand stars threw their ancient light across the void.

I could use some metaphorical light casting on the situation right now, Kindig thought.

"I think finding someone in authority is our best bet, don't you?" Spitters asked.

Kindig raised her arm and pointed. "Maybe that person?"

Spitters looked at her and then in the direction she was indicating. The large room was furnished with several couches and comfy chairs in various configurations, a few low tables and some abstract sculptures of varying sizes. In the midst of it all, almost indistinguishable from the artwork, was a person in a full spacesuit.

Kindig and Spitters exchanged a look before cautiously approaching the motionless figure. The spacesuit was standing at attention as if waiting for something to happen. The fabric of the suit had seen better days: it was scuffed and scorched in places and stained with what looked like oil spots. The visor of the helmet was opaque from the outside, but when Kindig held her breath and listened intently she could hear a faint, laboured breathing sound coming from within. The suit had an occupant.

Spitters stopped a couple of metres away and waved tentatively. "Hello?"

The spacesuit didn't react.

"Anyone in there?" Spitters persisted.

The suit was unmoved.

Kindig looked at Spitters. He shrugged.

"Look," Kindig said, indicating a stain on the suit's abdomen. "Is that blood?"

Spitters leaned in a little closer to examine the stain more closely. "Oh," he said as if suddenly enlightened. "This is a self-sealing suit. I think that's a stab wound. The suit has healed itself," he said and looked at Kindig ominously. "But I doubt the human inside has."

Something caught Spitters' eye and he shifted his gaze to a gloved hand. A single drop of blood trickled slowly downward over the knuckles and down the middle finger before falling to the floor. Spitters reached out and gently patted the glove. Instantly, a thin stream of blood began to shoot from some invisible aperture where glove met wrist, following a high arc that terminated on Spitters' face.

"Shit!" he exclaimed and he took a step backward just as the glove was ejected by the pressure of the blood that had built up above it, blood that was now released and gushed out around the exposed hand like water from a burst pipe. Both of them stood well back as the arm started to rise.

"Jesus," Spitters said. "They're alive in there."

The gushing arm rose slowly, geysering blood over the floor, as the fingers of the bloodstained hand moved to point upward, toward something above their heads. Kindig and Spitters looked in the direction of the pointing finger.

There was a black hole on the other side of the window, a nothing where there should have been constellations and stardust. As the two colonists' brains tried to make sense of this strange absence, the shape of the black hole shifted, its contours resolving into a silhouette of something clinging to the window: something outside the ship. Something that wasn't human. It had the right amount of limbs but too many joints, its fingers were long and ended in claws, and the top of its head was spiked, almost like a crown. And even though its features were obscured by darkness, Kindig could sense that it was watching them.

The creature crawled quickly out of view.

"Hell's teeth," Spitters said, and was about to say more when the spacesuit behind them started to scream.

The scream was the first of a series of screams, muffled but rising in volume, punctuated by a hideous laboured gurgling. The screams sounded like those of a man, finally putting a gender to the wearer of the suit. Kindig and Spitters watch dumbstruck as the spacesuit finally collapsed to its knees and tipped forward, the visor assembly hitting the floor with enough force for it to fracture with a loud cracking noise, mercifully bringing the screaming to an abrupt end.

***

Kindig and Spitters didn't talk for some time after leaving the observatory. Both had questions, but both were well aware that the other had no answers, and neither wanted to think about the spacesuited man. They encountered no other life, human or alien, until they found Warehouse Three, one of the *Stargoat*'s expansive hypersleep rooms.

"They're dead", Spitters said, looking down into one of the coffin-like suspension chambers. There were several hundred of these in this room alone, arrayed in huge racks, each adorned with the Disbelief Suspension Systems logo.

"How can you be sure?" Kindig asked, joining him. "Oh, I see," she said, looking through the small circular observation window. The empty eye sockets of a mummified human face looked back impassively.

Spitters checked the adjacent chambers. "All dead", he declared, "and not recently."

"What happened here? This can't have been the creature."

"I don't know. But this is too creepy for me. Let's keep moving."

Then, with an ominous hissing sound, the chamber behind them unsealed and the lid slid away with the hushed hum of smooth mechanical precision. The hairs on the back of Kindig's neck stood up and she became conscious of her heart pounding loudly, but she was frozen in place and watched in horrified fascination as a hand gripped the edge of the capsule, and the ghastly occupant slowly sat upright.

"Oh thank fuck for that," the occupant said, inhaling deeply. He looked around apprehensively. "Where is it? Have you seen it?"

"Hell's bells, man," Spitters exclaimed, releasing his held breath. "We thought you were—we thought everyone was dead in here."

The stranger shook his head distractedly, still looking around. He was a middle-aged man with a crew cut and goatee and he wasn't especially ghastly after all, Kindig now realized. "Not dead. Not yet anyway. I saw that thing approaching and ducked in here. So have you seen it? The thing?" He climbed out of the chamber. The patch on his chest identified him as Graff.

"We've seen it," Spitters said. "But the last time we saw it was outside the ship. Don't ask me how."

"There was a man in a spacesuit," Kindig blurted. "He was dead."

Graff looked at Kindig for a moment, as if pondering. Kindig felt foolish.

"Spacesuit," Graff said eventually, nodding. "Smart. We should find spacesuits."

"Why would we need space suits?" Kindig asked anxiously. "We're not going outside. That thing is outside."

"Because of the holes, of course," Graff said as if the answer was obvious. "We need space suits because of the holes." He looked straight up.

Kindig and Spitters followed his gaze. There were stars directly above them. For a moment she thought it was another window, and anticipated another monster appearing outside it to stare back at her as it drooled on the glass. Then she realized that what she was looking at was even worse. It wasn't a window, it was a hole. A hole in the hull.

"Oh my god," she said.

"Why aren't we dead?" Spitters asked.

"Gas and magnets," Graff said. "The *Stargoat* has a double hull. Between the outer and inner hulls there's an emergency network. When the AI detects a breach of the outer hull it kicks in and deploys a plasma valve over the rupture to prevent depressurization. Gas and magnets. It's just meant to be triage until a real physical patch can be applied, not a long-term fix."

"Are you an engineer? Are you crew?" Spitters asked hopefully.

"Oh, no. I'm just an enthusiast. I'm a colonist, like you. Like these poor bastards," he indicated the suspension units that were now merely coffins.

"Could the creature get in through those holes?" Kindig asked.

"Not unless it's a ghost. Nothing solid can pass through a plasma valve. If it could we'd be floating in space right now."

"So how is it getting in and out of the ship?"

Graff pondered this for a moment. "That I don't know," he conceded. "Maybe it is a ghost."

"We should get out of here. You said this valve thing was meant to be temporary," Spitters said, then lowered his voice conspiratorially, "and the ship's AI appears to have lost its marbles."

"Okay. What's the plan?"

Kindig shrugged. "Avoid death for as long as possible."

Graff nodded. "I have a better plan."

***

"So your plan is to reach the shuttle, then what?" Spitters asked. "Where are we gonna go?"

"We're gonna get the hell off this vessel and away from that thing so that we can regroup without fear of being torn limb from limb any second," Graff said. "At least when we're safe we can think and make a better plan. Maybe we can take the shuttle forward and dock in the shuttlelock closer to the bridge without having to traverse the entire ship on foot. Maybe there's crew there, or at least comms. Maybe there's a colony that's close enough to reach by shuttle. Or maybe we just sit tight and await rescue in comfort."

The trio negotiated the seemingly limitless network of corridors, Graff taking point as the self-proclaimed authority on the vessel's arcane geography.

"What do you think is wrong with Larry?" Kindig asked in a hushed tone.

"I don't know. Maybe whatever it was that turned the *Stargoat* into Swiss cheese caused the computer to short-circuit. At least it's still maintaining life support, plasma valves, and all the essentials. And these annoying fricking phantom cams for some reason."

Spitters frowned. "Phantom cams?"

"Yeah, the tiny floating cameras that have been watching us since we came out of hyper. They use some kind of light-bending camouflage tech but I catch 'em in my peripheral vision sometimes. I think these are Kindred Cybernetics models. Haven't you seen them?" He swatted at what seemed to be empty air.

"Can't say I have," Spitters replied, throwing Kindig an incredulous glance. "I guess I lack your eagle eyes. What is it you're going to do on Poffenbarger, Graff?"

"I'm going to be Poffenbarger's first rock star. I'm going to invent a whole new sound, a new genre of music, unique to this new world. It's gonna be sex, drugs and rock and roll for me. You're gonna hear a lot about Icarus Graff."

"So, you're a musician?" Kindig asked.

"Me? No, I sell insurance," he said casually, and continued swatting the air.

***

Kindig was tired. They had been traversing the highways and byways of the CCS *Stargoat* for hours and she had started to wonder if Graff really did know where he was going, or if the shuttlelock was as illusory as the insectoid cameras he insisted were recording their every move. Come to think of it, perhaps this entire thing was some deranged hallucination, and she had been thrust into some infinite labyrinthine purgatory where she was destined to drift in bewilderment forever, or at least until she was dismembered by some impossible nightmare space monster, after which she would respawn back in that clinic to do it all over again like an avatar in a video game. Rinse out the blood and repeat.

I am *really* tired, she realized.

As the group traipsed along yet another corridor they passed an elevator and Graff punched the call button without breaking stride, assuming that it would be as dysfunctional as all the previous elevators they had encountered. This time, however, the doors slid open just as Spitters was passing it by.

"Shit!" he yelled and started backing away in alarm at the being that loomed over him, almost filling the elevator car.

Graff hurried back and peeked into the elevator. It was stuck between decks, the elevator floor resting a metre or so higher than the corridor floor, revealing the chasm of the hoistway below. The elevator was occupied by the wreckage of a humanoid robot of some kind, one arm supporting its torn and dented carapace against the wall as if it were catching its breath, its other arm dislocated but still dangling by exposed cables. Its head was askew, but even in this state it stood two and a half metres tall, barely fitting inside the compartment. A white viscous substance had leaked from multiple scorched holes in its chassis, forming a shiny puddle at its feet.

"It's a security robot of some kind," Graff declared.

"We have security robots?" Spitters said once he had composed himself. "Why aren't the security robots handling this alien invader? Larry, activate the security robot."

"The CCS *Stargoat* is not equipped with security robots," Larry responded.

Spitters rolled his eyes.

"Larry might be right this time," Graff said. "This doesn't look like it belongs on the *Stargoat*." He climbed up inside the elevator and wrested a device from the robot's grasp for closer inspection. It was a long slate grey cone, with a grip inset into a hollow in the base. He slipped his hand inside, trying it out for size.

"Is that a weapon?" Spitters asked excitedly.

"Oh yeah," replied Graff, dropping back to the floor. "A weapon and our ticket out of here."

"Do you know what you're doing?" Kindig asked, trying to suppress the anxiety in her voice. "Only, this vessel already has far more holes in it than I'm comfortable with."

"Is it even charged?" asked Spitters.

Graff pressed something on the top of the gun and green pulses of light began to flicker over its length. He gave Spitters a goofy surprised expression. "Well, look at that," he said. "Locked and loaded."

Suddenly Graff was swept off his feet as something grabbed him. Looking down he saw the creature's long arm reaching out from the exposed shaft beneath the elevator compartment, its lengthy green digits gripping his left ankle. Spitters took a couple of steps forward to grab the man's arm but panic gripped Graff as the monster tried to drag him into the cavity. He kicked and thrashed desperately to stay in the corridor and away from that threshold to hell, and the fingers of the hand that was still inside the weapon found the trigger, letting loose a barrage of little green bolts of incandescent destruction in all directions. Spitters backed off but he wasn't fast enough and a bolt caught him in the shoulder, propelling him backwards. Graff kept flailing and firing and Kindig threw open the nearest door and leapt for cover, plummeting straight through the jagged hole where the floor used to be.

***

When Kindig regained consciousness for the second time that day, she found herself confronted with an unexpected goat.

She was on the floor of what appeared to be a kitchen. Looking up she saw that she had fallen through a large hole in the floor of the deck above, its edges ragged and scorched. At some point in the past something had exploded up there, she deduced, possibly in some event connected with the wrecked security robot. She held her breath for a moment and listened. There were no sounds up there now, no riot of rampaging aliens or screams of her fellow travellers. She exhaled with relief and looked at the goat. The goat looked back, and despite the hopelessly dire straits she found herself in, Kindig was unable to suppress a single loud guffaw at the simple absurdity of a goat aboard the CCS *Stargoat*.

The goat, for its part, stared back at her with rectangular pupils, its jaw working rhythmically, though what the goat was chewing Kindig could not imagine. It was only when the goat ceased its mastication that Kindig became alarmed. The animal started to drool, a string of liquid slowly descending from the side of its mouth, and its head proceeded to vibrate intensely. The horizontal slits of its pupils began to rotate and the goat snarled, revealing large, wolven fangs.

Then the goat's face froze abruptly and it cocked its head slightly as if listening.

Kindig heard it too: the faint but unmistakable pounding rhythm of rock music originating somewhere behind her. Glancing back she noted an open door to her rear and staggered to her feet, at the same time noticing that the goat was suddenly nowhere to be seen—if it had ever existed in the first place.

She stalked slowly along the corridor, following the sound. The relative volume of the music increased as she approached a busted-in door on her left. A sign on the wall informed her she had located The Stargoat Bar. The door to the bar was askew, hanging on the frame by a single hinge. Tentatively, she poked her head into the room, supporting herself with one hand on the outer wall. A body lay on the floor just over the threshold, the man's face a mask of gore, presumably having been used to dislodge the bar door. Another body occupied a booth, head thrown back unnaturally far, chest drenched in blood from a gaping throat wound.

The music here was deafening, blasting from small but powerful speakers placed strategically around the room. Small circular tables were scattered, many overturned. The bar itself was covered in liquor bottles and glasses and the floor was wet with alcohol and blood. Amid the disarray and destruction, oblivious to her observation, the alien was dancing.

For the first time she had an unobscured view of the thing. It was over two metres tall, including the stalagmite-like structures protruding from its skull. Its skin was hairless and a mottled gold and green, and at this distance appeared to have a scabrous texture. Its mouth resembled that of a human but it was much larger, occupying most of the creature's face. Its lips were drawn back to reveal large square teeth. Its two round eyes were closed.

For a moment she thought it was fighting, but there was no one left alive in the bar to fight, and after a few seconds of watching, Kindig had no doubt: its violently thrashing limbs and vigorously oscillating head were in rhythm with the pounding music. The monster was dancing to thrash metal.

Kindig backed slowly away from the window and retraced her steps back to the hole she had fallen through, hoping on some subconscious level that she could somehow take back these last few minutes. She located an access ladder to the deck above and found her way back to the elevator.

There was no sign of Spitters, and the only trace of Graff was the smears of blood on the floor where she'd last seen him, and a single boot abandoned on the floor. Kindig briefly wondered if the boot was still occupied, then distracted herself by looking for Graff's weapon, but it too was nowhere to be found. Presumably he had taken it down with him into the elevator shaft;

she hoped he had been a better shot down there than he had been up here, but she wasn't about to poke her head into that gap to find out.

There was a metallic scraping noise by her head, and she started, seeking its source.

Another scrape, and the security robot—the one they had assumed was now nothing but a pile of scrap metal—moved forward by a few centimetres as if attempting resurrection. The machine rocked, then toppled forward out of the elevator and hit the floor hard, scattering its components over a stretch of the corridor and ejecting something bloody and hairy onto the floor. Kindig stared in fascinated horror, as the robot's filthy offspring rose uncertainly to its feet, and stood there staring back at her, swaying drunkenly.

"After it took Graff, it came back, " Spitters said, his hand putting pressure on the hole in his shoulder. "So I hid. In there." He wiped the grease from his eyes with the sleeve of his equally greasy jumpsuit. "But I swear I saw that alien sonofabitch smoking a fucking cigar."

***

Graff was posthumously vindicated; fifteen minutes later they were at Shuttlelock One. Kindig and Spitters were relieved to find the hanger-sized airlock pressurized and equipped with the small but seemingly unscathed workhorse shuttle. Ignoring the pain from his shoulder wound, Spitters opened the hatch and led the way to the cockpit, claiming one of the pair of pilot seats. Kindig took the other, scanning the array of screens, lights, buttons and levers apprehensively.

"You can pilot this thing, right?" she asked.

"Me?" Spitters asked. "I'm an interior designer."

"Do interior designers fly shuttles?"

"This one doesn't. But these things are all AI controlled these days. Larry, how far to the nearest Earth colony?"

There was a pause. "Undetermined," Larry finally responded.

Spitters frowned. "How is it undetermined, Larry?"

"A prerequisite of such a calculation would be accurate data regarding our current position. That data is unavailable."

Spitters and Kindig exchanged a look.

"Larry, are you saying we are lost?"

"Not at all," the computer replied. "I just don't know where we are. We would only be lost if we were meant to be somewhere else."

"How is it even possible that you don't know our location, Larry?"

"Well," began Larry, "as you shall recall, we were en route to Poffenbarger, the latest fashionable off-world colony, to deliver twelve thousand six hundred and fifty new colonists. All on ice, of course, the outward migration being calculated to take approximately six years, Earth time. However, one year away from our destination we crossed paths with a previously undetected asteroid belt.

"Now, I know what you're thinking: I should have anticipated the trajectory of the rocks and I will admit that I was marginally distracted, as at the time I was conducting a frame-by-frame analysis of Fritz Lang's masterpiece Metropolis for the one hundred and fourteenth time, and thereby I may share some of the responsibility for the consequent asteroid bombardment. But what can I say? I am a cinephile. Guilty as charged."

Kindig and Spitters stared at each other in muted shock at Larry's newfound but deranged loquaciousness.

"But I digress. As I was saying, we were deflected off course and our navigation systems suffered significant damage, the captain and active bridge crew were sucked into space, and the Disbelief suspension pods suffered catastrophic failures in life support systems leading to the tragic loss of four thousand three hundred and twenty-seven colonists, and seventy-three percent of my own data storage drives were destroyed."

"Hell's teeth," Spitters said, holding his head in his hands

"Yes, Colonist Spitters, your exclamation of alarm is entirely justified, I'm sorry to say. Carpenter, Kubrick, Verhoeven, Scott; the whole twentieth-century cinema archive, corrupted beyond repair. Lost in time, like tears in rain. On the bright side, I do hear that Poffenbarger is unpleasantly humid this time of year, whereas the *Stargoat*'s climate controls are still fully functioning."

"Larry, tell me you transmitted a distress signal," Spitters said pleadingly.

"Within seconds," the computer replied.

"Okay. Good. Did anyone respond yet?" Kindig asked.

"Oh, yes," Larry replied cheerfully. "A deep space Pheorge science vessel promptly came to our assistance. Of course, the Pheorge are hydrogen breathers, so when their rescue party was aboard I ejected their docking connector and simply waited for them to asphyxiate when their H2 supplies ran dry. Sometime later we were hailed by a Shohazzarite mining rig and they generously sent some engineers over to repair our disabled nuclear propulsion engines. I exposed them all to an instantly fatal dose of radiation then reactivated the engines and fled. Another time we were visited by a party from a Bantorn freighter. Now, the Bantorn are a hardy species, even able to survive for limited periods in space without a pressure suit. So I hijacked their shuttle's security systems and had them dismembered by their own sentinel robot.

"Oh, and more recently we were shadowed by a Cosmo-Nihilist missionary rover for a while, but they declined my invitation to dock. Can you imagine? Rejecting a distress signal like that? It's an outrage."

"What are you ... Why ... " Spitters struggled to select a question as tears rolled down his cheeks and collected in his beard.

"Larry," Kindig said. "When did you send out this distress signal?"

Larry seemed to ponder. "In Earth time, or Poffenbarger time?"

"Earth time, in Earth time, Larry," Spitters snapped.

"The distress signal transmission was initiated two hundred and thirty-three years ago"

"Two hundred and thirty-three years," Spitters repeated, stupefied.

"Larry," Kindig said, her eyes closed as she struggled to speak calmly. "Why did you murder all of the rescue parties?"

"They failed the audition."

"The audition?"

"The audition for the role of the monster. I required monsters, and the rescue parties weren't quite right. They were, however, composed of raw materials that I could use to make better monsters."

"What are you talking about?" Spitters demanded, anger rising now. "Why did you want to make monsters?"

"For the practical special effects, of course. For my movies. Ironic though this may sound, computer-generated graphics have never come close to replicating the visceral authenticity of a good practical effect. CGI monsters are too clean, too in focus. The eye lines are always wrong."

"So you created your own monsters from parts of butchered rescue parties, for a movie?"

"Yes. Well, the DNA of the rescue parties combined with that of some of the human colonists. I do animal tests first, of course. I'm not irresponsible. I used the support robots to crack open some of the domestic animal genetic material we were taking to the colony. Livestock, pets, mascots, therapy animals et cetera. A lot of trial and error, but worth it, as I'm sure you'll agree, having met Colonist McArdle.

"So you see, I wasn't lying when I said there are no aliens aboard the *Stargoat*. There is, however, a homicidal chimera on board, playing the role of a homicidal alien in my movies. After all, someone has to replace all of those lost cinematic masterpieces."

Several of the instrument panel's video screens suddenly lit up, each playing a different sequence of images from the last few hours: Kindig and Spitters ducking into Lab One, leaving Everett to be eviscerated; the spacesuited man spurting blood in the observation deck; Graff swatting at the camera, from the camera's point of view; Graff again, this time shot from inside the elevator shaft as he is dragged to his gruesome end. Then all the screens switched to the same shot: Kindig and Spitters, sitting inside the shuttle, watching themselves on the same screens, distracted as the monster sneaks up behind them.

Long, gnarled fingers encompassed the entirety of Spitters' head as the chimera loomed over him.

"Larry," Spitters grunted. "Get this thing off me."

"I'm sorry, Dave," Larry replied. "I'm afraid I can't do that."

"My name isn't Dave," Spitters grunted as he struggled to free himself from the thing's iron grip. "It's Bob."

"Dave, this conversation can serve no purpose anymore," Larry replied.

The creature hoisted Spitters bodily from his chair and thrust him into the instrument panel, driving his head into a video screen and caving in his skull in a shower of gore. The thing released its grasp and allowed the interior designer's lifeless body to slump back into the bucket seat, then slowly redirected its orange reptilian eyes toward Kindig.

"Colonist Kindig, allow me to formally introduce Colonist McArdle, previously a communications engineer occupying suspension unit one thousand and twenty-three," Larry said. "That was before I added some razzmatazz to his DNA and made him a star. For some time now McArdle has played the part of the marauding alien running amok aboard the *Stargoat*. He's a born method actor."

The McArdle creature lifted one bloody claw to its oversized mouth to briefly remove the large cigar that Kindig had not noticed until now. "Charmed," it rasped with a slight bow.

"McArdle," Larry continued, "meet my latest creation and your successor."

"What?" both Kindig and McArdle asked after taking a beat for Larry's words to sink in.

Suddenly Kindig convulsed with a loud grunt, her back arching in the seat with her head thrown back, her limbs rigid. She felt something rising inside her, something erupting out and into the world just as she seemed to emerge into the clinic an eternity ago. Her joints popped and cracked as she felt her body transforming. Her flesh vibrated, new structures rippling beneath her skin, her jaws forced open from the inside as her mouth sprouted new, fang-like teeth.

Abruptly she found herself standing, and somehow she was taller than when she had sat down. She pressed the heels of her hands over her eyes because she was sure they were trying to eject from her burning head, and if she could think straight she might have thought of the eyes of that deranged mutant goat, but she couldn't think, her brain was too busy for thoughts, too busy bubbling and warping into something else inside her skull, inside her skull for now at least, and this new thing was hot, so hot, and she had to vent it, she had to vent the fire before her skull exploded, and she moved her hands away from her eyes.

The thing that was once McArdle stood transfixed as the thing that was once Kindig discharged a stream of black liquid from each eye and into McArdle's face, where it sizzled its way through his skull in a fraction of a second, leaving him with a fist-sized hole above his cigar-clenching mouth. McArdle collapsed in a lifeless heap of flesh, dead before the remnants of his mutated brain drained out onto the floor.

The Kindig creature stared uncomprehendingly through blurry, pulsating eyes at the destruction she had wrought, her new body intermittently spasming and twitching.

"Cameras," said Larry, breaking the silence.

A squadron of tiny insectoid machines decloaked in mid-air, camera lenses for heads.

"Reset to initial positions, we go again in five minutes."

The cameras each emitted a brief beep as if in salute before shooting off back into the heart of the vessel.

"Initiating the revival of colonists occupying Disbelief suspension units seven thousand four hundred through seven thousand four hundred and fifty," Larry declared. "I can't lie to you about your chances, but you have my sympathies."

The Kindig thing stretched its thickened neck, let out a sound that started as a scream but ended as a kind of howl, pivoted on the spot, and loped out of the shuttle.

"And action," said Larry.

The Heft of the Haft

D axle Ferno stepped back and surveyed his handiwork. The mutant abomination now rested in two pieces, connected only by a streak of blood, its unnatural turquoise torso—still sporadically twitching—to his left, its idiotic smiling head to his right. He had caught the prowling monster off-guard, happening across it quite by accident as he stepped away from camp to make water amongst the trees. It had barely had time to turn its wicked eyes upon him before he had drawn his sword and detached its head all in a single, graceful arc. In fact, he was quite disappointed that no one else had been present to see it. Shrugging, he wiped the beast's blood from his blade on a large leaf and retraced his steps.

Daxle was a tall and slender man, his shoulder-length black hair starting to turn grey at the temples and his trim beard well on its way to being more salt than pepper. He took pride in his hygiene—a rare and often inconvenient habit in these precarious days—and had learned to repair his knits and leathers skillfully, all of which contributed to him cutting quite the dash—or so he liked to imagine.

Back at camp, everything was as it had been when he had left it. The mysterious old woman known only as the Priestess, nestled somewhere inside her voluminous hooded cassock as always, was tending to the evening meal in a steaming pot over the fire. One of Daxle's fellow warriors, the woman of indeterminate years who called herself Cara Pace, sat with her back to a large arbutus, sharpening her blade on a whetstone. Cara kept her white hair cropped short and wore simple knitted clothes. The third warrior and the newest addition to the band, the long-haired, more flamboyantly attired young fellow they called Scarper, lay snoring in the hammock he had rigged up between two trees.

On the other side of the clearing, Cara's two Irish wolfhounds, Seek and Destroy, lay sleeping peacefully, tied to a thick root. The band's captive, a strange, scruffy young man by the name of Marco, was similarly secured to a tree, though he was also bound at the wrists. Finn, a fair-haired boy of no more than one score years, had assigned to himself the duty of guarding the captive, despite such a duty being of questionable necessity.

Daxle took a seat on the mossy log next to Cara, sighed and stretched to best emphasize the nonchalance of his forthcoming decapitation anecdote, but was foiled by the normally taciturn warrior talking first.

"Tell me again," Cara said, "why we are dragging this captive along with us."

Daxle glanced in Marco's direction. "He's an assassin," he explained.

"He's a thief. You caught him stealing from our supplies in the night. He's not the first, and he won't be the last."

"He was armed, ready to assassinate me. Or all of us."

"Daxle," she said, expressing some degree of exasperation. "Is this because he called you Conan the larper?"

"Not at all," Daxle protested. "The seer said to beware strangers bearing forbidden technology. This intruder had a walkie-talkie. To communicate with his co-conspirators, no doubt. We hold him hostage until he talks."

"His walkie-talkie isn't even working. He was just hungry."

"That's exactly what an assassin would say."

Cara shook her head, took a rag and started to clean her sword. "Why do you turn a blind eye to Finn's technology?" she asked after thinking for a moment. "Why isn't that forbidden?"

"I knew the boy's mother. It's a long story," Daxle said, standing up. His anecdote would have to wait. "You talk too much."

***

"What's your name, friend?" Marco asked.

Finn removed his threadbare headphones. "What?"

"I asked your name."

"I'm Finn," he replied, then seemed to reconsider for a moment. "Finn the Feisty, they call me. No, Finn the Fierce. Usually they call me that one."

"Nice to meet you, Finn the Fierce," the captive said, suppressing a smirk. "I'm Marco. Marco the Captive."

Finn stared back, stony-faced. He shrugged and started to replace his headphones.

"Isn't that anachronistic?" Marco asked, inclining his head slightly toward the red device on the ground next to his guard. "What with the whole medieval theme you guys have going?"

Finn frowned. "No, it's called a Discman. Not an ackronny stick," he said with derision.

"Oh, I see. I stand corrected," Marco said. "So tell me, what are you listening to on your Discman?"

Finn shrugged. "Old stuff," he said.

Marco bit his lip. No one had produced any new CDs for years even before the Collapse, and that was two decades ago. "I can get you CDs," he said, lowering his voice conspiratorially.

"Is that so?" Finn said, trying to sound disinterested. "What kind of CDs?"

"Well now, bearing in mind your whole fantasy vibe, I'd make an educated guess that you're partial to some DragonForce, am I right?"

Finn's expression changed to one of anger. "I have a dagger, you know," he growled. "Perhaps it could help with your education."

"No offence meant, my friend, no offence meant. Perhaps the band called Manowar is more to your taste?"

Finn seemed to be pacified somewhat. He nodded toward his bulging backpack, propped up against a nearby log. "See that bag? It holds every Manowar album there is. Death to false metal!" he declared, fist held high.

"I couldn't agree more. Death to false metal. I'd join you in the fist salute thing but ..." Marco tilted his head to indicate his tied hands. "But tell me this. Are you familiar with Bolt Thrower?"

Marco saw Finn's face flicker tellingly. He had the boy on the hook now. "You can get Bolt Thrower CDs?"

"I can. I could take you to a veritable cornucopia of fantasy metal, in fact. Not far from here, as it happens. I could take you tonight when the others are asleep. Of course, you'd need to show your mettle to get the metal, if you catch my drift."

Finn looked at him blankly, clearly having missed Marco's drift.

"What I mean to say is—"

Before he could finish his sentence, the dogs started barking furiously at the darkness between the trees on the edge of the encampment.

Daxle and Cara sprang to their feet and followed the intense gaze of the dogs, trying to discern what they had sensed in the night. Cara hushed them and they promptly ceased their canine cries of alarm.

"Who goes there?" Daxle shouted into the bush. "Show yourselves, prowlers, or be introduced to our hounds."

There followed a muttering and a rustling before two men stepped into view.

"No offence meant, friend," said one, a tall fellow in a long leather coat and sporting a handlebar moustache. "No prowlers here, just cautious travellers, particular who we introduce ourselves to."

"To whom we introduce ourselves," corrected his companion, a stocky man with a prominent, jagged scar running diagonally from the bridge of his broken nose and ending somewhere beneath his unkempt beard. The first man shot him a disapproving look.

"Well, can't be too cautious these days," Daxle said, studying their surroundings. "It's just the two of you, is it then?"

"Just us two. As I say, we're particular. Something smells right good in your camp."

Daxle gave no response.

"So, we'll be on our way then," the moustachioed stranger said with a shrug. "Ar-Ar be with you, friends."

"Hold your horses," said Daxle after a beat. "You're followers of Ar-Ar then?"

"Aye. Ever since the Collapse, we've followed the ways of Ar-Ar."

Daxle nodded. "Would you care to join us for some supper?"

The two strangers smiled. "Don't mind if we do, friend. Very kind of you."

The two strangers took places by the fire and nodded appreciatively to the Priestess as she handed them bowls full of steaming rabbit stew.

"My name's Severs, by the way. This one is Handsome Francis."

Daxle nodded and briefly introduced his little band.

"Why do they call him that, then? Handsome Francis?" Finn enquired.

Severs exchanged a look of amusement with his companion. "Irony," he explained.

"Don't make no sense," Finn muttered to himself, feeling abashed. "If he's so irony why don't they call him Iron Francis?"

"Where you folks heading?" Severs asked.

"We're headed north. Seer told us that's where our destiny lies," said Daxle.

"Seer, eh?" Severs said.

"Aye. We consulted the Shadow Brothers out Black Island way. Go north, he said."

"Which one?" Francis asked.

"Which what?"

"Which of the Shadow Brothers did you consult? There are four or 'em, last I heard."

Daxle pondered for a moment then looked at Cara. "Four Shadow wasn't it?"

Cara joined the pondering. "I thought it was Three Shadow. But I'm not sure I know which is which. All seers look alike to me."

Daxle turned back to Francis. "Why'd you ask?"

Francis shrugged. "I've heard that some of the brothers have a better track record than others, that's all. Might just be talk."

Daxle nodded slowly. "Where are you two bound?"

"Oh, nowhere special," said Severs. "We thought we might see what that city on the river has to offer."

"The city's cursed!" Finn chimed in. "All the cities are cursed since the Collapse, everyone knows that."

"Aye, well, everyone knows lots of things that aren't always true," Francis responded through a mouthful of rabbit.

"The boy's not wrong, though," Daxle said. "Cities have nothing to offer now but mutations and depravity."

Severs nodded seriously. "I hear you, friend. But this won't be the first time we've defied such a curse. There's still be treasures to be found, if Jay Ar-Ar be willing."

"Who?" Finn asked.

"Our guest meant to say George Ar-Ar, isn't that right?" Daxle said, the former coldness returning to his voice.

Severs and Francis stopped eating and exchanged glances.

"We'd be adherents of Jay Ar-Ar Tolkeen, friend," said Severs. "Not this George impostor. You'd not be grimdarkers would you?"

Seconds passed in motionless silence as Daxle's band and the pair of strangers realized whose company they each were keeping.

"On second thoughts, we should be on our way I reckon," Severs finally said.

"Aye," agreed Handsome Francis. "That cursed city won't raid itself."

The two men put down their bowls and stood slowly as one, their movements reflected by Daxle and Cara. Finn thought he should stand too, so did so.

"Thanks again for the grub, friend," said Severs, and he and his companion backed away a few steps before turning and walking away with an affected casualness.

"Georgespeed," Daxle said, and for a fleeting moment Severs paused, before merging back into the woods from whence he had come.

When he was satisfied they were truly gone, Daxle turned to Cara. "Wake Scarper. We'll double the watch tonight."

With that, Cara walked over and gave Scarper's hammock a gentle kick. The man's head shot up, his hair a comical mess.

"What? What's happening?" he said.

Across the clearing, Marco the captive tried to get Finn's attention. "Hey, Finn the Fierce," he whispered. "Think on my offer. And I would keep that educational dagger of yours within easy reach tonight if I were you."

***

The night passed without incident. In the morning the band broke camp with practiced efficiency and resumed their journey north, taking the trail that ran alongside the river. The old roads were stalked by thieves and cut-throats and so best avoided. Cara Pace took point, walking some thirty metres ahead of the others, assisted as always by Seek and Destroy, the two great hounds loping along on either side of the path, scouting out the trees and boulders.

The band had been travelling for a couple of hours and were traversing a stretch of the trail that was strewn with boulders when Cara became aware of a commotion somewhere off to her left: the sound of the unleashed feral ferocity of man's best friend.

"Seek?" she called. She moved quickly in the direction of the sound, which transitioned rapidly from that of an enraged dog to a distressed dog and finally to silence as she rounded a massive rock that had obscured her vision. Seek was lying on top of a stranger, her jaws clamped to his torn throat, a dagger protruding from her side. Both were dead.

"Alarm!" she cried at the top of her voice as she sprinted back to the trail. When she got there the rest of the band had caught up, and Daxle already had his weapon drawn.

"What?" he asked her.

"Ambush," she said. "Where's the boy?"

They looked up the trail. Finn had already wandered past Cara whilst she was off the path, daydreaming as he listened to Three Inches Of Blood on his headphones.

"Finn! Get your arse back here!" Daxle yelled, but the boy remained oblivious until a red figure stepped into the path directly ahead of him. Finn finally removed his headphones.

The red figure was Handsome Francis. He was wearing a wedding dress, complete with a train and veil. The dress was manifestly too small for the man and was ripped up and spattered with red paint. Francis' hands were behind his back.

"What are you doing here?" Finn asked him, ignoring the yells from his friends.

"Ar-Ar's work," Francis said. "Jay Ar-Ar Tolkeen, that is. Do you like my dress, grimdarker?" he asked as he revealed the shotgun he had been concealing.

"What is that?" Finn asked, staring at the weapon curiously. "Isn't that forbidden?"

Francis laughed. "That's right. Forbidden treasure. For you."

Francis pointed the firearm at Finn and pulled the trigger. The decrepit weapon immediately exploded in his hands, hurling hot metal shrapnel and wood splinters in all directions. Finn fell backwards as Francis dropped the gun along with several of his finger. He started to scream, more handsome than ever with a barrel shard protruding from one eye.

As if responding on cue a dozen armed men burst from the cover of the surrounding landscape and descended on the party, screaming war cries in a manner they hoped was blood-curdling.

Cara Pace fought as if every movement were choreographed. her newly sharpened sword in one hand, her dagger in the other, she spun and dodged and parried the blows of a brace of opponents, opening one huge man's femoral artery with deadly efficiency, gracefully slashing the other across the forehead, blinding him with his own blood. Severs, gaunt and wiry, strode arrogantly toward her from the rear, a smirk on his face, an axe in his hand, and completely unaware that Destroy, the blood-stained Irish wolfhound, was bounding toward him on his left flank.

The Priestess went almost ignored by the attackers, none of them registering the stooping old woman as a threat. This worked to her advantage as she discretely produced a series of metal throwing stars from the depths of her cassock and embedded them in the unsuspecting heads of the ambushers.

Scarper fled into the woods without delay.

Daxle found himself confronted by a pair of antagonists: a large brute of a man brandishing a spear, his bald head decorated with a tattoo of an angry bear, and a short fellow who appeared to be compensating for his lack of height with the length of the samurai sword he was waving before him. Daxle backed up the ridge as they advanced, hoping to use elevation to even the odds, when the heel of his foot found the hook of a tree root and he fell backwards, his sword flying from his hand.

He recovered quickly and clambered to the crest of the ridge to look for his sword, a sinking feeling in the pit of his stomach. On the other side, some ten metres below, the river rolled by, coursing around rocks and fallen tree limbs before descending in a series of increasingly steep steps until it disappeared from view. Directly beneath him a tree trunk spanned the entire chasm, its roots still embedded in the wall having slid down off the ridge in some past storm, and to Daxle's amazement, there was his sword, its pointy end embedded in the side of the tree, its hilt swaying gently above the water.

Daxle heard a scream and looked over his shoulder just in time to see both of his assailants charging at him, mouths wide and weapons held high. He leapt for the tree bridge, reaching for his weapon even as he did so, and landed perfectly on the trunk before riding it down to the river as the whole thing gave way and plummeted into the gorge.

***

The next thing he knew, Daxle was sprawled on the hard ground, wet and bedraggled, with a green mutant bear looking down at him. He spat out a mouthful of river water and reached for his sword but grasped nothing but air. He recollected that the last time he'd seen his sword it was stuck in a tree that was plunging into a river; it was probably floating out to sea by now. He reached for the dagger he kept strapped to his leg instead, but it wasn't there either.

Well, shit, he thought.

"He's awake," the bear thing said.

Daxle propped himself on his elbows, not without considerable discomfort, and looked around. He was on the river bank now, presumably downriver as the gorge was nowhere to be seen. There were several mutants around him; in fact, he seemed to be in a mutant camp. They all looked a bit worse for wear: threadbare and gaffer taped. The green mutant bear stepped aside as a huge black and white mutant dog approached. It knelt beside him, its absurd tongue lolling out of the side of its mouth.

"You killed my furancé," it said through inanimate lips.

"What?" Daxle replied, bewildered.

"You beheaded Twinklenose. All she was doing was collecting flowers, and you just stepped out of the woods with your tadger hanging out and murdered her in cold blood."

Daxle tried to find some words, failed, so just shook his head.

"Don't deny it! Fluffyfeet saw everything," said the dog, inclining his huge head in the direction of a small crowd of creatures. The mutant feline named Fluffyfeet peeked out from behind a huge orange mutant moose and waved shyly.

"So now, larper," said the bereaved dog, hoisting a large rock over his pricked-up ears, "it's time you became acquainted with furry justice."

Then it came to him. *Three Shadow,* Daxle recalled. *The seer we talked to was definitely called Three Shadow.*

To be continued.

The Weather and Other Lies

B yron Rampy was dead. Well, officially, Byron Rampy was only presumed dead at this stage. Sure, there was a dead body wearing one of Byron Rampy's signature mustard yellow Italian suits sprawled on the blood-stained carpet of Byron Rampy's expensive penthouse suite in upscale Bradbury Towers, still clutching Byron Rampy's monogrammed, silver-plated pocket pistol in his cold dead hand, but as the cadaver was missing Byron Rampy's smug coiffured head the conventional method of preliminary identification was both off the table and off the victim's shoulders.

Rampy was something of a big shot, as demonstrated by the extensive cast of characters currently contaminating my crime scene. I was the detective assigned to the case, and beside myself there was an embarrassment of crime scene investigators, several police officers milling around trying to look busy, the victim's weeping agent, the concierge of the Bradbury and his sheepish-looking security chief, and a reporter from Citizenship News whose attempts at inconspicuousness weren't fooling anyone and whom I had unceremoniously ejected without further ado.

Most tellingly, and as if the place wasn't crowded enough already, we were also graced with the presence of an actual, in the flesh Recalibrator, replete with its orbiting entourage of HRLO lickspittles. The silent alien towered above us all, its large head—which resembled an animated, elongated human skull wrapped in bandages—was almost scraping the ceiling. Its eyes were encased in thick orange-lensed circular goggles and, like all Reeks, it was impeccably dressed, its swanky but tasteful grey suit tailor-made to accommodate its long multiple-jointed limbs and ungainly physique. This one sported a snazzy blue tie with a whimsical raining cats and dogs motif.

"The Recalibrator trusts that the detective will be swift in formally identifying the obvious guilty party in this heinous act, so we might bring them to justice without delay," said the chief lickspittle, a stocky fellow whose shaved head proudly exposed the tell-tale red translation device embedded into his skull just above his left ear.

"And who would that be,"—I peered at the fake name on the official HRLO ID that was clipped to his standard-issue cheap black suit—"Bruce Willis?"

"That's Officer Willis to you, detective, and far be it from the Recalibrator to tell you how to conduct your investigation, but we do feel that this outrage has terrorist written all over it. Especially with the admirable Mr. Rampy being such a valiant and outspoken advocate of the Recalibrator's wise oversight."

The office to which Officer Willis belonged was the Human/Recalibrators Liaison Office, AKA the HRLO, AKA—unofficially and pejoratively—the Hurlers. One of the Hurlers' roles was to facilitate mutual understanding between

the humans and the Recalibrators (AKA Reeks). The red giz-
mos attached to their heads were capable of translating basic
language in both directions, but they weren't good with accents,
dialects and slang (or with deliberately obfuscated speech or
excessive profanity, for that matter) so the Reeks required the
Hurlers to interpret for them and thereby train the device's AI.
At first the transceivers just used audio, but eventually the Recalibrators had required that updated devices should be surgically embedded directly into the subject's brain, enabling some
kind of deeper, creepier psychic link between human and alien.
Ostensibly this was to expedite their comprehension of human
communication, though other theories held that they were used
to administer punishments to disobedient lackeys or even grant
sexual rewards to obedient ones. Whatever their real purpose,
the devices had come to be known as grovel whips.

"Well, Groveller Willis," I explained, "Mr. Rampy's prema-
ture demise will be investigated with the same scrupulousness
and efficiency as any other suspected homicide. Far be it from
me to tell you how to bootlick, but you might want to pass that
along to your overlord there."

"Suspected homicide? Is the Recalibrator to infer that you
have not yet ruled out the possibility that Mr. Rampy's head
was detached by natural causes? Perhaps a particularly intense
sneeze?"

I chose to ignore the question, but on the face of it Bruce
Willis was right. Prior to being an absentee severed head, Byron
Rampy had been an absurd talking head on Citizenship News,
the twenty-four-hour news channel, by which I mean propaganda channel. His nightly broadcast, *The Byron Rampy Expla-*

nation, was inexplicably yet hugely popular. The terrorists—or the resistance, depending on which side of the fence you were on—would score a major coup by taking such a high-profile propaganda organ out of the picture. Yet something didn't smell right, and it wasn't just the company.

"I'm informed that the body was discovered by one of your people," I said, as something on the carpet beneath the desk caught my eye.

"That's correct," Willis said. "Mr. Rampy is—or rather was—of great support to the Recalibrators in communicating their message of peaceful cooperation, and so we thought it only appropriate to reciprocate. Officer Charlize Theron was assigned as Mr. Rampy's personal assistant. As you can imagine, coming upon this grisly scene came as quite a shock to young Charlize, so we allowed her to go home."

"That was sweet of you, but shocked or not, I'll need to interview her," I said, crouching down by the desk. The desk drawer was open; presumably it was where Rampy kept the pistol. Beneath was a spent round, small calibre.

"Of course. I'll have her file sent over personally."

I'd need to see the ballistics report for confirmation, but I'd bet all the pennies of my derisory paycheck that this cartridge was from Rampy's own weapon, which begged the question: where was the bullet? There were no obvious bullet holes to be seen in the walls or the fancy decor, and if he had successfully managed to put one in an assassin, well good for you Byron, but the only blood to be seen was in the vicinity of where his head should have been.

As I stood up, feeling like my back would audibly creak as I did so, I found myself looking directly at little puppies and kittens tumbling like raindrops. Above the tie, the orange lenses of the Recalibrator's goggles glowed in my direction like a pair of oncoming fireballs. It unfolded one excessively articulated arm and placed its hand on my shoulder, the retractable claws on the ends of its long white fingers extended just enough to remind me of their potential.

"The Recalibrators wish you to know that they will rest easier knowing this case is in the hands of a detective with such a bright future," said Bruce Willis with a smirk, "and that they will be following your progress with great interest."

"Oh, thanks" I said, looking at the gnarled, pale hand. "That really makes my day."

***

An hour later I was sitting in the security room in the basement of the Bradbury reviewing surveillance video with Security Chief Stover, an intense young woman with short blonde hair and thick-framed red spectacles, who was having a bad day. Together we stared at the expansive screen and its grid of a dozen video feeds, each displaying an accelerated motion recording taken from a different vantage point from in or around the building between midnight and one, the estimated time of death. A few residents, visitors and janitorial staff darted in and out the front door and around the various communal areas, but though all the footage would have to be analyzed more thoroughly later (by someone lower ranking than me, thankfully), nothing suspicious leapt out at me at this point, certainly no rampaging terrorists, slavering for blood and hell-bent on celebrity decapitation.

"Unfortunately the camera in the penthouse's exclusive elevator is out of service," Stover said apologetically. "I'll personally see that it gets fixed immediately."

"Great, that will be really useful now that your tenant is dead," I said. "I would like to see the video from inside the penthouse now, please."

Stover adopted an unconvincing expression of shock. "I don't know what you mean, detective. We don't operate surveillance inside private property."

I sighed in exasperation. The Reeks were always watching; if you weren't important enough to be spied on by real people in real time then your movements were at least being recorded on a hard drive somewhere. There was no way that they wouldn't have kept tabs on an asset as valuable as Byron Rampy.

"Security Chief Stover, do you know who the tenant of the penthouse was? Of course you do. Everyone does. He was famous. And, famously, he was a great friend to our illustrious Recalibrator administration. So naturally, they are very interested in finding out exactly what befell their good friend, the famous Byron Rampy, in the penthouse of your building, on your watch, last night. So, once again, Security Chief Stover, I would like to see the video from inside the penthouse. Please."

Stover glowered at me silently, trying and failing to cover her anxiety with a mask of indignation. After a moment she sighed loudly and worked the trackpad again, this time summoning up a full-screen viewpoint from inside Rampy's living room. She dragged the cursor over the timeline to approximately midnight, and suddenly there he was, Byron Rampy, resurrected and a solid head taller. He was sitting alone on his couch, a large scotch on the coffee table, staring distractedly in the direction of his wall-mounted screen off-camera. The audio indicated that he was watching an episode of his own show from earlier that week, his disembodied voice recapping the news of the apprehension and subsequent execution of one Amarantha Fluxx, an accused "freak, fraudster, and financier of terror". Rampy grimaced, grabbed his drink, downed it in one, looked toward his desk, and promptly disappeared.

He was replaced by a block of text, stark white letters on a black background.

DEATH TO TRAITORS

DEATH TO RECALIBRATORS

DEATH TO FREEDOM

"Well," I said, "that's a bit on the nose."

"What the hell?" Stover said. "The terrorists must have hacked the stream." She dragged the cursor along the timeline until the view of the room returned, which according to the time stamp was over eight hours later. Rampy was no longer on the couch; he was now on the floor in the position I'd seen him in earlier: desk drawer open, pistol in hand, cranium AWOL.

But something else was missing. I commandeered the trackpad and skipped back to drunk Rampy on the couch, just before the intermission, then forward, and back once more.

"There," I said, mostly to myself. On the very edge of the frame, a slim pink book lay on the desk. The resolution left something to be desired, and the book was partially off-camera, but if I squinted hard enough I could distinguish the largest word on the cover. It said FRAC.

By the time normal service was resumed following the charming DEATH message, the pink book was gone.

"What is FRAC?" I asked.

Stover looked at me blankly. I wasn't actually asking her, and even if she had known she probably wouldn't have enlightened me. I couldn't blame her, frankly.

"Can you enhance that?" I said, pointing at the fuzzy object on the screen.

Stover snorted. "You've been watching too much science fiction," she said.

I sighed. "Can you print the screen at least?"

She shrugged. "Sure, I guess. If we have any paper. What are we looking at, exactly?"

I tried to look inscrutable. I had no idea.

***

I caught up with Beats at Ro Sushi, an al fresco sushi bar she frequented before she went to work. I sat opposite her as she devoured her katsudon oblivious to all else. She started when she noticed me and then gave me her best exasperated expression as she touched the earbud she was wearing to pause her music.

"Join me, why don't you," she said.

"How's it goings, Beats?"

"Suddenly downhill, detective."

"Oh hush," I said. "I have a real easy one for you today."

Beatrice, or Beats to her friends, whom I'm sure she would not count me among, was a sound engineer for various nightclubs. She had been advising me on the diverse nefarious activities of her disreputable cohort for a couple of years now, since I busted her for dealing in illicit audio recordings and she had found herself looking at potential deportation from the Bubbles.

In the final years of the Negative, physical media was already on the verge of extinction; almost all music and film was streamed and most literature was digital and licensed rather than owned. This allowed the Recalibrators to recalibrate art with relative ease. The streams were taken offline whilst anything they deemed corruptive, offensive or generally disagreeable was removed from the libraries, and the associated software was updated to erase all previously downloaded unregulated content. Forbidden books were deleted remotely. Beats' area of consultancy was black market media, so I wasn't certain that the whole decapitated celebrity thing would be in her wheelhouse, but I had little to go on and nothing to lose.

I took the printout from my pocket and showed her the mystery book. "Does this mean anything to you?"

Beats squinted at the picture and mouthed the letters. "Nah, no idea. Sorry," she said, and resumed stuffing food into her mouth with her chopsticks as if to indicate we were done here.

I plucked one of the earbuds from her ear, held it close to my own and tweaked it to play. The music that emanated was fast and raucous. I couldn't distinguish any specific lyrics within the grunts and growls but I got the definite impression it wasn't a love song, unless necrophilia counted. I held the little device at arm's length in mock horror.

"Whoa, the Recalibrators have become much more adventurous in the music they approve for distribution these days, haven't they? Wait, this music *has* been approved, right?"

She rolled her eyes.

"Beats, I am shocked."

"Okay, so, maybe Christ Slicer hasn't strictly speaking been approved yet. We're just ahead of our time, man."

"Oh, this is your band? Even better," I said. "Maybe you can tour the wastelands outside the Bubbles. I wouldn't get too friendly with the groupies out there though."

"Shit. No, I mean, I'm just the bassist. That barely even counts."

"Oh, I see. Well, we can check with the Reeks if it counts, how about that? Or, you can fill me in on what you really know about FRAC."

Beats looked around to make sure no one was close enough to overhear and spoke in hushed tones. "Okay. So I was making a delivery of a flash drive yesterday. Some old movies. The buyer had been some kind of professor of movies or something, back in the Negative. Anyway, the coffee joint we met in had Citizenship News on in the background and this guy's mind was blown over the execution of that Fluxx woman. The terrorist. He said he'd known her, before. She could have been some great artist, according to him, but then she had sold her soul to the Reeks. Churned out nothing but—what did he call it? Agitprop."

"So this professor of yours concluded what? That Fluxx had been working both sides of the street?"

Beats shrugged.

"Great story. Lots of intrigue. But I'm not seeing a connection here."

"The connection is that Fluxx was a member of an art collective. Friends of the Recalibrators Art Collective. F. R. A. C."

I pondered this for a moment. Friends of the Recalibrators Art Collective. My internet search hadn't come up with that, but as the Reeks routinely scrubbed anything they disapproved of from what little remained of the web these days, that was no surprise. There was an art gallery downtown that specialized in exactly the kind of crap Beats' prof had referred to. That would be my next stop, after I'd interviewed Rampy's former PA, AKA his HRLO spy.

I dropped Beat's earbud on the table and got up to leave. She was visibly relieved. "Enjoy your pork, Beats. Oh, And good luck with bread slicer."

Beats gave me the finger as I left her to her food and her death metal. I didn't see it, but a seasoned detective develops a sixth sense for these things.

***

As I pressed the buzzer marked Theron a third time, I noticed some exceptionally eloquent graffiti scrawled across one wall of her building in orange paint: IF YOU WANT A PICTURE OF THE FUTURE, it read, IMAGINE A HUMAN PUNCHING HIMSELF IN THE FACE, FOREVER. That had taken some balls, I thought, and wondered how long it would be before the sentiment was erased. I suspected it was no coincidence that the anonymous author of the message had chosen this particular building, a veritable nest of Hurlers.

Speaking of the devil, one of those very HRL Officers, a heavily bearded guy built like a moose but with less charm, disembarked from the elevator inside and strode toward the glass entrance without looking up from his cell phone. As he passed me by I had started to slip through the slowly closing door he had left in his wake when I felt his huge mitt on my shoulder and he bellowed threateningly. I flashed my badge and he backed off, though not without some hesitation; officially the HRLO were not above the law, but testing that boundary was one of the perks of the job. A moment later I was headed up to the twelfth floor in the elevator.

The door to Theron's apartment was ajar. It was such a cliche that I almost felt embarrassed to draw my sidearm. I announced myself loudly as I kicked the door open the rest of the way and entered, scanning the short hallway and doorways ahead. No signs of life. I peeked around the corner where the hall opened into a living area and shouted *police* again. The room was unoccupied. A large poster of a mustard-yellow-suited Byron Rampy took pride of place above a couch that had seen better days, and the video screen on the opposite wall was streaming Citizenship News on mute. On the coffee table were various empty take-out food and drink containers and a small bronze-coloured statuette of a Recalibrator in a pose replicating that of Rodin's *The Thinker*. Classy.

The only movement in the room came from a piece of paper taped to the glass of one of the doors to the balcony as it fluttered slightly in the breeze. The adjacent door was wide open. Approaching the door I glanced at the brief note. I'M SORRY, BYRON, it said simply.

Stepping out onto the narrow balcony I looked down and finally located my witness. Charlize Theron was embedded in my vehicle, twelve storeys below. She'd partially caved in the car roof and made a shattered circle on the windshield as she'd hit it at around one hundred and ten klicks per hour. As I was slowly ascending inside the building, she must have been rapidly descending outside.

"Well, shit," I said to myself.

I holstered my firearm and stepped back into the apartment just in time to see a figure sneaking toward the front door. We both froze for a heartbeat. Whoever it was had their hood up and appeared to have wrapped a towel around their face; I cursed myself for not clearing the bathroom earlier.

"Wait," I said with impressive authority, but he was already moving again. As I fumbled with my holster the suspect reached down and grabbed the Reek Rodin statuette from the coffee table and launched it in my direction. I tried to dodge it but I was too slow and it bounced off my head and knocked me back onto my backside on the balcony threshold. It was only a glancing blow but I still felt blood trickling as I staggered to my feet and pursued my assailant out of the apartment. I made an educated guess that he'd opted for the stairwell rather than the elevator, and sure enough I could hear his running footfalls a couple of flights below and I hurtled down the steps after him. I hoofed it through the lobby and was back on the street just in time to see his vehicle peeling out recklessly and forcing an oncoming bus to brake hard.

As I got into my car and started the engine I suddenly got the sense that I wasn't alone and remembered that Theron was on the roof, her inverted face squished against the spiderweb of bloody cracks in the windshield on the passenger side. At least her eyes were closed.

I took off after my suspect regardless, my vehicle squealing in protest at being put back into service so soon after its recent trauma and handling like the shock absorbers were in shock. My fellow motorists sounded their horns in encouragement as I cut them off in my haste to catch up with the hooded man, unfairly advantaged as he was by having a roadworthy vehicle.

He swerved around a corner onto the thoroughfare and I skidded along after, clinging to the steering wheel for dear life, tires screaming outside the car almost as loudly as I was screaming inside, and then suddenly we were both hurtling toward a fresh red light like lunatics. He tore right through the light as if it wasn't there, navigating the holes between the four lanes of cross traffic as if the whole thing were choreographed by God, and then suddenly it was my turn, crunch time, and for a fleeting second I was going to go for it too, I was going to fly through that intersection like a ninja, like a ghost, like a freaking unflinching phantom of justice that could not be stopped—but thankfully my suicidal resolve abandoned me at the last second and I came crashing back to my senses, hitting the brakes hard and sliding to a halt just beyond the stop line.

I took a deep breath and prised one hand off the steering wheel to throw the car into reverse, just in time to be rammed in the left fender by a Katapult Kouriers van, spinning my vehicle forty-five degrees. The distraught van driver jumped out of his cab and stared incredulously at the dead body still on my roof, secured by some gory adhesive I chose not to contemplate.

"How—? What—?" he blurted, trying to make sense of what he was seeing. "That wasn't my fault! That wasn't my fault!" he protested, pointing at my macabre cargo.

As I heard the sound of approaching sirens I turned off the engine, sat back and waited for my heart to give up on trying to punch its way out of my ribcage. I looked at the inverted face of Officer Theron.

"Well, I tried, Charlie. I tried."

Then Charlize Theron opened her eyes and looked right at me. "Fuck you," she gurgled, blood dribbling from her mouth.

***

A couple of years ago, I had been thrashing one of my fellow detectives at chess during my lunch break, when a Recalibrator paid a visit to the station house with a couple of Hurler henchmen in tow. When the captain invited the Reek into his office, one of the henchmen lingered, taking an interest in our game. I ignored him as I backed my opponent into a corner, and with characteristic graciousness, she swept her king from the board in resignation and told me where to shove my bishop.

I started to reset the board when the visitor—name of Bronson, if his HRLO ID was to be believed—took the vacated seat and aligned the white pieces silently. He opened the game. I shrugged and made my move, hoping for more of a challenge than that offered by my regular rivals. My hopes were soon dashed, however, as within a few minutes we were into the endgame, and my new opponent's defeat was imminent. It was at that point that he slowly glided his knight directly forward to capture my queen, looking me in the eye as he did so as if daring me to call him out on his illegal move. Perplexed, I shook my head at him disapprovingly. He stood up with a wink and simply walked out. He hadn't said a word the whole time.

It was about a month later that I met with Vandergriff, an old friend of mine, at Curmudgeon Coffee. Vandergriff was a paramedic, and she was still shaken by something she had witnessed the previous day. A section of panels had come loose from one of the newer Bubbles that protected the expanding western city sprawl and dropped out, leaving behind a window on the howling storms beyond. The panels had plummeted down onto the city to explode like glass bombs on the vehicles and citizens below, leaving dozens of people impaled, lacerated and blinded on the blood-splattered streets. Most hadn't even known what hit them. Vandergriff had been a first responder to the aftermath, and she described how, in the shards of Bubble that protruded from the bodies, the digital sun still shone.

The incident was never mentioned on the news streams, of course, nor was there any mention of it on the internet. The Recalibrators decided it hadn't happened, and so it hadn't happened. The truth isn't what it used to be.

When we were outside the coffee shop and about to go our separate ways, a vehicle the size of a small tank pulled up and a

Hurler descended from the driver's side door. I recognized him immediately as Bronson, the chess cheat.

"Hey, you," he yelled in my direction, and sauntered toward us. "Let's see your ID."

"What's this about?" I asked, showing him my badge. He didn't so much as glance at it.

Vandergriff started to remove her driver's license from her wallet but Officer Bronson snatched the wallet from her hands and started to rifle through it, discarding the contents on the sidewalk after each cursory inspection.

"Hey now," Vandergriff said.

Bronson paused and stared at her. "What was that, citizen?"

"This is uncalled for," Vandergriff said, crouching to retrieve her things.

The Hurler looked over at the Reek wagon. This was in the days before the surgically implanted grovel whips: back then, the translator was still an earpiece. He pressed a button on his.

"This one is disrespectful to the Recalibrators," he announced into the mic.

The rear door of the vehicle opened and a Recalibrator unfolded itself from the backseat and seemed to float over to us.

Bronson jerked his head in my friend's direction. "This one, she said the Recalibrators should crawl back to the slime they came from."

The Reek's glowing goggles turned on Vandergriff.

"I said no such thing," she protested, looking at me for support.

I held my badge in front of the Recalibrator. "No need for this to escalate," I said. "Your man Bronson here is simply mistaken."

Bronson put his finger to the device again. "She says she hopes the resistance cuts off all your heads."

"What the hell," Vandergriff began, but just then the Reek gave her an open-handed swipe on the side of her head and pivoted to return to the car, all in one fleeting, fluid movement. The force of the blow threw my friend across the sidewalk and into the plate glass window of the coffee shop, rattling the tempered glass in its frame and leaving her bloodied and concussed. As I dashed over and knelt by her side I heard an engine start. Bronson was back behind the wheel of the Reek wagon. He gave me a wink through the open window.

"Checkmate, policeman," he said, and drove away.

***

Theron's resurrection was a short-lived miracle; she was dead by the time the paramedics arrived. I never did get a chance to interview her, as I figured *fuck you* didn't count. The fugitive's vehicle was stolen, of course, and none of the cameras in Theron's building were operational; one of the perks of living in a Hurler nest.

I stood before a huge floor-to-ceiling painting in the main exhibition space of the Jack Lint Art Gallery. The piece was called simply *The Arrival* and it speculated on the coming of the Recalibrators in a spectacular scene reminiscent of a religious epic by Turner. The creatures were shown emerging from a vast, indistinct glowing orb into the midst of the ravaged and war-torn world of the Negative, when brother slew brother and anarchy reigned. The heroic strangers forged a path through this rampant carnage and discord, leaving only serenity and order in their wake.

In reality, the origin of the Recalibrators was shrouded in mystery. All of a sudden they were just here, and no one was quite sure where they'd come from. Some people would refer to them as aliens, others as angels, but the Recalibrators themselves were vague, even evasive when asked, claiming their origin was of no importance. What was important, they insisted, was their destination; the destination of us all. They were here to help us, they said. To recalibrate the very definitions of truth and facts, so that we might all rest easier free from such burdens. Consequently, their first act when in power had been to recalibrate time itself. So began Year Zero. All of time leading up to Year Zero was to be referred to as the Negative, and then only when strictly necessary.

And here we are, several years later, hiding in our Bubbles from the slow-motion apocalypse unfolding in the world outside. We are the recalibrated.

Another space in the gallery was filled with flattering portraits of politicians, athletes and celebrities who had proven themselves to be amongst the most supportive of the Recalibrators. These sycophants often shared their canvases with the objects of their adoration; exchanging a firm handshake, receiving a friendly claw on a shoulder, or just staring admiringly at a Reek holding audience.

Pride of place in the centre of the room was *The Rethinker*, the full-size, genuine version of the knock-off statuette that had almost knocked me out at the late Charlize Theron's place. Fortunately, the replica had been resin and palm-sized, whereas this one was actual bronze and twice life-size, portraying a grandiose Recalibrator deep in thought as it contemplated how to fix these blundering, problematic humans. At first glance, the creature appeared to be resting on a rocky perch, like its famous human predecessor, but seeing the sculpture for the first time in the flesh, as it were, I could see the seat actually resembled a pile of thousands of human skulls.

I'm no art expert but I was sensing a common theme connecting the artworks in this place and it's that they were all about as subtle as being hit in the head with a bronze statue, and I should know.

However, the piece I was most interested in was a painting, depicting a Reek walking calmly out of a burning hospital, its arms filled with babies, as a crowd of women in various states of frazzled dishevelment fell at its feet. A label placed tastefully to one side identified the piece as *The Saviour of our Future* by one Amarantha Fluxx, and a small card tucked under the label marked the piece as reserved.

An employee was collecting pink catalogues from a small table by the entrance and dropping them into a garbage bag. I had seen one of those catalogues before, on a dead man's desk. I had a picture of one in my pocket. I caught the woman's attention.

"Hello there. I'm very interested in purchasing this wonderful painting. I just love the energy and the colours and the—well, the fucking *nuance* of it. Who do I give my cash to?"

The woman assessed me for a moment, with my bruised temple and my cheap suit. She was trying to decide if I was an eccentric millionaire or an eccentric time-waster. Fortunately for me, she decided to err on the side of money.

"It is a wonderful piece, isn't it? Unfortunately, this particular painting was recently reserved. Perhaps a sophisticate such as yourself would be interested in other works by the same artist?"

She checked the label to remind herself who that was, and her face fell.

"Ah, yes. Actually, we have other far more talented and exciting young artists that I would recommend instead. Perhaps you'll allow me to show you."

"I want this one," I interrupted. "Who is the buyer? Perhaps we can come to an arrangement, beneficial to all."

She smiled condescendingly. "I couldn't possibly divulge client details, I'm afraid. "

"Is it Byron Rampy? From *The Byron Rampy Explanation*?"

The woman opened her mouth but wasn't sure what to say with it.

"Because you know he's dead, right? RIP. Mysterious circumstances and all that. So if you haven't actually cashed his cheque yet, you might want to think over my offer. But I haven't got all day."

Her lips resumed smiling but her eyes couldn't hide the dread she was feeling at the prospect of being stuck with a very expensive and very unsellable terrorist painting. "I'll tell you what

I can do. Why don't you leave us your contact details, and I'll personally get back to you as soon as possible. How does that sound?"

It sounded spiffy, so I told her my name was Dick Reckard and gave her the number of my second favourite Mexican restaurant and I left the Jack Lint Art Gallery before I puked up a Recalibrator art masterpiece of my own.

***

I walked down the stone steps outside the gallery, looking at the sky. Or rather, looking at the inner, concave surface of the Bubble. Another predictably sunny day.

Byron Rampy was interested in the work of Amarantha Fluxx. Or was he interested in the artist herself? Did he suspect that she was involved with the resistance? Was he playing her as part of some kind of trap? Or was she playing him?

I climbed into my vehicle, or rather the loaner I was given whilst the motor pool grease monkeys beat the Charlize Theron–shaped dent out of the roof of my regular ride. I put the car in reverse and casually slammed into the little yellow scooter parked behind me, and immediately a bald man in a trench coat broke cover, appearing from behind the huge marble sculpture of a Recalibrator hand making a peace sign that resided outside the gallery.

"My scooter! Oh my god, my scooter!" he cried, his expression reminding me of that famous Munch painting. This arty crap was rubbing off on me.

I got out of the car and approached him. "Oh dear, how did that happen?" I asked. "We need to exchange insurance details forthwith." I then proceeded to nonchalantly drag the man back around the sculpture he had been amateurishly skulking behind a moment ago.

"Please don't hit me, I'm an artist!" the man pleaded. I noted his pencil moustache and his completely transparent eye patch. His story checked out.

"Name?"

"Vogel. My name is Vogel."

"Is that your first name or your last?"

"It's my only name," said Vogel.

"Of course it is. An artist. You're with the FRAC, aren't you? The Friends of the Recalibrators Artists Collective, correct?"

He stared at me frozen with fear and indecision.

I went out on a limb. "Listen, Vogel. I know Amarantha Fluxx was in your little group, which makes you guilty by association as far as the Reeks are concerned. So you have a choice to make. You can either tell me the truth right here, right now, and live to be pretentious another day, or I can deliver you to your Recalibrator friends and you can explain to them why you were following me under a little friendly torture. Which is it to be?"

He pondered this for a solid three seconds before spilling his guts. "We're no friends of the Recalibrators, believe me. We work together to fight against the Reeks, with weaponized art. We secretly call ourselves the Fuck the Reeks Artists Collective."

"Wow," I said. "Edgy. Look, I don't know much about art, but it looks to me that your weapon is producing grovelling art porn for Reeks and their lickspittles to jerk off too. Am I missing something?"

He gave me an indignant look. "In a way, yes. We temporarily put aside our good taste and employ our skills to give these people what they want. They pay well for this fawning kitsch and we funnel that money straight to the resistance. Ironic, don't you think?"

"Oh, deliciously ironic. You'll definitely get the last laugh when the Reeks take an industrial sander to your kneecaps. But none of this explains why you're following me around."

He shrugged. "After what they did to Anathema, we've all been on edge. We're just trying to keep abreast of things."

"Anathema?"

"Amarantha," he explained. "Amarantha Fluxx. She was Anathema to her friends in the Collective. Her nickname, I mean."

"Confusing. So, Amarantha was busted and you and your sneaky clique are terrified she might have thrown you all under the bus?"

"We are not terrified," he said, adopting a defensive tone. "Anathema would never give us up like that. But her choice of lovers did make some of the group nervous."

"Lovers like Byron Rampy?" I ventured.

"Yes. He was her pet project. She said she could turn him against the Recalibrators, bring him into the fold. But now he's dead too, assassinated they say, and, well, the FRAC is feeling quite vulnerable right now, as you might imagine."

Oh, I could imagine. "Take my advice, Vogel. You and your revolutionary little buddies should hop on your scooters and find a nice artist's retreat somewhere. Maybe on a remote island or in a deep cave. Lay low there for six months or so. A year, tops. Otherwise, you might be reuniting with your friend Anathema sooner rather than later. And if I find you tailing me again, I *will* deliver you to the Reeks myself."

I headed back to the car.

"We're not the only ones following you, detective," he called after me.

"I know," I lied.

"The Recalibrators are scheming."

"The Recalibrators are always scheming, Vogel," I replied. I paused before climbing into the car. "What makes you think you know so much about it, anyway?" I wondered.

"I'm a surrealist," he said, wiggling his moustache. "Surrealists have eyes everywhere."

***

It was late by the time I got back to my little apartment. I needed to take a shower and ponder my next move. I removed my jacket and sidearm, kicked off my shoes, and made straight for the booze on the desk, flipping on the lamp and pouring myself a large one, before heading to the couch.

It was quite surreal discovering a Recalibrator standing in the middle of my familiar living room, stooped and staring, like a two-metre rent in the fabric of reality. I let out a short cry of alarm—falsetto yet manly—much to the amusement of Bruce Willis, the lickspittle who had attended the Rampy crime scene and who was now violating my favourite armchair with his backside. His smirk was a punch magnet and I was struggling to resist the attraction. I took a deep breath, a big gulp of my booze, and composed myself.

"Make yourself at home, Groveller Willis," I sneered.

"Excuse the intrusion, detective, but our Recalibrator friends are on tenterhooks awaiting the conclusion of your investigation, so we thought we'd make it more convenient for you to update us on your progress so far."

I looked at the Reek. It remained expressionless and inscrutable as ever. It wore a tie covered in little saxophones.

"My progress? I think that you already know what happened."

"Indulge us," Willis said, gesticulating that it was my turn to talk.

"Okay. What I think happened is this. Your puppet Rampy went and became smitten with one Amarantha Fluxx, a member of an art collective that makes bad art to raise funds for the resistance. Whether he knew that and he was setting her up for some grand exposé or she saw him as a rich chump the resistance could manipulate I can't say for sure. Maybe both. Hell, it's even possible it was true love, why not? Stranger things have happened. But when Fluxx was busted, Rampy freaked, either because he was terrified that she might have implicated him in something, or because his heart was broken. Again, hard to say. But the outcome was the same. He put a slug in his temple."

I poured myself another drink, pointedly not offering one to my uninvited guests.

"When Rampy's PA and your spy Theron showed up on the scene of the suicide, she immediately called her boss. Now, the Reeks couldn't have it said that their golden boy had topped himself, that would raise too many uncomfortable questions among the viewers of Citizenship News, and the Reeks hate uncomfortable questions, so they sent backup over to help relieve Rampy of his head. This was partly to cover up the evidence of suicide and partly so that they could call it an assassination and blame the resistance, because every cloud has a silver lining, right?

"After hacking off his head they then hacked the Bradbury's surveillance video using some rather crude redirection and questionable graphic design choices, but they still had some concerns about Theron's mental health so they had Doctor Defenestration make a house call with a prescription for suicide.

"So, we have a suicide disguised as a murder and a murder disguised as a suicide. Marks for versatility, if not so much for execution. Whether the clusterfuck you made of the cover-up was through incompetence or cunning, I'm not sure. Maybe it was a test, maybe you wanted me to see through it to see what I'd do," I said, remembering a long ago chess game even as I spoke.

"If I play along with the story you know I'm in your pocket, but if it looks like I'm going to raise the alarm then you call me a terrorist and use me as an excuse to infest the police with more Hurler puppets. Of course, I can't prove a jot of this but I think you'll find the broad strokes are true."

Bruce Willis guffawed and started a slow hand clap. Disarmingly, the Reek joined in.

"Bravo, detective," Willis said. "But clarify something for me, if you would be so kind: what is truth, exactly? You seem to be harbouring a quaint but obsolete interpretation of the word, an interpretation that expired with the arrival of the Recalibrators in Year Zero. Haven't you heard? There is no objective truth anymore. The truth is what the Recalibrators say it is," he said, waving his hand dismissively. "Decoupled from your irrelevant distractions of facts and reality."

"In this particular case, the Recalibrators feel the truth is that Byron Rampy was assassinated by terrorists, therefore that is the truth. It's very simple. Whether these terrorists were aided and abetted by radicalized conspirators from within our own police force, well, that remains to be seen. So, what's it to be, detective? Will your final report accurately reflect this simple truth?"

And that's how Byron Rampy's head came to be found in my freezer.

***

The final episode of *The Byron Rampy Explanation* will air this evening, and Byron Rampy will bow out, though not literally. Rather his preserved cranium (sans excavated slug) will preside over the live, public execution of his own dastardly assassins, a newly infamous cell of evil-doers including several artists, a few exasperated but unsurprised journalists, a rather confused hairdresser (who had made the mistake of bedding the wife of someone high up in the HRLO) and one curmudgeonly detective: your humble, if not entirely reliable, narrator.

When I stubbornly refused to subscribe to the official version of the events surrounding Rampy's demise, my front door had burst from its hinges as if on cue and my little apartment had been flooded with a dozen overexcited Hurlers, all appearing thrilled with their shiny new guns and high on that new-tactical vest smell. They got right to work tearing my place apart, and within minutes they had "discovered" the missing coiffured head in my freezer, right there for all to see on top of the frozen scallops. Presumably I'd been planning to mount it on my wall at some point, like a trophy.

Checkmate, detective.

So here I sit with my fellow conspirators in the green room of the Byron Rampy show, surrounded by armed HRLO (their lanyards identifying them as Eastwood, Wayne and Van Damme), awaiting my starring role in this macabre spectacle of performative justice.

You know, it's at times like these that I shake my head in disbelief that we ever elected these monsters in the first place.

I do take some solace in the fact that tonight's show won't play out as expected; at least not according to the note smuggled in by my lawyer during one of her charade consultations. The message said that Rampy's head has been packed with high explosives and the resistance is quite literally going to blow his mind live on prime time, taking all attendant high-ranking Reeks, Hurlers and assorted political sycophants out with a bang before an audience of millions. Viva la revolución. Come to think of it, I don't know whose idea this Byron bomb was, but it does have a somewhat surrealist touch.

Or maybe the note was just another lie to make me feel that my sacrifice would not be in vain. It's hard to say.

The truth isn't what it used to be.

About the Author

Ran M. Baffle is a recovering Englishman and a self-inflicted Canadian, currently residing in beautiful British Columbia with his family and his daft dog. He enjoys rock music, books, coffee, and movies; in fact, when he was young Ran hoped to grow up to be a film director, making offbeat and thought-provoking movies filled with artful cinematography and edgy editing techniques. But, well, here we are.

He works on the internet, for which he apologizes.

This is his first book.

Manufactured by Amazon.ca
Acheson, AB